THE MOUNTAINS
won't remember us

Other books by Robert Morgan

FICTION

THE BLUE VALLEYS

POETRY

ZIRCONIA POEMS
RED OWL
LAND DIVING
TRUNK & THICKET
GROUNDWORK
BRONZE AGE
AT THE EDGE OF THE ORCHARD COUNTRY
SIGODLIN
GREEN RIVER: NEW AND SELECTED POEMS

THE MOUNTAINS
won't remember us

AND OTHER STORIES

ROBERT MORGAN

PEACHTREE PUBLISHERS
ATLANTA

To the memory of my father,
Clyde R. Morgan (1905–1991)
storyteller, rememberer

Published by
PEACHTREE PUBLISHERS, LTD.
494 Armour Circle, NE
Atlanta, Georgia 30324

Design by Candace J. Magee
Cover illustration by Margaret deNeergaard

Manufactured in the United States of America

First printing (1992)

Library of Congress Cataloging-in-Publication Data

Morgan, Robert, 1944-
    The mountains won't remember us and other stories / Robert
    Morgan.
      p. cm.
    ISBN 1-56145-049-9
    1. Blue Ridge Mountains--Fiction. 2. North Carolina--Fiction.
    3. Mountain life--Fiction. I. Title.
    PS3563.087147M68 1992
    813'.54--dc20   92-7010
                                          CIP

CONTENTS

ACKNOWLEDGMENTS

Epoch: "Poinsett's Bridge"
War, Literature, and the Arts: "Watershed"
Pembroke Magazine: "Death Crown"
Iron Mountain Review: "Frog Level"
Southern Review: "The Bullnoser"
The Nightshade Short Story Reader: "Mack"

The author would like to thank the National Endowment for the Arts and the John Simon Guggenheim Memorial Foundation for grants which were of great help in the completion of this book.

POINSETT'S BRIDGE

Son, it was the most money I'd ever had, one ten-dollar gold piece and twenty-three silver dollars. The gold piece I put in my dinner bucket so it wouldn't get worn away by the heavy silver. The dollars clinked and weighed in my pocket like a pistol. I soon wished they was a pistol.

"What you men have done here this year will not be forgotten," Senator Pineset said before he cut the ribbon across the bridge. "The coming generations will see your work and honor you. You have opened the mountains to the world, and the world to the mountains."

And he shook hands with every one of us. I still had my dirty work clothes on, but I had washed my face and hands in the river before the ceremony. The senator was as fine a looking man as you're ever likely to see. He wore a striped silk cravat and he had the kind of slightly red face that makes you think of spirit and health.

The senator and all the other dignitaries and fine ladies got in their carriages and crossed the bridge and started up the turnpike. There was to be a banquet in Flat Rock that evening to celebrate the road and the bridge. I shook hands with the foreman, Delosier, and started up the road myself for home.

Everything seemed so quiet after the ceremony. The warm fall woods was just going on about their business, with no interest in human pomp and projects. I carried my dinner bucket and my light mason's hammer, and I thought it was time to get home and do a little squirrel hunting. I hadn't spent a weekday at home since work started on the bridge in March. Suddenly two big, rough-looking boys jumped out from behind a rock above the road and run down into the turnpike in front of me.

"Scared you?" one said, and laughed like he had told a joke.

"No," I said.

"We'll just help you carry things up the mountain," the other said. "You got anything heavy?" He looked at my pocket bulging with the silver dollars. I had my buckeye in there too, but it didn't make any sound.

"Yeah, we'll help out," the first one said, and laughed again.

Now I had built chimneys ever since I was a boy. Back yonder people would fix up a little cabin on their own, and make a fireplace of rock, then the chimney they just built of plastered mud and sticks. Nobody had the time or skill for masonry. Way back yonder after the Indians was first gone and people moved into these hollers a wagonload at a time coming to grab the cheap land, they'd live in any little old shack or hole in the ground with a roof over it. The first Jones that come here they said lived in a hollow tree for a year. And I knowed other families that hid theirselves in caves and lean-tos below cliffs. You just did the best you could.

My grandpa fit the British at King's Mountain and at Cowpens, and then he come up here and threw together a little cabin right on the pasture hill over there. You can see the cellarhole there still. And where we lived when I was a boy the chimney would catch fire on a cold night, or if pieces of mud fell off the sticks, and we'd have to get up on the roof and pour water down. You talk about cold and wet, with the house full of smoke. That was what give Grandpa pneumonia.

That was when I promised myself to build a chimney.

Nobody on the creek knew rockwork then, except to lay a rough kind of fireplace. Only masons in the county was the Germans in town, the Doxtaters and Bumgarners, the Corns, and they worked on mansions in Flat Rock, and the home of the judge, and the courthouse and such. I would have gone to learn from them but I was too scared of foreigners to go off on my own. People here was raised so far back in the woods we was afraid to go out to work. So I had to learn myself. I'd seen chimneys in Greenville when Pa and me carried to market there, and I'd marveled at the old college building north of Greenville. "Rockwork's for rich folks," Pa said, but I didn't let that stop me.

After the tops was cut and the fodder pulled one year I set myself to the job. First thing that was needed was the rocks, but they was harder to get at than it might seem at first. They was rocks in the fields and pastures. Did you just pry them up with a pole and sled them to the house? And the creek was full of rocks, but they was rounded by the water and had to be cut flat. That was the hardest work I'd ever done, believe me, getting rocks out of the creek. It was already getting cold, and I'd have to go out there in the water, find the right size, and tote them up the bank. I had to pry some loose from the mud, and scrape away the moss and slick.

They was a kind of a quarry over on the hill where the Indians must have got their flint and quartz for arrowheads. The whole slope was covered with fragments of milkquartz and I hauled in some of those to put in the fireplace where the crystals could shine in the light.

I asked Old Man Davis over at the line what could be used for mortar and he said a bucket of lime mixed with sand and water would do the trick. And even branch clay would serve, though it never set itself hard except where heated by a fire.

Took me most of the fall, way up into hog-killing time, to get my stuff assembled. I just had a hammer and one cold chisel to dress the rock. Nobody ever taught me how to cut stone, or how to measure and lay out. I just learned myself as

I made mistakes and went along.

Son, I remember looking at that pile of rocks I'd carried into the yard and wondering how I'd ever put them together in a firebox and chimney. My little brother Joe had already started to play with the rocks and scatter them around. Leaves from the poplars had drifted on my heap and already it looked half-buried. I waited until Ma and Pa and the other younguns had gone over to Fletcher to Cousin Charlie's. In those times people would visit each other for a week at a time once the crops was in. I stayed home to look after the stock. One morning at daylight I lit in and tore the old mud chimney down. I knocked most of it down with an ax, it was so shackly, and then I knocked the firebox apart with a sledgehammer.

Well, there it was, the cabin with a hole in the side and winter just a few short weeks away. That was when I liked to have lost my nerve. The yard was a mess of sooty mud and sticks, and my heaps of rocks. I thought of just heading west and never coming back, of taking the horse and going. I stood there froze, you might say, with fear.

But then I seen in my pile a rock that was perfect for a cornerstone, and another that would fit against it in a line with just a little chipping. So I shoveled out and leveled the foundation and mixed up a bucket of mortar. I put the cornerstone in place, and slapped on some wet clay, then fitted the next rock to it. It was like solving a puzzle, finding rocks that would join together with just a little mud, maybe a little chipping here and there to smooth a point or corner. But best of all was the way you could rough out a line, running a string or a rule along the edge to see how it would line up, so when you backed away you saw the wall was straight in spite of gaps and bulges. I worked so hard selecting and tossing rocks for my pile, mixing more clay and water, setting stone against stone, that I never stopped for dinner. By dark I had the hole covered with the fireplace, so the coons couldn't get inside. I liked the way I made the firebox slope in toward the chimney to a place where I could put a damper. And I set between the rocks the hook Ma's pot would hang from.

It wasn't until I was milking the cow by lanternlight I seen how rough my hands had wore. The skin at the ends of my fingers and in my palms was fuzzy from handling the rock. The cow liked to kicked me, they rasped her tits so bad.

But by the time Ma and Pa had come home from Cousin Charlie's I had made them a chimney. I made my scaffold out of hickory poles and hoisted every rock up the ladder myself and set it into place. It was not the kind of chimney I'd a built later, but you can see the work over there at the old place still, kind of ragged and taking too much mortar, but still in plumb and holding together after more than sixty years. I knowed you had to go above the roof to make a chimney draw, and I got it up to maybe six inches above the comb. Later I learned any good chimney goes six feet above the ridgepole. It's the height of a chimney makes it draw, makes the flow of smoke go strong up the chimney into the cooler air. The higher she goes the harder she pulls.

People started asking me to build chimneys, and I made enough so I started using fieldstone, and breaking the rocks to get flat edges that would fit so you don't hardly have to use any mortar. They just stay together where they're laid. And people asked me to steen their wells and wall in springs and cellars. It was hard and heavy work, taking rocks out of the ground and placing them back in order, finding the new and just arrangement so they would stay. I had all the work I could do in good weather, after laying-by time.

Then I heard about the bridge old Senator Pineset was building down in South Carolina. Clara—we was married by then—read about it in the Greenville paper which come once a week. The senator was building a turnpike from Charleston to the mountains, to open up the Dark Corner of the state for commerce he said. But everybody knowed it was for him and his Low Country kind to bring their carriages to the cool mountains for the summer. They found out what a fine place this was and they started buying up the land around Flat

Rock. But there wasn't hardly a road up Saluda Mountain and through the Gap except the little wagon trace down through Gap Creek. That's the way we hauled our hams and apples down to Greenville and Augusta in the fall. That same newspaper said the state of North Carolina was building a turnpike all the way from Tennessee to the line at Saluda Gap.

The paper said they was building this stone bridge across the North Fork of the Saluda River. It was to be fifty feet high and more than a hundred feet long, "the greatest work of masonry and engineering in upper Carolina" the paper said. And I knowed I had to work on that bridge. It was the first turnpike into the mountains and I had to go help out. The paper said they was importing masons from Philadelphia and even a master mason from England. I knowed I had to go and learn what I could.

Senator Pineset had his own ideas about the turnpike and the bridge, but we knowed there'd be thousands of cattle and hogs and sheep drove out of the mountains and across from Tennessee as well as the rich folks driving in their coaches. That highway would put us in touch with every place in the country you might want to go to.

I felt some dread, going off like that not knowing if they would hire me or not. I had no way of proving I was a mason. What would that fancy Englishman think of my laying skill? And even if he took me on it was a nine mile walk each way to the bridge site. I knowed the place all right, where the North Fork goes through a narrow valley too steep to get a wagon down and across.

They's something about the things a man really wants to do that scares him. He's got to go on nerve a lot of the time. And nobody else is looking or cares when you make your choices. That's the way it has to be. But it was a kind of fate, too, and even Clara didn't try to stop me. She complained, as a woman will, that I'd be gone from sunup to sundown and no telling how long it would take to finish the bridge through the summer and into the fall. And she wouldn't have no help around the place except the kids. "They may not do any more hiring," she said. But I knowed better. I knowed masons and stonecutters of any kind was hard to come by in the up country, and there would be thousands of rocks to cut for such a bridge. And when I set off she give me a buckeye to put in my pocket for luck. She'd didn't normally hold to such things, but I guess she was worried as I was.

Sometimes you get a vision of what's ahead for you. And even if it's what you most want to do, you see all the work it is. It's like foreseeing an endless journey of climbing over logs and crossing creeks, looking for footholds in mud and swamp-land. And every little step and detail is real and has to be worked out. But it's what you are going to do, what you have been given to do. It will be your life to get through it.

That's the way I seen this work. Every one of that thousand rocks, some weighing a ton I guessed, had to be dressed, had to be measured and cut out of the mountainside, and then joined to one another. And every rock would take hundreds, maybe thousands, of hammer and chisel licks, each lick leading to another, swing by swing, chip by chip, every rock different and yet cut to fit with the rest. Every rock has its own flavor, so to speak, its own grain and hardness. No two rocks are exactly alike, but they have to be put together, supporting each other, locked into place. It was like I was behind a mountain of hammer blows, of chips and dust, and the only way out was through them. It was my life's work to get through them. And when I got through them my life would be over. It's like everybody has to earn their own death. We all want to reach the peacefulness and rest of death, but we have to work our way through a million little jobs to get there, and everybody has to do it in their own way.

The Englishman was Barnes, and he wore a top hat and silk tie, though he had a kind of apron on. "Have you been a mason long?" he said.

"Since I was a boy," I said.

"Have you ever made an arch?"

"Yes sir, over a fireplace," I said.

"Ours will be a little bigger," he said and looked me up and down.

"Let me see your hands," he said. He glanced at the calluses the trowel had made and sent me to the clerk, who he called "the clark."

I was signed on as a mason's helper, which hurt my pride some, I'll admit. All morning I thought of heading back up the trail for home, and letting the fine Englishman and crew build whatever bridge they wanted.

And if I thought about leaving when the clerk signed me on as an assistant, I thought about it twice when Barnes sent me away from the bridge site up the road to the quarry. It was about a mile where they had picked a granite face on the side of the mountain to blast away. One crew was drilling holes for the black powder, and another was put to dressing the rock that had already been blasted loose.

I had brought my light mason's hammer and trowel, but I was give a heavy hammer and some big cold chisels and told to cut a regular block, eighteen inches thick, two feet wide, and three feet long. The whole area was powdered with rock dust from the blasting and chipping.

"Surely you don't want all the blocks the same size?" I said to Delosier, the foreman from Charleston.

"The cornerstones and arch stones will be cut on the site," he said. "In the meantime we need more than five hundred regular blocks, for the body of the bridge." He showed me an architect's plan where every single block was already drawed in, separate and numbered.

"You're cutting block one aught three," he said.

Some of the men had put handkerchiefs over their noses to keep out the rock dust. They looked like a gang of outlaws hammering at the rocks, but there was nothing to protect their eyes. I squatted down to the rough block Delosier had assigned me. After the first few licks I felt even more like going home. It would take all day to cut the piece to the size Barnes required. I wasn't used to working on rocks that size and shape.

After a few more licks I saw where the smell in the quarry come from. I thought it was just burned black powder, but it was also the sparks from where the granite was hit by the chisels. Every time the steel eat into the granite it smoked and stunk a little. With a dozen people chipping, the whole place filled up with dust and smell.

But I kept at it. I had no choice but to keep working because I would never have another chance like that. And even then I knew that if you don't feel like working in the morning, it will get better if you just keep at it. You start out feeling awful but if you work up a sweat the job will begin taking over itself. You just follow the work, stick to the job, and the work will take care of you. I put my handkerchief over my nose and started hammering along the line I'd measured and scratched on the side of the block. I was already behind if I was going to finish that block in one day.

"You want a drink, boss?" The slave held a dipper from the bucket of water he'd just carried from the spring on the mountainside.

I pushed down the handkerchief and wiped the dust from my lips. The cold water surprised me. I had been concentrating so hard on work I'd forgotten I was thirsty. And I wasn't used to being waited on by no slave, nor called boss neither.

When we stopped for dinner everybody washed their hands in the creek and we set in the shade and opened our lard buckets. Clara had packed me some shoulder meat and biscuits. My arm was a little sore from the steady hammering. My block was cut on only one side. Delosier inspected my work and spat without commenting. I had made a clean face, but I'd have to speed up to finish that evening.

The slave that carried water had a harmonica in his pocket which he began playing. There was a slave boy named

Charlie that carried tools and messages between the quarry and bridge. "Hey Charlie," somebody was always calling, "Hey Charlie, get this bit sharpened."

Charlie started dancing to the harmonica music right there in the clearing. He started to move the toes on one foot, and then the foot itself. You could see the music traveling up his leg, up to his waist, and then out one shoulder and around till he had his hand dancing. You never saw such a sight as when he started dancing all over. The harmonica played faster, and the boy started dancing around in circles and the first thing you know he was doing somersaults all over the clearing.

Then the harmonica player moved back in the shade and slowed down and the boy slowed down too. He danced backwards getting slower, like he was winding down, slower and slower, until he stopped and the music went down one arm and through his body and down a leg until only the foot was moving, then the toes. And he stood still all over when the music stopped.

Now the funny thing was Delosier had been watching and enjoying the dancing as much as any of us. But as soon as the music stopped he said, "That's enough of that. You're wasting energy on my time. You boys can play and dance on your own time."

I didn't see no call for what he said, since it was dinner hour. But we all put our dinner buckets down to go to work, and the boy, sweating something awful from the dancing, run to sharpen more chisels. I hunkered down over my block.

"Never mind what our names are," the older boy said.

"No, I won't mind," I said.

"We'll just walk along with you a little ways, to keep you out of trouble."

I tried to remember if I'd seen them anywhere before. Chestnut Springs even then had a lot of rough people, liquor people and all. Names like Howard or Morgan kept coming to mind, but I couldn't place them. Our folks had come from South Carolina and I knowed a lot of people from Landrum and Tigerville, but I couldn't place them.

"You just got paid down at the bridge," the older boy said.

"I worked on the bridge," I said. I could have said I walked this road every morning and evening for nearly five months, and I'd never seen them.

"You wouldn't fool us," the younger one said. "We watched all them big shots from up on the mountain. And we seen all of you'uns standing around before they cut the ribbon."

"You should have come down and had some punch, and some sweetbread," I said. "One of the carriages from Greenville brought a basket of sweetbread and a keg of punch, along with a big bottle of champagne for the dignitaries."

"We got our own bottle," the older boy said.

"Can't we help you carry something," the younger brother said. He lifted a side of his vest and I seen the pistol in his belt.

"I'm doing fine," I said.

"Ain't you got something just a little too heavy for you to carry," the older one said. I noticed he had a knife about eighteen inches long stuck in his belt.

If only another carriage would come along, or if we'd meet a wagon coming back from mill, I could ask for a ride. I prayed that somebody I knowed would be walking down the mountain. But they was nothing ahead but the road through the holler, built while we was building the bridge, winding up toward Saluda Gap.

"What you got in there, Boss?" the older brother said, and prodded my pocket with the pistol.

"You got something a-ringing a regular tune," the younger one said.

"You wouldn't lie to us?" the other one said.

I stepped back, and just then I seen the rock in the younger one's hand.

11

After the first day I was almost too tired to walk back up the mountain. And the next day I was nearly too sore to lift a hammer. But I made myself keep going, and after a while I worked the soreness out. It took about a week for me to learn to cut a block a day, getting surer and ever closer to the measurements. It took ten men to slide one of those blocks up on an ox cart to carry to the bridge site. Delosier showed us how to do things with rollers and skids and pulleys you never would have dreamed of. I had never handled big stuff like that before. It looks like there ain't nothing a man can't do if he just takes time to study it out.

I got a little bit of a cough from breathing the rock dust, but after seven or eight weeks we had most of the blocks cut and moved down to the bridge itself. They had put up a frame of poles and timbers to build the arches on, and I looked close to see exactly how Barnes and Delosier done it. If a giant could pick up all the rocks of an arch and drop them into place at once you wouldn't need a frame underneath. But with regular men moving in a rock at a time, there was no other way. Delosier built a big A-frame with pulleys to hoist the stones into place. It was something to watch.

They had a spot right down by the river where we did the final dressing of blocks before they was lifted into place above. Once the arches was built we could roll everything out onto the bridge as we went, but the arches had to be put in place first. It was convenient, and cooler by the water. We wet the drills and rocks to keep down the dust.

"Everything will be fine unless there's a flash," I said to Delosier.

"What do you mean a flash?"

"A flash flood," I said. "On ground this steep it can come up a flash tide pretty quick."

"It's not the season for flash floods," Mr. Barnes, who had overheard me, said.

12

"A flash can come anytime," I said. "All you need is a cloudburst on the slope above."

"You mountain folk are so superstitious," Mr. Barnes said. "All you ever do is worry about lightning, panthers, snakes, floods, winds, and landslides."

I knowed they was truth in what he said, but it was like he was saying that I, as an assistant mason, didn't have a right to an opinion either. But I let it go and went back to work.

But along in July it come up the awfullest lightning storm you ever seen. You know how it can thunder in South Carolina, there at the foot of the mountain, after a hot day. It was like the air was full of black powder going off. We got under the trees, until we saw a big poplar on the ridge above turn to fire and explode. Splinters several feet long got flung all over the woods. We got under the first arch then, knowing the rock wouldn't draw the lightning.

"When the Lord talks, he talks big," said Furman, another mason's assistant.

The slaves got in under the cover of the arch, saying nothing. Lightning struck up on the ridge again, and it was like the air had jolted you.

"The Lord must have a lot on his mind," the harmonica player said.

"Maybe telling us how sick he is of us," another slave said.

The storm passed over for a minute and then come back, the way a big storm will. Lightning was dropping all around on the ridges above. It was so close you could hear the snap, like whips cracking, before they was any thunder. Snap-boom, snap-boom. The air smelled like scorched trees and burned air.

"This old earth getting a whippin'," the harmonica player said.

After about twenty minutes the worst of it passed, and we could hear the thunder booming and rattling on the further mountains. While it was still raining a little we got out and stood in the drizzle and the drip from the trees.

"What is that roar?" Delosier said.

"Just wind on the mountain, boss."

"No, it's coming closer."

It did sound like wind on a mountainside of trees, and my first thought was we was having a little twister. They don't come often to the mountains, but they have been known to bore down out of the sky and twist up trees.

And just then it hit me they was a flash tide coming down the valley. "It's the creek," I hollered, but no one seemed to notice.

"It's the river," I hollered again. "Let's get the tools." Must have been a dozen hammers and chisels, several T-squares and rulers, levels and trowels under the bridge. And there was an extra set of block and tackle. Only Charlie and the harmonica player seemed to hear me. They run down and got five or six of the sledgehammers, and I got one end of the big block and tackle and started to drag it up the bank.

Then everybody all at once saw the water coming. It was gold colored from the red clay and frothy as lather. The river was just swollen a little bit, as was normal after a hard rain when nearby runoff spilled into the stream. But somewhere higher up a valley had been drenched all at once, with the cloud's insides dropping into a narrow branch holler. It was not like a wall of water exactly. It was more like a stampede of furry paws rolling over each other and slanted down to a frothy front that swerved and found its way through trees and bends. Besides the foam you could see sticks and leaves and all kinds of trash tossed up and tumbled around.

Everybody pulled back from the banks at once and I had to wrap the big block and tackle around a tree. Then I run back up the hill with the rest.

That big cowcatcher of water come through the narrow valley tearing saplings loose and bending trees over till they pulled out by the roots. There was a wind with it too, a cold breeze swept down with the tide. I thought at first the bridge was going to go, the frames we had put up for the arches. But

I guess there was enough weight on them now to hold them down. The bridge was far enough along to stay intact.

"The Lord have mercy," the harmonica player kept saying.

"Oh blast, oh blast it all," Mr. Barnes said, and took off his hat as he watched the charge of water swirl through his frames and pilings and suck through the arches.

"Oh blast it all," he said.

"Everybody safe?" Delosier called.

We looked around and everybody seemed to be there, wet from the rain and white-faced with shock. The body of a mule shot by in the current, and then a chicken coop. A cart that had been used at the quarry come down. And a big black snake passed, spinning around as it tried to swim.

"The Lord almighty."

The water rose to the groin of the biggest arch, and slapped at the stones a while, then began to recede. Once the high mark was reached, the flood begun to drop quick, pulling back from the banks, drawing most of the debris with it, letting go of roots and stumps. As fast as it had come the flash shrunk back to the river bed, leaving sticks and trash in the tops of bushes and the banks scoured. You could tell how high the water went because the ground there was bare as a plucked chicken. Roots and rocks was exposed in the dripping slope.

Many tools had been washed away, and some of the blocks we was cutting had been carried down by the tide. Several logs and saplings had been lodged against the pillars of the bridge.

"Why look at that," Charlie said, and pointed to what looked like a seedbox. "Boss, I don't want to look at that," he said to Delosier. It was not a seedbox, but a pine casket, half rotted away. Everybody crowded to the box, but there was nothing in it except some rotten rags and bones.

"Don't that beat all," Delosier said.

Mr. Barnes directed four men to carry the box up the hill

and bury it above the road.

"Shouldn't we find out who it was and return it to the family?" Delosier said.

"And how do you propose to do that, sir?" Mr. Barnes said. "This could have come from anywhere upstream, and we have work to do."

As soon as they had started up the hill Mr. Barnes turned his glare on me. "Jones," he said, "You could have warned us."

"I told you it might flood," I said.

"Jones, you might have warned us effectively," he said. "From what you said I understood there was only the remotest chance of a flood, and that after days of rain."

"A flash can come up quick," I said.

"So I notice," he said. "You folk never know how to say what you mean."

The other time I saw Mr. Barnes lose his temper at me was when I put on the hoist a block that had been overchipped. The rock was already cracked a little and when I tried to smooth it up, a chunk two inches wide come off. But in a big block that didn't seem to matter. We could turn it inside and no one would know. I didn't see Mr. Barnes come up behind me as I was fixing the ropes.

"You know *perfectly* well that won't do," he said. He tapped the rock with his cane.

"We can turn that side in," I said.

"Jones," he said, "I'm disappointed in you. Hiding shoddy work. Very disappointed."

I was taken by surprise. Nobody had talked to me like that since I was a little boy. It was not what he said but the tone of his voice that was so shocking and humiliating. I had heard him scold others but it was different when he turned his scorn on me.

"Jones, if you can't meet our standards you can go back to your chimneys," he said. "Go back to your stick and mud. No one requires your presence here."

"I'm sorry, sir," I said. And immediately I was more humiliated to have apologized. It was as though his manner and his rage had pulled the apology out of me with no decision on my part, as if I had been hypnotized by his glare and his anger and had no choice.

"Well then," he said. "You'll get rid of that block and go back and cut another."

It was after he strode away that the anger and hate began rising in me, pushing aside the surprise and embarrassment. He has no right to talk to me that way, I kept saying to myself. Everybody on the job, including the slaves, heard him tell me off for almost nothing. It was like a public whipping. And not only had I felt helpless to defend myself, I had actually apologized to that limey lord-over-creation. That's why my grandpappy fit the Revolution, to get rid of such strutting peacocks, I said to myself.

"Massa Barnes sho like to have his say," the harmonica player said as we carried the hammer and chisels back to the quarry to cut the new block.

He's going to tell off one man too many, I thought to myself, and end up with a hammer in his brain. All that morning while I was chipping at the new block, measuring and marking, sweating with the excitement of my anger as well as the work, I kept running through my mind plans for revenge. The thing I wanted most was to sink my hammer through his top hat into his skull. I saw the silk collapse and blood spurt as the bones crumbled. I chuckled with pleasure at the image.

And then I saw myself doing it all with my hands, fighting fair.

"A fist in the gut and a knee in the face when they double over," my cousin Nary liked to say. While chipping that extra block I must have kneed Barnes in the face a thousand times and seen the blood gush from his nose. I hammered until my eyes was filled with sweat and my breath was coming short. I hammered like it was Barnes's head I was cutting down to size.

Of course what some fellows would do was just walk away from a job where they talked to you that bad, then come back with their gun and shoot the rawhiding foreman. And I saw myself coming back with my shotgun and filling Barnes's belly with buckshot. It would take him days to die of peritonitis as he swelled up and screamed with the pain.

I worked so hard I was plumb exhausted by dinner time, when I had to walk back down to the bridge to get my dinner bucket. And as I walked I thought I was so mad because I didn't know how to talk back to Barnes. He had took me by surprise and the cat got my tongue. And it was only words. Sticks and stones, I kept saying, sticks and stones. His hardness was what made Barnes such a good builder. I had learned a lot about masonry, and also about how to run a job—how you demand that everybody meet the standards. By the time I got to the bridge I was feeling better about the whole thing. I got my dinner bucket from the spring and set down on the bank with Delosier and the other masons. It was midsummer, and the jarflies was loud in the trees all around.

"They do sound like rattlesnakes," somebody said.

"Except a rattlesnake's not up in an oak tree."

"You can't always tell where a sound's coming from in the woods, especially if they's a big rock nearby."

Barnes come out of the little shed he used for an office. The men lived in tents, but he boarded in the Lindsay house down the river. He kept all his plans and instruments in the little office.

"Jones," he said. "We won't need that extra block after all. We've already used the block you chipped on the inside." Then he strolled away toward the spring. It was so hot he had taken his jacket off, and his armpits was wet.

I was instantly mad all over again, that he had made me waste a morning's work on that extra block. I imagined sinking an ax into his spine as he walked away.

"I never knowed him to change his mind before," Furman

said.

"He could have changed it before I wasted a morning's work," I said.

"Don't get riled up again," Delosier said. "That's the closest I've ever seen Mr. Barnes come to an apology."

That evening I went back to dressing blocks before they was hoisted into place, and was more careful than ever not to overchip a corner or side. But I didn't like Barnes anymore, and I wished the job was already over.

When I woke up on the turnpike my head hurt like thunder. My pockets was empty. I looked around for my dinner bucket. They had throwed it down the bank, and my ten-dollar gold piece was nowhere in sight. I set back down where I had crawled to and held my head, which throbbed like it was in a vise. After a whole spring and summer's work I had nothing to show. Clara had put the corn in pretty much by herself, with a little help from the kids and from my brother Joe. She was now drying peaches and apples on the rooftop, and on sheets spread out on the bank behind the house. The stock would have less fodder for the winter, and there was no money for shoes or coffee. I'd have to find another job building a chimney or springhouse wall. I had wasted half a year and all I had to show for it was a bloody knot on my head.

"You seen the big ceremony," Clara would say, "And the rich folks going up to Flat Rock for their banquet. I guess that's your pay. You can tell everybody that."

I was just going to set awhile, to catch my breath and stop my head from swimming. They was tracks all around me in the dirt, but I knowed I could never identify them big rough brothers from their tracks, which could have been made by anybody's big brogans.

My head hurt so bad I thought it must be cracked. And I felt thirsty. They was a spring in the bend about a mile ahead. I'd have to stumble up there if I was to have a drink. I was about to gather my strength and try to stand when I heard somebody holler.

The mountainside was steep there, and it was hard to tell where the sound come from. But while I was looking and holding the back of my head this cow come around the bend ahead, this big red cow, and then another, and two more, and three or four others, and still more behind them. Boys with switches run along beside them. They just kept coming down the turnpike like a flash flood of beef, hooking and slobbering.

"Stand aside," one of the boys called. "Hey mister, stand aside."

I stumbled to my feet and backed over the edge of the road and stood in the leaves as they trotted past. They was men behind popping their whips, and the boys with hickories run alongside hollering, "Aye, aye" when one of the animals slowed or started to turn aside.

You never seen so many cattle. They must have passed for twenty minutes, raising the dust and bawling, lifting their tails and spraying the ruts. Finally along come the end of it, a wagon loaded with cooking gear and blankets.

"Where you coming from?" I asked the driver.

"Why friend, we've driv these cattle all the way from Tennessee," the man said.

"Where you going?" I said.

"Wherever they buy cattle," he said. "Augusta, maybe Atlanta."

Then they was gone, and the dust settled in the late summer light coming through the trees.

Son, I stepped into the road and started back up the mountain. But I hadn't took more than ten steps when somebody hollered behind me, "Step aside, sir. Step aside."

I looked back and there was the prettiest carriage you ever seen, with a black driver all in livery carrying his long stiff whip. They was lanterns of polished brass and glass on the corners and shiny black fenders. You never seen people dressed up like them inside, ladies with parasols and dresses so low you could nearly see the nipples on their bosoms, and men in top hats and silk cravats. And behind that carriage was other carriages, and buggies, and a whole bunch of wagons carrying supplies and servants. It was some big party from the Low Country coming up for a picnic in the mountains. I've heard Fremont, the general and governor of California, was in that party. He was just a boy then. I stood back and let them pass, and they ignored me just like I was air.

Then when I did get started up the turnpike finally, stepping around cowpiles and horse apples, my strength coming back a little at a time, I met more drovers coming down the mountain. It was like they had opened a flood gate and flocks of sheep came along, baaing and pushing and jumping over each other, turning the road to dirty wool. And then a drove of hogs came, nosing and grunting, squealing when prodded by boys with sticks. I thought I had seen it all by then, but all of a sudden around the bend come a flock of turkeys, all gobbling and squawking. And behind them a bigger flock of geese come waddling, driven by more boys and followed by an old woman who carried a sack on her back.

"We's come all the way from Kentucky," she said.

Finally I thought I had the road to myself. I knowed I'd have to hurry if I was to get home by milking time. Clara was going to be mad, but they was no point in putting off the bad news.

"Watch out, watch out, sir," somebody called behind me.

It was a man in a buggy pulled by a shiny Morgan that just clipped along. He had a sack on the seat beside him. And I recognized Sam the peddler from Spartanburg. He used to come around with a pack on his back, and we almost always bought cloth and buttons and such from him and asked him to stay for dinner. And now he was driving a fine buggy with a carriage horse.

After he passed it seemed late in the evening. The road was already nearly in shadow. They was a buckeye laying in the tracks, but I couldn't tell if it was mine. It had been stepped on by a cow and I let it go. But I seen something shiny in the dirt ahead. It was my light mason's hammer. Them big rough boys had dropped it there as they run away. They didn't have no use for a mason's hammer, and thought it was too heavy to carry. I picked it up and wiped the grit off the handle and head, then started again for home.

WATERSHED

Boy, what I'm about to tell you I ain't told nobody for a long time and I probably won't tell it again, 'cause them that know it are gone and them that come after don't need to know, for that time is past. It was a time of building up this valley and clearing land. But I want somebody to know these things. It's the war now and all the outlawing and bushwhacking that has remembered them to me. The air has the smell of burning and every patch of woods seems dangerous.

It is the memory of the face of that Cherokee girl brings it back on me all of a sudden, the march and the hollering. She wasn't no bigger than you are now. I was just big enough to carry a gun.

They's things we do we never did plan on nor think we could do. Sometimes it's good we don't know what we have inside us, things that are just happens in the heat of the moment, you might say. When these outliers we got coming around here now started out, they didn't mean to be outlaws I would say, most of them. It was just a happen. They never made any decision to be outlaws when they deserted or was wounded and got left behind. My guess is, after taking the first chicken they found it easy to take a ham from some unlocked smokehouse, and after that ham a whole pig or cow, and a horse to tote their loot away. They never made a choice, until they later realized a choice had been made. Next they was stealing corn from widow women and slapping little kids to make them tell where the silver was buried. And now they'll kill a man for a pound of shot or an ounce of salt.

Boy, I don't want you to think them are devils that held you against the wall and took your pocket knife and hurt your arm to make you tell them where the powder was hid.

Only people around here's got any shot these days is the McBains, and everybody knows the Cherokee told them where the secret lead mine was. You can make powder from charcoal and saltpeter and a little brimstone. But lead can't be made out of nothing but lead, and it just comes out of the ground and has to be melted down.

Guns was long and heavy in them days, and Pappy had just give me my own which he bought when he took some hams down to Greenville. And I'd already done a little hunting, for squirrels and wild turkeys. They was deer then aplenty, and panthers back in the coves, and bears using all around on Olivet and in the Flat Woods.

The Cherokee never lived here much. It had been their land since they took it from the Catawbas, but all their towns was over on the Tuckasegee and Little Tennessee and some down in Georgia and South Carolina. This was their hunting ground where they come through once or twice a year to run deer with fire and to fish. They had trails and camps all up and down the valley, and even a few Old Fields where they must have raised corn to eat when they camped here. You'd see these clearings in the woods when the white people got here that must have been used by the Indians since the beginning of time. And some of the fields they might have played ball in too, for they was like kids playing ball for days without stopping.

But our people poured into this valley after the Revolution like flies going to molasses. The new state didn't recognize it as Indian land and sold it off in big tracts to Colonel Davis and such as your great-great-grandpa. Some people, like the McBains, who had been Loyalists and was hiding out, had already come and had doings with the Indians and learned herbs and witchcraft from them, as well as the location of the secret lead mine.

The Cherokee had sent a party to raid the settlements. They's no doubt that's what they come for. They had a camp right up at the head of the river, upper edge of what we call the Abe Jones Flats. And boy, I'm telling you them Indians was wild. It was liquor they liked most to steal, but the truth was they'd steal anything, stock out of the woods, chickens out of a henhouse, guns and powder.

They'd been any number of people that lost sheep and hogs to them. They burned the Revis cabin up on Rock Creek, and took Charles MacDowell's girl where they caught her by the spring and ruint her. Nobody knowed where they might show up next.

So word went out—Old Man Bayne was kind of the organizer—for all the men to meet with their rifles up at the ford where Cedar Springs Church is now. They was no church in all the valley then.

I was both hoping and fearing I would get to go. I was about eleven or twelve. That was near the turn of the century.

"No, you can't let David go," Mama said. "He's my baby boy."

"He's old enough to carry his own gun, and he can go," Pappy said.

It was dark when we left home, the clearest night in November. It would have been perfect for coon hunting except the moon was only in its quarter.

I remember saying to myself as we left the milkgap that I might never see the place again. It was hog-killing time and Mama give me a hot biscuit with tenderloin to eat on my way out.

It was a strange night. I skipped along gripping my cold gun. We went by lantern light up the river road, which was just a track. And they was lights all over the mountains. You might have thought they was stars except they moved around. And they was a blue light in the hollow above Cabin Creek.

We seen lights hovering in the woods on Thunderhead, and lights gliding along over the river. The night was so quiet you could hear somebody stumble way up on the ridge, or a horse shake its bridle half a mile away.

What's that? Sure I was scared, and shivering with excitement at the same time.

There at the ford all the men stood around a fire, hardly talking. Some was loading their guns and sharpening long knives. Somebody had a jug of whiskey but Old Man Bayne said, "Stopper that thing up. We ain't gone have no drinking till the job is done. Then you can fill your skin all you please."

It was long before daybreak when we started up the river on the north side. You know how the valley gets narrow there above the Ward place and winds back into the mountains. Sometimes the valley is so pinched the road has to go through water. We sloshed along quiet as we could. I remember Phil Bailey who was my own age was along, but he didn't say much either. It was about eight miles from the ford to the headwaters and we didn't want to get there after daylight.

I can still smell the witch hazel blooming along the river. It blooms after the leaves have gone. You've seen the pretty blossoms like parched corn in the November woods, sometimes even blooming after a snow. Something would plop into the river from time to time, but I don't think it was trout feeding at that time of the year. It must have been a muskrat or mink dropping into the water when we scared it. One time we smelled a skunk ahead, but I'm glad it never throwed its juice on us in the dark. You couldn't surprise nobody with polecat fumes all over you.

Boy, what I'm saying is this march felt like something out of the Bible, a mission, a crusade on the orders of the Lord. When they ruint the MacDowell girl the Indians signed their doom in this valley. I weren't even sure how she was "ruint" but I knowed it was bad. They was a long line of men on the trail and you could feel their fear and determination. Yes, it was mostly fear. In the dark woods they was many a heart

26

running away with itself.

The headwaters of the river is one of my favorite places. Don't you like the way the stream kind of winds and shimmies back into the high mountains, like it was bouncing off one mountain wall and then another? And the voice of the water echoes in the narrow gorge so it sounds like people are calling to you, or drowned people are wailing and talking inside the shoals and trout pools. The tall hemlocks go right down to the water's edge and reach up toward the cliffs. And they's a big rock that one time rolled down the mountain and lodged right by the river, which we call the Prayer Rock. The first time I reckon it was called that was when we stopped there and Old Man Bayne took off his hat and prayed.

"Lord aid us in our struggle against the heathen, against the children of darkness," he said. "Guide our hand as it is raised against thy foes."

"Amen," the men all said. And I said "Amen" too for the first time.

"We're going to run them out of the watershed," Pappy said when we started out. And all that time we was walking up the river I kept rolling that word on my tongue and around in my mind. You know how it is when a word gets caught on your tongue and you can't stop saying it. I must have heard the word "watershed" a hundred times before that night, but I'd never noticed it before.

First, the word suggested some kind of building, like a spring house or well cover. And I had heard the term "water closet" but knowed it was something different. But "watershed" sounded like a place where great barrels of water might be stored.

I heard Pappy say a "watershed" was all the region that drained into a river when it rained. It was the big curved and wrinkled bowl of land that fed its runoff into a stream, gathering from the branches and seep springs all the way up to the line of dividing water along the ridge top. That was the words I already knew before that night, "dividing water," the place where rainfall and runoff was parted and some sent one way all the way to the Atlantic coast while a drop adjoining it goes all the way to the Ohio and down the Mississippi to the Gulf of Mexico. I seen it as the place a decision is made close up in just a matter of a fraction of an inch yet it has such a long-range consequence.

As I walked along the dark trail beyond the Prayer Rock, thrilled by the sound of whitewater, I kept thinking about a drop that might lay right on the very top of the ridge for a while, not able to make up its mind which way to go, until slowly, so slow you wouldn't notice it, the droplet edged to one side of a leaf and was caught for a long time until others going around it pushed it along. It would be a while, at that elevation, before it was clear what decision had been made, where it was going.

That night I heard Old Man Bayne talking to Pappy and the others, saying things like, "The rascals is camped almost right on the watershed," and it occurred to me the word could mean the very line of dividing water itself, not just the area that drained into a river. And I thought if they was camped right at the lip of the watershed, it might be like we could just tip them over, tilt them a little, and they would run down the other side into the French Broad valley and go all the way to Tennessee. Maybe it would take just a little nudge to make them vanish over the rim of the mountains and never come back.

The long rifle seemed to weigh a hundred pounds in my arms by the time we got halfway up the river. I carried it in my hands and I carried it in the crook of my arm and then I toted it on my shoulder.

"Don't point that thing at me," the Jones boy behind me said. I think he must have had something to drink because he kept stumbling over every rock and root and turn in the path. My gun was loaded and I knowed his was too. If he stumbled and hit the hammer he could fire right into my back. It was me that should be worried.

What's that? No, I'd never seen an Indian except twice. By then they was mostly gone from the river valley. We seen one down at the store at Crossroads when we went to trade eggs for some cloth. Mama said, "Look, there's one of them red devils," and I expected to see a tall man with feathers on his head. But it was a man dressed pretty much like us except he had long hair. He had a pistol in his hand and looked like he had been drinking. Preacher Jarrett was there at the store and he said, "Halfmoon, you go on home now. Ain't nobody gone bother you. Go on home."

But the Indian had a grin. I don't know if he was a normal Indian or not, or if maybe he was just drunk. But he had that grin that scared me because they was no reason for it. I think he was afflicted somehow.

But the other time was when I was out looking for ginseng. They was plenty of it there on the ridge at the jump-off into South Carolina and way back in some of the coves. You have to dig it when the leaves is on, otherwise you can't find it. And that meant if you did any digging, if you did any digging at all, it had to be after the corn was laid by in July and before fodder-pulling time in August and early September. That's why revival meetings was held then, and baptizings, when they was a preacher come through, which wasn't too often back then. But if you waited till after fodder-pulling time, say into squirrel season, you risked a frost coming and the leaves falling off, and you couldn't find any sang to save your soul.

So I was out in the Dog Days, in the snake-crawling time and the spider web time, when I was scared every jarfly I heard was a rattler and every twig a sting worm. You couldn't see far in the woods with all the leaves, so you felt closed in.

I was going along looking at the ground, looking for sang, maybe looking for bear tracks too. They was bears using on the upper edge of South Carolina. And I was swatting at bugs and knocking cobwebs out of the way when I looked up along the ridge and there was this Indian standing among the trees so still you couldn't tell if he was there or not. I figured it was an Indian 'cause I could see this braid down the side of his face and he didn't have no shirt on. He stood there and I thought it might be the stump of an old tree or something I just dreamed.

But he was looking at me, like an owl when you see him is already looking at you. I froze to my tracks like I'd seen a rattler. The sweat was coming down into my eyes and I had to brush it away. My temples was sweating and I thought my heart was going to leap out of my chest. Maybe I could start running down the mountain and beat him back to the settlements. My eyes distorted with the sweat in them, like when you've been crying and the world bulges and blurs, or is kind of magnified like you're looking under water. I had to wipe away the sweat that was stinging my eyes, and when I looked again the Indian was gone. That was the scariest part of it all. One instant he was looking at me and then the next he was gone just like that. I looked all up and down the line of the ridge and there was nothing but trees, and no tree big enough for him to hide behind. I run up to the top and looked down, and they was a little slick of laurel bushes a hundred yards down and he could have been hiding in the laurels. But I didn't even see any kicked-up leaves where he run down there. The trash on the ground looked untouched.

It was like he had been a ghost that just flitted away. I've often thought the woods was haunted by the Indians. Every ridge and creek was named by them, you know. "Green River" itself is the English of whatever they called the stream. And they've buried so many dead in the ground you're might nigh afraid of turning up a bone when you dig in it. Every time you hear a waterfall or shoals you think you can hear an Indian talking in it. The mist coming up out of hollows of an evening looks like smoke from their fires. In fall everything seems dabbed with warpaint.

Walking along that night every time we passed a shoals I thought I could hear Cherokees talking. I wondered if the other men was scared as I was. Surely the Indians would hear us coming. Maybe we was walking right into their trap. Maybe they was watching us from behind rocks and laurel clumps.

It was getting light when we stopped at the forks just below the Abe Jones Flats. The river had been broke into so many branches by that time it was just a little creek anyway. There one branch goes off into Sister Mountain, and the other, the main branch, goes right up through the flats toward the first spring this side of the divide where Blue Ridge Church is now. We gathered by the forks there in the first light, and it was hard to believe such a little stream could be the same as Green River. It was just a little fist of water knocking around on the rocks, the clear muscle rippling and foaming like lace around wrists of clear water. I could almost step across it. It seemed like a toy river, for a kid to play in, somehow shrunk down and made clearer.

"Sh-h-h-h," Old Man Bayne said. "We're going to surprise them in their huts."

"What if they's already up?" Jody McBain said.

"They won't be," Old Man Bayne said. "Indians is lazy."

"Let's burn them out," John Maddox said.

"No, we'll shoot first, shoot all we can," Old Man Bayne said. "Then we'll burn their huts out later."

He didn't pray again, and we started off, going quiet as we could. A mist was rising off the stream in the cold air. The poplars and chestnut trees had shed all their leaves and the wet leaves was quiet as long as nobody kicked them. We circled along the edge of the Flats. The Old Field there had grown up in briars and hogweed, but you could still see a few rotten corn stalks where the Indian women had farmed it at one time. I followed Pappy, and we stayed crouched down behind the hazel bushes. I must have been scared then, but I was too busy to think, now that we was there.

For the longest time I couldn't see a thing. There was just bushes, and mist rising off the branch. Then Pappy tapped me on the shoulder and pointed. And I seen at the end of his finger a cloth hung on a bush like it had been put out today. And they was a hut. It was more like a shack or lean-to, just propped up on poles and covered with bark. It looked like they had heaped leaves over it to make it hard to see. But you never seen such a crude thing for people to live in. It looked like it would smash down if a breeze come up. We stooped down there in the bushes trying to see how many they was.

They was a smolder where the fire must have been the night before. And then all at once we seen the girl. It looked like she was tied to a birch tree. Her feet and hands was bound and she was tethered to that tree. She was covered all over with dirt, like she had been rolling in a struggle.

Everybody thought the same thing at first, that it was a white girl they had captured and tied up there to hold for ransom. You couldn't really tell much about her, she was so dirty and covered with leaves.

"Kill every one of them," Old Man Bayne whispered. And we commenced firing into the huts. What happened next is like it's been magnified over the years.

In the still morning it sounded like a thousand cannon started firing as the echoes bounced off the mountains and rattled around. We run across the branch and shot into the huts, then stopped to reload in the field.

It didn't take more than two seconds for the yard to be full of Indians crawling out in the clearing and waving knives. One old man who had a pistol wheeled around and aimed at me, and I felt this hot itch on my shoulder. There was blood running down my arm and on my trigger finger. But I had reloaded and was running toward the tree where the girl was tied. They was firing and screams all around me, and so much smoke it was hard to see.

The girl had crawled around and was shivering against the birch tree, her legs drawn up. It was the first time I had seen a woman's private parts. She couldn't have been no age at all because her hair down there was just flossy. She was bound up so she couldn't run or defend herself.

Looking back through the years I still don't know if she was being punished or if she had been captured. But she was an Indian girl all right. And the chance is she might have been afflicted in her mind, or had tried to kill herself, and they had tied her up for her own good.

I must have just stood there and looked at her. She was about my age and she had dust and dirt all over her. They was the old dirt that looked black and gray on her skin and they was the new dirt stuck like flour where she had rolled over and crawled away from the shooting. She was dressed in rags so that even her little titties was showing.

But the look on her face I won't never forget no matter if I live to be a hundred. It was the look I still seen when it was all over and the camp just a smolder of sticks and trash and bodies laying around in the brush along the branch where they tried to run. It was the face I seen after the Indians was all buried in the Old Field below the head spring.

I've tried to make sense of things, boy, by talking to preachers when things troubled me. And I've tried to find out from the Bible what portents was listed and events foretold. And most times it seemed to work. Like when I was courting your grandma over on Willow and it bothered me was I doing the right thing. How was I to know what to decide? My mama didn't want no daughter-in-law from over that side of the mountain. She'd never be happy living away from her folks over here. Mama said a girl needs to talk to her ma. Pappy said he'd never been too sure of anybody with Nickelson blood. It was a line that was dangerous, going back to Severance Nickelson that killed two men in duels back in the early days of the county. You never knowed when the crazy or fittified streak might show up again. I worried about this and studied it for months. 'Cause I had my heart set already on that gal from Willow. But the preacher wasn't no help. And I opened the Bible just anywheres looking for a verse that would guide me. Nothing I put my finger on seemed to fit.

So it come this Sunday when I had to make up my mind. She was a popular girl your Grandma was. And she was a healthy girl that wanted a family.

"You make up your mind," she said. "'Cause my mind is made up." She knowed how much I cared for her but time was wasting and a girl is more concerned than a man about days slipping away. That was the awfullest week of my life. I knowed if I didn't go back by Sunday she'd know it was off and might marry one of the boys over there. They was lots would have been happy to have her.

Every night I'd lay there thinking about what to do. And I knowed the rest of my life would depend on what I choosed. Even while I was milking and while I was stripping tanbark and going through the motions of eating, I meditated on the decision. I fell off so bad Mama said I looked like a whippoor-will. Victuals didn't interest me. They's nothing as painful as being in love. Hate is almost peaceful compared to love.

One evening, it must have been a Friday, I was coming in from the barn and seen how red the sky was in the west. And I thought, I'll go by the signs. If it's rainy on Sunday the Lord means me not to go over on Willow to marry the Nickelson girl. And if it's clear weather he means me to go and I'll go no matter what my folks say or the preacher says. I felt better then 'cause it was decided, it was out of my hands. But the next day it was raining, and it rained all day. And when I milked and put up the stock it was still raining and foggy in the river valley. I didn't sleep a bit all that night thinking how I'd live my life without that girl. But when I tried to think about marrying another one, somebody from Green River, I knowed I couldn't. So I said I'll go marry her whatever it's doing. But soon after daylight the mist on the valley begun to rise up in rags and the sun cut through. I put on my best suit of clothes and walked over the mountain to get my girl and bring her back.

As we run into the little clearing where the Indian camp was, you could smell the stink of the place. I don't mean it was some awful smell like carrion, but it had a peculiar odor, the way I think of Indians smelling, like smoke and old grease and sour milk. And they had a bunch of hides stretched out on pegs in the ground, and meat drying on a rack of limbs.

I don't think nobody fired from his shoulder except for the first round. After we reloaded and run forward it was mostly firing from the hip at Indians on the run, or right into the chest of a brave or old woman if they stood to put up a fight. Out of the corner of my eye I seen the Jones boy run after one woman until she got almost into the pines. She was a fat woman and couldn't run fast. And she was carrying something like a bundle of sticks, but it must have been, now that I think about it, some skins or rolls of cloth which was her most valuable possession. She run to the trees with the Jones boy right after her and he wouldn't fire at her back. He was waiting for her to turn around. And just before she got to the pines she did turn around like she was maybe going to surrender. She had long gray hair that flung around over her face. I thought for a second she was just going to glare at her attacker, defying him to kill her. But she hurled the bundle in his face and he shot her down.

"Don't just stand there like a fool," Pappy called as he kicked and hacked at a bark hut, until a boy run out. Pappy shot him in the head and the body kept running for a few steps until it stumbled in a heap against a pole. Then Pappy kicked that miserable shed down to make sure nobody else was hiding in it.

The girl on the ground looked at me like a dog that has been cornered. She kicked at me with her tied feet and she would have hit or bit me if she had got loose. I wondered for a second if the thing to do was to cut her loose and let her run for it, or fight for it. Maybe I could take her prisoner. I couldn't hardly bring myself to just shoot her there against the tree. That wasn't what we had come to do: we had come to run them out.

My hands was trembling so I could hardly point the gun at her. She kept rolling around in the dust, getting out of the way of my aim.

"Let's go," Old Man Bayne hollered at me when he seen me pausing. He didn't mean "let's leave," but "let's get on with it. Hurry up and get the job done." Just then an Indian come up behind him with an ax and I seen the blade split right down through his hat and face. The face sliced like a piece of pine wood and blood poured out.

I turned just a little and shot that Indian so he fell almost on top of Old Man Bayne, both of them not more than twenty feet away.

So there I was unloaded. And the Indian girl thrashed around like a dead chicken, twisting her tether. She was sweating and picked up more dirt and pieces of leaves as she rolled. She tried to kick the gun out of my hand as I started to reload. I had to back out of her range.

I had a knife and could have cut her throat, or cut her loose. And there was the ax nearby sunk in Old Man Bayne's face. But I kept reloading while the furor continued around me. My hands shook so, powder spilled on the ground and on my wrists. I dropped at least one shot on the ground trying to place it in the barrel. Then the ramrod just seemed to not go in the mouth of the barrel. I backed further away and it must have took me two minutes to get the thing reloaded and cocked.

By then so many Indians had run out of the clearing and our men had followed to hunt them the place was about deserted except for bodies. I edged back up to the girl, still wondering what to do with her. Her dress had got torn worse and her breasts was sticking out and covered with dust. I was like somebody fascinated and unable to move. I stepped closer and reached out a hand and she heaved up at me and spit on my leg. I wondered if she had been bit by a mad dog and that was the reason she was tied up. I couldn't see any wounds on her, though with all that dirt and trash stuck to her legs, it was hard to tell. She looked at me with eyes like she might be in a fever. They had a glassy look you see in a cow's eyes when she's got milk fever. I thought there must be some way to let her go. Maybe I could just walk away and leave her. But then somebody else would shoot her and call me coward.

Just then an old man Indian come back into the clearing. He crossed the branch like he had escaped from his pursuer and wanted to see about his folks, or find out if we was still there. First thing I seen, besides his long white hair going down to his shoulders, was this musket he was carrying. I seen it all in just a smidgeon of a second. He raised the musket and I dodged sideways as a ball hit me in the thigh. It burned like a red-hot iron going through the leg. Just at the same time Pappy returned and hollered at me to watch out as he shot the old man in the back soon as he had pulled the trigger on me.

It happened so fast just as I meant to untie the afflicted girl. It was like I was following through my intentions of going to her. But as I got near her, the awful pain in my thigh, with Pappy calling as he run forward, I found myself aiming at her chest. Her eyes was neither defiant nor surrendering. She didn't exactly laugh at me, but she panted like somebody trying to laugh and nodding their head. I tell you she was a loony.

"Hey boy," Pappy called. And I shot her.

"We got them," Pappy said. "I think we got them all." But I didn't feel nothing but pain in my shoulder and in my thigh as the others returned and combed through the ruins. It was like the day had got dim. Pappy made me a kind of crutch from a maple fork and they cut a couple of poles to carry Old

Man Bayne's body on.

Maybe it was overcast. It was still so early in the morning we'd get back to the settlement by dinner time. Everybody went through the wrecked huts to see what they could find. But them people didn't have a thing but some corn and dried meat. They had some cloth that had been stole from the Bayne house, and a few pots and baskets. But I don't guess they was ten musket balls between them all. I brought back a boy's bow and arrows that smelled smoky. I had them for years, but your Daddy must have lost them when he was a little boy.

As we walked back down the river we seemed to go faster than we had come up, even though they had to carry me part of the way. I was hurting bad by the time we got to the ford, and Pappy bound my leg with a piece of buckskin. The river got bigger and wider, and several times Pappy give me a drink of cold water. I was glad to see tended land again.

You could see clear and far that morning, though the light was dimmer. It was November weather. The houses and barns and picked cornfields stood out sharp as we went on and groups broke off at their places or the mouths of hollers. It must have been the pain that made everything stand out sharp.

They seemed more cabins and clearings along the river than had been there the night before. We come to one after another. I don't reckon any had been built during the night, but it seemed they was more cleared ground and trails, and the houses and barns had multiplied.

THE SAL RAEBURN GAP

Soon as I came over the rise out of the Long Holler I thought I could see the whore's house. At least I could see a reflection on something, a window, a piece of mirror, a quartz rock shining its light through the trees.

"You can't hardly miss it," Pa said. "It's the only house on the trail beyond Big Springs."

The trail went down again into the laurels and I lost sight of whatever it was flashing up ahead. But I knowed I was close.

"When you get to the whore's house don't you go in," Mama had said. "You stand out in the yard and holler for Grandpa till he comes out."

It smelled different way back there. That far from the settlements there wasn't any scent of woodsmoke or plowed ground, or hogpens. It was all woods, the moldy smell of wet woods drying in the late winter sun. I'd never been that far back before. Grandpa and me once came sang hunting almost to the foot of the Long Holler, but then turned back because it was late in the day. There was ginseng all over the mountains back there. You could practically smell the roots in the wet ground under the brown leaves.

My feet was sore going down into the laurels, for the shoes Grandpa bought back in the fall in Greenville was near wore out and my feet had growed. And I wasn't used to walking that far. Another month and it would be barefoot time anyway. Meanwhile I had to get to the whore's house.

I hadn't seen a soul since I passed the Hince Anders cabin back before the Long Holler. A woman stood over a washpot beside the cabin, working her trouble stick in the column of smoke and steam, in the early morning chill.

"Where you going, boy?" she called.

"Going up to the Sal Raeburn Gap, to the whore's house," I said.

"You be careful, boy," she called. "Most people go up there never come back."

I shivered walking past her clearing. There was still frost on the ground that early, and a whirlwind had got loose in her little cornpatch and was stirring up the shucks and leaves in a twister that leaned toward the woods. And there was crows everywhere around, on the trees, and on the clothesline.

Hince Anders that used to live there had killed Arley MacDowell and disappeared. I'd heard the story ever since I was a baby, how Arley got on a drunk and said he was going up to the Gap to see the whore. And people warned him she was being looked after now by Hince. Well, Arley came all the way up here and saw the whore, and him and Hince got to drinking and gambling and got in a fight. And Hince up and shot him and disappeared out west, they said. They had to carry the body all the way down the trail, his family did, through the Long Holler and out by Big Springs because you never could get a wagon up that mountain. I shuddered just thinking about where I was headed.

There was somebody on the trail above. I heard a twig break, and a kind of tinkling sound. I stopped and everything was quiet. There was nothing but a peckerwood on an oak tree. But I had heard the tinkle. It seemed like the woods was watching me. I walked slow and careful on the trail, gripping the dirt with my old shoes. There was nobody on the trail. I breathed deep and went on.

Suddenly there was a shaking in the laurel bushes and a snake came flying at me and landed at my feet. I jumped back clear into the bushes on the other side of the path.

"If it was a snake it would have bit you," a voice said, and a man in a black hat stood up in the laurels and laughed. He held a sack full of something that tinkled like glass jars or jugs all knocking together.

"Scared you, didn't I boy?" he said, and laughed again. His hat had slid over sideways he laughed so hard, but he held onto the sack.

"Killed him just down the trail," he said. "But he was still sleepy from winter and didn't even rattle or coil."

The snake lay still in the trail, its head crushed. I stepped around it.

"You be careful, boy," the man called as he swung the sack over his shoulder and headed down the trail. "They's been a panther in the woods. And you watch out for the old gal in the Gap. She likes little boys. She eats them for breakfast." He disappeared around the bend still laughing.

I hurried on up the trail. It was getting steep again, toward the main gap, and I knowed I couldn't be too far from the cabin.

Why would Grandpa come all this way? I asked myself again. Why would he worry Mama and Pa and the whole family to come up here?

The trail wound around through the laurels and came out in a high clearing. Pa said the water from the Gap drained into South Carolina, and flowed all the way to the Gulf of Mexico. It seemed like a different world from the one I had left that morning. There was a little cornpatch around the cabin, and pokeweeds was punching up through the crust of dirt and stubble, same as back home, but it seemed different. There was just a woodshed behind the house, and a little chicken coop. The front window shined in the sun. Before I got closer than a hundred yards a dog commenced barking. It was a big cur chained to a post of the porch.

"Don't you go in that house," Mama had said. "You holler for Grandpa out in the yard."

I sure wasn't going to get even close to that porch.

I stopped by a tub where somebody had once made lye soap. It had been a while, but you could still see ashes scattered on the ground, and the staves was bleached white.

"Grandpa," I yelled. "I've come for you."

The cur growled and barked again, and ran out to the end of his chain. I felt out of breath from the long walk. I'd started before daylight. It must be ten miles back down to the river valley and the settlements.

"Grandpa!" I hollered loud as I could. "It's time to go home!" But my voice didn't seem to have any effect. The dog quieted for a minute, and I could hear the hens in the coop behind the cabin putting up a fuss. Seemed like something stirred behind a window, and then it was still. I felt strange standing there, so high on the mountain, a little breeze coming up the slope across the corn patch, pushing smoke aside from the chimney.

"You'll have to send Little Brad," Mama had said. They called me Little Brad because Grandpa was Big Brad and I had been named for him. "You'll have to send Little Brad 'cause ain't nobody else he'll pay mind to."

"It's dangerous up the Long Holler," Aunt Martha said. "I wouldn't send no boy of mine up there."

"Brad's near grown," Pa said. "A boy twelve years old's nigh grown. But he can take his gun."

"Can't take no gun," Mama said. "That's just asking for trouble."

"Nobody but Brad can fetch him when he gets like this," Pa said.

They sent me after Grandpa once before, when he got to drinking and running after a whore down at the cottonmill. I knowed Grandpa thought about women most of the time, but he didn't run after them but when he was drinking, which was maybe once a year. He'd stay sober and go to church and not even tell dirty jokes around the preacher for a long time. Then it would just kind of build up in him, especially in the early spring. He'd shave twice a week in front of the mirror on the porch, and keep his overalls clean.

I was his favoritest. Ever since I was a little kid he'd give me nickels and let me work with him. I set in his lap and explored the bib pockets of his overalls and counted the money in his pocketbook. He took me rabbit hunting and bought me a .22 rifle when I was eleven.

"Can't nobody get through to Grandpa when he's drunk but Little Brad," Mama said.

So I had to put on my old shoes and start out. Somebody had seen him going past Big Springs, so we knowed where he was headed. Sal was the biggest whore in the country, and I knowed Grandpa. When he got to studying on women it was like there was nothing he could do. And he had come here before, when both him and her was younger.

I'd heard about Sal Raeburn Gap since I was a kid, and it always give me a shiver to hear the name, for it suggested awful things that happened up there, way beyond Big Springs and the Flat Woods.

I remember Grandpa and a bunch of men talking around the store about how Kyle Goings had found this Spanish coin, a big thing of gold and heavy as a silver dollar. It had a face on it, and fancy writing. He took it to the school principal at Flat Rock and they said it was Spanish, from way back two or three hundred years ago, dropped there in the woods by explorers, or Indians that had traded with the Spanish. It was the prettiest thing, and Kyle said he found it back in the Sal Raeburn Gap.

"I'll bet you found something else there just as pretty," Grandpa said.

"I was looking for sang," Kyle said, his face turning red.

"I'll bet you was," Grandpa said, and laughed so hard he had to spit out his tobacco to keep from swallowing it.

"The principal said it was the king of Spain on that coin,"

Kyle said.

"Well the king of Spain will never get it back," Grandpa said. "How much was it worth?"

"He said it was worth two or three hundred dollars at least," Kyle said.

"Now you can afford to go to the Sal Raeburn Gap," Grandpa said.

When Grandpa got to drinking the first thing he wanted to do was go off and find him a whore. He took the wagon down to Chestnut Springs a few times, and one of the Hargis boys brought him back sick and laying in the wagon. Another time he went off on the train to Asheville, and Mama had to get her purse and hat and go over there in the train herself to find him. But when he came back nobody said much about it. Grandpa just rested a day or two, and then he was back out in the woods same as before, cutting stovewood and hewing crossties. Once it was over nobody talked about Grandpa going off, like it would never happen again. He'd stand up at prayer meeting maybe and testify he had been a sinner and was thankful the Lord had brought him back in the way he should go. But everybody in the family pretended like it had never happened. It was like Grandpa was a little child that done wrong and was brought back home.

"Grandpa, I come for you," I hollered again. The breeze had shifted and the smoke from the chimney found me. I had to brush it away to breathe. I thought I heard a racket inside the cabin. The cur growled again, its hackles stiff.

But nobody came to the window or door. I thought there was another rustling inside, but I couldn't be sure, not with the cur shaking his chain and the hens clucking behind the house.

"Grandpa, come on out," I hollered. I was mad at Grandpa for making me come all that way, and leaving me standing out there on my sore feet. I was tired and hungry too. There wouldn't be a thing to eat till we got back. And it was ten miles to go down the trail to the river valley. I picked up a rock and throwed it on the roof, but the shingles was old and mossy, and the rock just rolled off without making much of a noise.

The clearing in the Gap wasn't much bigger than an acre or two. The wind was just a whisper in the air, and you felt high up in the sky. I turned around and noticed for the first time how far you could see. From the yard you could look way down over the Long Holler to the Flat Woods. Big Springs was hid in its cove, but you could see beyond to the river valley. There was a little green, and the red of plowed fields way down there. I thought maybe I could see the roof of Grandpa's barn up by the pasture, but it was too far away. There wasn't nothing between me and Tryon Mountain that way; and Pinnacle loomed way over to the north. Whoever cleared this patch wanted to be high up and far away from anybody. I didn't see how things would grow up there, excepting wind-runted trees and a few snakes. But obviously somebody had put in a little corn.

Grandpa said in the old days people cleared off the mountaintops before the valleys, because the trees high up was smaller and fewer. In the valley it was all swamps and vines and poison ash. They'd cut down trees all winter and heap them in big piles. When spring came they set the logs on fire and you could see them terrible bonfires on the tops of mountains in the night, far as you could look. Folks had gatherings then, roasting potatoes in the coals and singing and calling to the groups on other ridges. Grandpa said the whole sky would be lit up red with the fires, and the piles was so big they burned all night and sometimes for three or four days.

I never seen a person who liked to cut trees as much as Grandpa. He'd been clearing land since he was a boy, before the Confederate War. Him and his brothers spent their lives clearing new ground above the creek. And sure as he seen a stand of big trees anywhere he'd say, "If I was a young man again I'd like to cut them down." He took more pride in seeing ground cleared for planting than anybody I ever knowed.

"Grandpa, I'm leaving," I yelled. I was mad at Grandpa for making me stand there hollering. Of course I didn't even know there was anybody in that cabin for sure. Except for the smoke from the chimnay you might think the place was empty. Maybe the whore and Grandpa had gone off somewhere, to Chestnut Springs or Wall Holler. Or maybe they was dead.

There was a trail leading down to the edge of the clearing and I followed it, knowing there must be a spring down there. I was thirsty and I wanted to get out of that spooky clearing with the dog growling at me.

There was a spring down in the laurel bushes, with a can hung on a broke limb. It wasn't much of a spring compared with Big Springs, or ours in the valley. It was really just a seep coming out of some rocks, and the basin was no bigger than a soup bowl. But the water was cold and clear. It tasted a little flat, compared to our spring, but maybe that was because it come right off the top of the mountain, instead of deeper in the rock. I dipped another drink with the can. Every dip lowered the water in the basin, and it took a few seconds to refill. It could take a long time to fill a washpot, I thought.

There was a pile of trash on the other side of the spring, in the bushes just up the slope. There was newspapers and tin cans and bottles and old magazines scattered around. I climbed up there to see what-all there was. There was lots of little blue medicine bottles in the leaves, and liquor bottles of all sizes, like somebody had had a lot of parties. And the magazines, all tore up and scattered around by the squirrels, had drawings of naked women, and nearly naked women, on almost every page. I set down and looked through one of them. The pages was yellow and crumbling from the weather. But there was all kinds of pictures like you'd never dream of, of women wearing garter belts and nothing else, and women laying flat on their backs and looking at you. I couldn't hardly get my breath as I looked, and my ears was humming. And there was some photographs too, eat up partly by worms and showing women riding bicycles with no clothes on, and just a fur draped over their shoulders. And some women had bullwhips in their hands and big boots on. I couldn't hardly figure it out, but I must have set there half an hour looking through the damp pages that come apart when you turned them. I forgot where I was completely until I heard a barking from the cabin. I pushed the pages away and stood up, feeling a little dizzy.

The sun was straight up above the trees. I'd have to get Grandpa now and start back if we was to make it before dark.

The clearing looked different with the sun shifted around. The field seemed more winter-bleached and the breeze had died down again. The chickens in the coop had quieted down. Hens make most of their noise while they are laying in the morning, unless they are riled up. The smoke from the chimney was now bending away toward the north.

"Grandpa," I hollered when I got in front of the porch. The cur barked and shook his chain.

"Grandpa, I'm going back without you. You'll have to stay here."

I thought there was another rustle inside. Then there was the sound of something splashing out back, like a pan of water had been thrown out. And the bang of a window being shut. I walked around the corner of the cabin, staying out of the cur's reach. There was a boxwood at the corner, and bare ground like where Mama swept our yard. But this yard had not been swept and it didn't have white branch sand sprinkled on it. The dirt was stained with chicken piles.

The hens in the coop set up another racket when I got to the back. There was nothing else around there but the woodshed and a washpot on some rocks. The whole place smelled like burned wood and moss and ground where a chamber pot has been emptied. There was an outhouse, but it was back up near the woods at the other side of the clearing.

I couldn't see anything else alive except the chickens behind their fence.

The ground right under the eave had been cut by the drip from the roof in a kind of trench of pebbles along the foundation. Standing in that trough I could just barely reach the window. I got a stick of wood from the woodpile and put it across the little ditch. Standing on the piece I could just see over the window sill.

At first I couldn't see a thing. Then I put my hands on the sides of my temples and I could see the dark room with a bed. And there was Grandpa and this woman both without a stitch on, looking awfully white. Grandpa was laying on his back on the bed like he was sick or dead. As the woman bent over him her big titties swung side to side. I stepped back off the piece of wood so confused I didn't even think to call out to Grandpa. I didn't know what was wrong with him, and the white bodies seemed like ghosts in that gloomy cabin. I stepped back and set on the chopping block to decide what to do.

Grandpa had always thought he would die from the Yankee bullet he carried in his hip. He got hit somewhere in Virginia and was left on the battlefield for dead.

"I never thought I'd see the morning," he liked to say.

But the Yankees found him and took him prisoner. The Yankee doctor didn't have time to take out the ball, so it healed up by the time the war was over, with the lead still in there. And all his life since it hurt him a little when there was a change in the weather.

"That ball tells me when it's turning cold," he'd say.

And it hurt him when he worked too hard or walked too far. That's why he never walked up to the homecoming at Cedar Springs when the rest of us did, and why he squirrel hunted down in the valley and didn't often go back to the Flat Woods beyond the ridge the way other men did. He would rarely walk this far except when he was drinking and after some whore. I didn't know how I'd ever get him home even if he wasn't dead.

I picked up a chip and throwed it at the window. "Grandpa, I seen you in there," I said.

The woman, pulling a gown around her shoulders, came to the window and raised it up.

"I've come after Grandpa," I said.

She turned around from the window and looked back into the room.

"There's a little boy here," she said.

"Grandpa, we got to go," I hollered. "Be dark before we get home."

The chickens was making their squawks again, and the cur was barking on the other side of the cabin.

"Grandpa, let's go," I said again.

"This ain't Grandpa," Grandpa said inside. That's when I knowed he was all right.

"Come on, Grandpa, we got to go."

The woman came back to the window and leaned out.

"Come on round to the front," she said. "I'll help him get ready." She held her gown closed across the chest just the way I'd seen Mama and Aunt Martha do. I run around to the front, careful to stay out of reach of the cur.

It wasn't only that Sal Raeburn was a whore that made people think she was bad. On her mama's side she was a McBain, and the McBains was always thought of as queer, going all the way back far as anybody could remember. I've heard Daddy say the McBains fit for the British in the Revolution, and then got run out of the Piedmont by the Americans. So they came up here in the mountains where it was nothing but Indian country. There wasn't another white man for a hundred miles when they settled on top of the mountain and cleared theirselves a patch of ground.

I've heard they lived with the Indians, even intermarried

with them. And the Cherokees taught them all their magic knowledge about herbs and spells, and about singing a rattle-snake its own song to keep it from biting.

I was going to stay outside that cabin like Mama told me to. When the door opened Sal leaned out and said, "Would you like something to eat? You must be nigh starved, coming all this way."

I was awful hungry, but I wasn't going in that house even if I starved to death.

"No thank you, ma'am," I said. "I'll just get Grandpa and go."

The cur started to bark again.

"Hush up there," Sal said. "He won't hurt you, but he might scare somebody to death I reckon." She took the dog chain and wrapped it around the porch post so the dog couldn't move more than a yard.

"Here, that'll keep him close," she said.

The funny thing was, Sal looked just like any other woman when you seen her close up. Her hair was straight and black, but her skin wasn't very dark.

"You can come on in and rest your feet," she said. I wondered if my feet's soreness showed.

"No ma'am, I'll just take Grandpa and go."

"Ain't nobody gone hurt a big strong boy like you," she said. She disappeared into the cabin and returned with a fried pie in her hand.

"Here, take this," she said. "You don't have to come inside to eat it." The dog barked again.

"Hush up there, Beelzebub," she said. I still stood beyond the steps.

"This here is apple. I just made it this morning," she said. I could smell the cinnamon on the turnover. I was plumb empty.

"Ain't gone poison nobody," she said. "Sure not a handsome boy like you."

In the sunlight you could see she was pretty. She must have been near forty, but she was still pretty. She smelled like some flower perfume, and her hands was all white and smooth.

Grandpa stumbled out onto the porch, with one hand on his walking stick and one on the door frame. "You better eat something, Little Brad," he said.

I took the pie from her hand and eat it while Sal helped Grandpa button his shirt and slide on his coat. It was his Sunday coat and it looked all wrinkled. The pie was good.

I wouldn't tell nobody that I had eat her pie though. Nobody would know. While she was helping Grandpa her gown fell open and I could see her titties. I turned away before she seen me looking at her. She led Grandpa down the steps.

"You all come back and see me," she said.

Grandpa leaned his right arm on the walking stick and I held his left arm. He needed a shave, but he had combed his hair with some kind of toilet water and he smelled like a perfume bottle.

"You all come back and see me," Sal called again from the porch. I looked back and the wind was flapping her gown. She waved to me but I had hold of Grandpa's arm and couldn't wave back.

"We're gone be mighty late," I said.

"Don't matter," Grandpa said.

"It'll be dark before we get to the river," I said.

"I know the way," Grandpa said. "I've walked the whole country in the dark, coon hunting and possum hunting. When I was your age I stayed out all night more times than I was home in bed."

"You gone be mighty tired."

"I ain't tired," Grandpa said, as I helped him around a rock in the trail. And it was true that as we went along he seemed to limber up and get better use of himself. Every step seemed to bring the life back into him.

"You want to slow down?"

"No I don't want to slow down. You?" he said.

After his drunks Grandpa was always agreeable, like he had made up his mind to be humble and go back to work. Whatever contrariness had drove him off was gone. I fancied I could smell liquor in his sweat, but maybe it was just the toilet water.

The weather changed as we went down the Holler. Cloud shadows crossed the valley, and by the time we reached Big Springs it was overcast and muggy-like. The clear weather of the Gap was gone.

"Gone to rain, a spring rain," Grandpa said, not slowing down.

"And you don't even have a raincoat," I said.

"I've been wet before."

You could feel the rain forming in the air as we passed the Hince Anders cabin. I didn't see anybody in the clearing, or in the window, this time.

"We could stop here for the night," I said. It was getting dark early because of the clouds. Grandpa stalked on with his walking stick, stumbling from time to time.

The first drops hit us when we came out into the Flat Woods and descended to the head of the river.

MARTHA SUE

The first time I seen him he was stringy, looking stooped down in his clothes from that awful camp in Elmira where they kept the boys in pens and sheds in mud along the river. He later told me about it, but you could tell he was starved, from the camp and the long ride home in cattle cars and the walk up the mountain from Greenville. I had no use for rebels. Pa and all my brothers slipped over the mountains into Tennessee to fight for the Union. But you couldn't hardly look at Ben Peace without feeling sorry for him then. He had that gray-green look from hungering in the prison and from the diphtheria he had there.

Still I found myself red all over my face, and red all over the rest of me too if that could have been seen, when he turned to look at me in church. Pa said Uncle Cyrus was going to bring him to meeting on Sunday and then home for dinner. And I thought, another silly boy to feed and then have to talk to in the parlor while he looks foolish and tries to talk of love things when I don't hardly know him and just want to yawn.

But even in the dim light of the churchhouse you could tell Ben looked different. He was old for one thing, already twenty-seven, and had fought in Virginia all them years, and had been sick in the prison camp. I counted the times he glanced back at me, which was three, just because I knowed he was studying on me. I could tell, even when he swallowed and looked at the preacher. I'd wore my blue sateen dress, which was enough to make anybody look.

And walking home ahead of him and Pa and Uncle Cyrus I could tell his eyes was on me, all the way in that bright April sun. When we got home me and Mama was putting on the dinner and I couldn't hardly glance at him. He set there at the table looking poor and hunched over his plate and didn't glance at me. I took off the apron and set down in my blue dress and tried to eat chicken without getting grease on my face. I thought I'd tell Pa to never bring another boy home or I would die, or just leave. And I did tell him that, but it was for a different reason. By then I was in love.

They left us in the parlor, after the dishes was done, like they always did when a boy come home with us. And I just hoped he wouldn't say anything too silly, because already I liked him a little. Already I had a feeling.

But he wasn't looking at me no more. He was looking at the mirror on the organ, maybe at something reflected from the window.

"Would you like some lemonade?" I said.

He smiled and said, "They all say I can't do it."

"Do what?" I said.

"They all say I can't build a house down by the river because of the moisture which will rot the sills and the mists that will give you TB."

He paused and leaned toward me in the parlorlight.

"But I've seen houses all over Virginia by river banks, big houses that had stood for over a hundred years. You just have to put creosote on the sills."

I nodded. They seemed nothing I could say.

"And they say I'm too weak to build a chicken coop, or even put in a crop, after the prison camp and diphtheria. But it's work that'll give me my strength back."

I nodded again, all my resentment and resistance gone out of me. He was the first boy who ever come to the parlor who had something to say, and I was listening.

"They say the house place is too far from the spring and

I'd waste half my time just carrying water," he said. "But I can pipe it down. I'll bore out pumplogs like I saw in Virginia and lead the water right down into the yard. I'll build a spring house and a box to put the milk and butter in right at the edge of the yard. They say it won't work."

"Who does?"

"My brothers Hiram and Columbus."

I was listening.

He told how he walked up the mountain from Greenville after the Yankees put him off the train, and how he stayed overnight with the Lindsays in Traveler's Rest. And the next day he climbed up Gap Creek and over Painter Mountain, and by late evening was coming down Bob's Creek toward the river. When he seen the Peace land across the valley, the sun struck at just the right angle to make the poplars seem more gold than ever. Where the trees clustered at the foot of the pasture hill was a shining spot and he knew that's where he'd build his house. As a boy he used to cut arrows for his bow among the sourwood sprouts there.

And he talked about how when he was in that jail at Elmira he built in his mind every day the house he wanted on the hill. To keep from going crazy in the cold up there, he thought through the whole job of building, from cutting down the pines and snaking logs to Johnson's sawmill, to riving the three cedars below the schoolhouse for shingles. In his thoughts he made that house board by board every day, while the boys around him coughed and cried out in delirium. He had to help carry out the bodies, to the gate where the Yankees put them in wagons to take to the cemetery. So many died they lost all count, and most was from North Carolina.

"I don't want to talk the war," I said. "You know Pa and my brothers fit in Tennessee for the Union."

"I don't hold no grudge," he said. "My family's all Republican."

"I just want the war to be bygones," I said.

"Everybody knows Dr. Johns and his boys went to Tennessee," he said. "I don't hold no grudge."

Then he commenced to telling me again about the house he was going to build at the foot of the hill above the bottomland, how the porch would get both the morning and the late sun. In his mind in the camp he had a hundred times dug out the place there, shoveling down through leaves and woods litter, after cutting the trees and burning stumps, shoveling down through gray topsoil and leveling out a shelf in the orange subsoil. He said when his shovel blade hit a rock he could smell the spark that singed the grain of granite. What about a man could talk like that, thinking of the smell of new dirt at home while the blizzards banged on the walls and seeped around the cracks in that prison shed?

He said even before he reached the footlog across the river, when he was limping home, his cur, Satan, run out to meet him, splashing through the river and wagging hisself end to end. His mother and father said that dog had took on something terrible for days, and they said, "Ben must be coming home."

None of the letters he wrote from Elmira ever got through the lines and they didn't know he was still alive.

"What did you write on and with?" I said.

"I got pencil and paper by catching rats and birds and selling them for four cents apiece. And stamps you had to get from the guards, paying double or triple the three cents."

And from what he said then I should have knowed we'd have trouble, though what young girl would know the nature of the trouble when she's falling in love. I allowed as to how his ma and pa must have been happy to see him.

"All mother said was, 'We knew you were safe. We prayed every night and had assurance.' And my first thought was anger," he said. "How could they have known I would survive the smallpox and scurvy, the pneumonia and amputations, living on potato peels and corncob soup, carrying out the dozens of bodies every day. I shouldn't have been mad, but I was mad."

How could I know from that what would be the nature of our troubles later? But I should have knowed.

And then he talked about the local business men of Elmira who built towers in the fall while the weather was still mild for the ladies to stand on and watch the Confederate prisoners. For fifteen cents they could climb the stairs and sip lemonade, holding handkerchiefs over their noses for the stench from the mud and the big puddles. Some watched for hours as the rebels carried bodies to the gate, or held gospel singings and prayer meetings to pass the time.

I forgot the time while he talked, and first thing we knowed Uncle Cyrus come in and said he had to go. Ben took my hand and said, "Miss Johns." And I invited him to come back next Sunday, and he said, "Ma'am, I will."

I watched him and Uncle Cyrus walk out of the yard, past the lilac bushes and into the road. I felt a humming in my shoulders and neck and behind my ears. Even my big hands didn't seem so ugly anymore.

I had decided years before that I would never have no man. I didn't want somebody pawing over me at night and ordering me around all day. Somebody sitting on the porch smoking while I had to fix supper after hoeing corn all day. Better to wash your feet at the back door before coming in from the patch, and then rest by yourself. A man and kids would give you no peace.

All through the war I had wanted some rest. Pa and the boys gone to Tennessee and left me and Mama to do everything. Even patients sent word wanting pills Pa had left in his cabinet. But the supplies got gone, and we hoed and plowed same as men, and put up dried apples. I learned to hitch up the horse good as any man.

It was the bushwhackers and outliers that give us no rest. They lived in the mountains in bands and raided the rich people in Flat Rock and decent people everywhere. They was just trash, deserters and outlaws, using the war as an excuse to rob. There was no man on the place but Grandpappy, who was near blind and fit only to sit on the porch chewing his tobaccer. We worked all summer putting up sacks of dried apples and peaches. We pulled the fodder, which blistered my hands, and I was stung by a packsaddle. Mama and me was near in rags, as we didn't have time to sew none until cold weather. Then just when frost hit the ridges, Bearwallow red and gold all over though it was still green on the flat ground, and after we redug the potato pit and lined it with leaves and shucks, put in twenty bushels of spuds and sweet taters, and the corn was gathered in the wagon and throwed up in the crib—I done the hitching and driving mostly—along before daybreak one rainy morning we was boiling water for grits and burnt-bran coffee (nobody seen any real coffee in them years) and this gang on horses rode into the yard. We knowed pretty much who it had to be and just latched the door and stayed inside. You could tell from their hollering they was drunk, been out all night plundering the big houses in Flat Rock and was on their way back to the Green River Cove or Dark Corner, likely. They just kept riding around the house hollering, "You got breakfast ready for us yet?" and some would say, "You girls got anything hot in there?"

And they would just ride around the house again. One poked on the door with his rifle and said, "You all come on out, you hear. We don't hurt no girls or womenfolks. We got our own at home." And another called, "Smells real good. You keeping it warm for us?" They all laughed and rode among the outbuildings, it sounded like.

It was still dark so's you couldn't see a thing. Then it sounded like one rode his horse against the chicken coop because we heard a crash and the hens set up a terrible racket. "Let's at least get us a chicken or two," one said, but another answered, "I don't want to get down to catch them. I'm too cold-stiff."

Then we heard them knock out the back of the crib and ride their horses over the spilled corn, still arguing about what to take. One suggested they hitch up the wagon and our horse and carry the corn with them. "They's a hundred gallon in that pile to be made." But the others showed how that would slow them down, if the militia was following.

They kept talking as it rained harder and the breakfast got cold. Grandpappy kept asking if they was gone. And finally after half an hour we didn't hear nothing and I got my shawl and stepped out to look. And they was gone. But most of the corn had been ruint, and they took the horse. And the potato hole had been opened and rained in so we lost a lot to rot by Christmas, though we covered all we could in dry leaves.

And I said right then I never wanted no man that would go off to war and leave me. It was in a man to tear down what a woman works to make. I felt the truth of it then. And a woman who has a bunch of children will die young most times.

I knowed the story of the Capes up on Olivet too. How Mr. Cape's woman had died and left him with a boy and a girl. They called him into the army and he had to leave Fidelie, who was eleven, and his sister, who was nine, to run the place. That far up on the mountain the outliers took their stock one winter night, even the chickens and guinea hens. They carried away most of the corn in sacks and scattered the rest on the ground for their horses. Fidelie and his sister stood in the door and watched them work by pine torch, loading hams from the smokehouse on the wagon. Before leaving, one—he recognized the man, a neighbor and deserter—held him while another took his pocketknife out of his pocket. "You don't need no knife unless you're up to meanness, boy," he said.

"You'll boil in hell," Fidelie called after him. The man driving the wagon hollered, "Whoa," and they come back. Holding his pine torch close to the boy's face the man said, "What was that you said?"

"I said you'll boil in hell like lard fat."

Before he finished the man slapped him against the door.

"Now we don't hurt kids," the man on the wagon shouted. They pushed Fidelie and his sister out of the way and swept

THE MOUNTAINS WON'T REMEMBER US

into the house, gathering up pans and dishes, blankets, and the rifle that had been without powder for months. But the Capes made it through that winter on the few potatoes the bushwhackers hadn't found, and on rabbits Fidelie caught in his gum. When Cape come back from the war his kids was nearly growed up.

I didn't want to be thinking about no man. But I did. All week long I thought about Ben Peace in spite of myself. Joseph Benjamin Peace, Uncle Cyrus said was his full name. I worked harder than ever, washing clothes by the well, mixing up pills for Pa. And I tried not to think about Sunday. And when we all got dressed up that morning and walked to the meeting house, I tried not to look for him and talked to Auberine before the singing started. When I saw Ben come in with the men and sit down, then turn back and look at me, I knowed then I was a goner because I felt such relief. Just to know he was there. I was ashamed of myself, and I didn't care.

So we was married, and I could tell Pa was relieved. He hated to lose my work around the place, and he didn't want to have me gone, but he was relieved. He thought he would never get me married. He thought I would be his old maid assistant.

Was I a man and not a woman I could have been a doctor as good as Pa, but it wasn't to be. Like most things you think you want, it was not to be.

That we Johnses was Hardshell and him Free Will didn't seem to matter then. And everything Ben said about his place I found out was true. It was near two hundred acres, with half a mile on the river bottom, and the old place his though he was making a new house. And that new place was pretty to me as it was to him.

Everything he had told me was true, about the perfect exposure, there above the fields. When Father Peace bought the square mile of land in 1840 he built his house right in the center, near the spring. And the log barn was down at the milk gap. Hiram and Columbus had already been give the tracts running all the way up to Cabin Creek in the northwest corner and joining the Bane land at the southwest corner. Ben was the baby, and stayed home to take care of Mother and Father. Nobody thought he would ever marry either.

That first day after we was married in the church at Upward, Ben drove me in the buggy across the ridge and down into the river valley. I'd never seen no prettier place. His land had the river front, then cornered and run all the way back to the ridge on Olivet. He and Father had cleared and set out an orchard on the mountaintop there, and plowed a wagon road up the slope. That high ground got the most sun, he said, yet kept the trees cold in winter, and needed only a few days' work each year. It was one of his favorite spots.

I never got tired of hearing Ben explain in those early days. It was the thing I loved most about him, the way he could describe things. He had thought and read so much, and seen so much in the war. He could talk for hours and I would listen.

The only disadvantage of the place, his one worry, he kept saying, was its distance from the spring. The Peace spring suckled in the hollow under the east flank of the pasture hill and was cooled even in July by the big hemlocks. It was the best spring in the community, he said, and come from four or five pores at once into a basin several feet across, so clear the quartz and gray sand and lizards seemed on the surface. He took me down for a drink from the coconut shell, and I tasted the coldest water I'd ever had on my tongue. I knowed it was the water I'd be drinking the rest of my life.

The spring run a full-sized branch over the lip of rock and through the floor of the cooling box where the milk and butter was. It was only a hundred yards from the old house, but near half a mile from the new place.

Ben was nervouser than I was when we got out at the old house. But I felt breathy and a little weak, stepping out of the buggy, until I seen his mother and father, who come out on the porch and down the steps to welcome us. They was old and giggly, and wouldn't be no trouble except to look after I thought. I lit in and made a supper right then and there and baked a pie from dried apples. Mother hardly touched the kitchen after that.

Afterwards Ben walked me down to the new house place, along the ridge above the spring. The skimpy rations, exposure in the prison sheds, the long winter in Elmira, and the rough ride in the cattle cars had made Ben weaker than I realized. He stopped twice on the walk and complained of dizziness, of feeling cold. I didn't hurry him.

That week him and Father had plowed out the bottomland for corn, and from the hillside we could look down on the new broken fields. That was the moment I first saw what I'd got into.

From high up on the hill the plowed fields looked like a brindled cow. The ground by the river was almost black, where years of floods had built the loam deep and rich. That ground was higher than the middle of the field, and Ben said the old channel of the river had been right down the middle of the bottoms, and when the river overflowed that's where the current still ran. That river dirt looked like gunpowder.

Ben said hoeing there as a boy when the black dirt multiplied the sun's heat, he would dig into the damp under-dirt and stand in the hole to cool his bare feet. That ground would pack down and give under pressure like baking soda. Corn growed there even in a dry year because the moisture was just under the surface. He said it was the perfect ground for cucumbers and watermelons. But bull nettles also growed there worse than any other place, becoming, if left in the baulks, waist high, with fancy lavender and yellow flowers. They produced yellow seedpods that Ben and his brothers used to throw and burst, leaving a mess of slime and seeds on each other's clothes.

The color of the bottomland changed back from the river,

the satiny loam blending into coarse brown dirt, what Ben called a zone of topsoil fattened by swamp vegetation before the land was cleared and the underground spring ditched and piped away. That's where the water stood in the rainy season.

Above the low ground a streak of silver clay run through the field, bright now from the fresh plowing. Above that clay belt the dirt become lighter brown, with a sprinkling of rocks. And then near the foot of the hill and below the house place the soil got brilliant red. Frank said the hard clay was good for sweet potatoes and rhubarb, but with runoff from the new hogpen he hoped to sweeten it enough for a regular garden in a few years.

"Hiram says I ain't got strength enough to plant corn, much less build a new house," Ben said. He kicked the undergrowth and twisted a sourwood sprout until its fiber broke. "I'll put the porch right here," he said.

I seen then what his problem was. It wasn't just the weakness from the war and prison. It was the way his brothers had run over him, and the way Mother and Father had always expected him to do for them. He was the youngest, and he had to stay on the homeplace. But he was the smartest.

"Ben's always off with a book," Mother had said at supper.

And it wasn't anything that I could say would help him. I had to let him know I would be there to help him. I stood close against him for the first time there at the house place. Wasn't anything I needed to say.

There wasn't nothing to say that night either, when we went to bed in his room. It was still cold then, in early May. We put the lamp on the table. It was just a little room. Ben looked weaker than I had ever seen him as he set on the bed and pulled off his boots. Mother and Father had long gone to bed in the other room, and the house was dead quiet, except that he kept on talking, about how he wanted a big attic in the new house where he could put his books and read on a rainy day.

He wanted to build a step ladder in the closet, to not take up the space with a staircase.

When he took off his shirt I could see how poor he really was from starving in the prison camp. His hands trembled a little as he slid down his galluses.

"I have bad dreams at night," he said. "I dream I'm carrying out bodies in the snow at Elmira and the snow keeps falling and getting deeper. And we walk on, carrying the stretcher as the snow piles up on the body and gets heavy so we can hardly hold it. And the snow gets up to our straddles, but we have to keep going."

I was only half listening, and my breathing was a little short again.

"Better put out the light," he said. But I didn't blow out the lamp.

"When I have that dream I'm afraid I talk in my sleep," he said.

"It won't bother me none," I said. I took my blue dress off and hung it on the chair. I stood in my petticoat with my bare feet on the cold floor.

"My buddies in the army said I snore something awful," he said.

I could see him then as just a little boy, sitting there in the lamplight. Maybe all men are just little boys.

"I'm going to put in the pumplogs as soon as we move in," he said. "You won't have to carry water for washing but from the spring house. I don't want you to hurt your back carrying no water."

"You can carry it for me when you get stronger."

"Columbus says I'll get TB if I keep working this spring," Ben said.

I didn't answer him no more. The time for talking was over.

"Columbus was always critical of me," Ben said. "Did I ever tell you about the time I tricked him into falling into the branch?"

I turned the lamp up a little.

"Ben," I said, standing full in the light. I slid down my petticoat and left it on the floor, and as I slid down my step-ins I stood close to the burning lamp.

"Touch me," I said.

The first thing any woman learns about children is that every one is different. By the time the house was built and we moved down to the river, I had Florrie. She was little and dark as Ben and eat like a hog from the first day she was sucking. She never stopped except when asleep. Even when she laid in her cradle she swum from side to side like something too full of life to contain itself. I said to Ben she would be trouble. She would be a vexation to him and me someday, and before I come to die I'm already beginning to see it's true. She had a spark of the devil in her from the first; she can't help herself.

Now Joe was just Joe from the start. Big and dreamy. He'd go to sleep sucking, lost in his own thinking. I'd come in at night and he'd be laying there in the dark just staring and not crying. I think he had a stutter even when he cried, which wasn't often. He had the same stutter when he started to talk that he always had. He'd start to say something and get confused as his thoughts run on ahead. And he'd give up for a moment and then start again, stomping his foot to relieve the tension.

And Virginia, who come next, the year the pumplogs was put in, the year the typhoid went around, was also a solemn child from birth. Even while she suckled you could tell she thought on serious things. And as a little girl she was fussy and careless by turns. She wouldn't eat a piece of bread unless its edges was cut even. Nothing broken rough went in her mouth. She constantly asked questions about God and death, about heaven and things in the Bible. And she could read by the time she was four, asking what this word meant and that, saving her money to buy a Testament of her own. I worried how the boys would ever like her, if she didn't relax some.

Now Locke was a little Johns. He liked to laugh and from the first he was interested in medical things. He'd do anything to get a laugh, make faces at prayer times, fall down on the floor, put crumbs in his hair. And he was born with a natural concern for the sick, like Pa and all the doctors in the family before him. Even when he was three years old and Ginny was sick with croup he brought her broth to drink by the fire, and magazines from the attic. He was a dark little feller, quick as Florrie, and his head was always full of plans and talk of the far places he wanted to go. It worried me that he seemed so impractical, but who can tell how a little boy will turn out. I hoped he wouldn't have the Johns weakness for liquor.

One thing I could not fault Ben on was drinking. He kept a bottle of corn liquor in the cabinet for medicine, but except when he was sick he never tasted it. He would pour out a spoonful and set it on fire to burn away part of the alcohol, then give it to one of the kids for croup, along with pneumony salve.

Now Pa always ordered whiskey for patients. He'd say, "What this case needs is a little whiskey." Then he'd send for a pint and test it hisself to see if it was good, then test it again. He come back from his rounds too drunk sometimes to hold the reins, the horse finding his way along the ruts. I've seen him lurch out of the buggy with his doctor's bag at sundown. Mama always said she was afraid he'd kill somebody when he was drunk. But his pills was mostly harmless and the remedy he prescribed most was liquor, for hisself and the sick. I don't reckon he ever did much harm, but whether he did any good I couldn't say.

Ben was drunk in a different way. For such a smart and reading man, he had a curious love of revival meetings. After working in the bottoms all day he'd wash on the back porch and head off to a meeting. I've always gone to church and believed I was a Christian since I was saved at fourteen. But

I never liked services where everybody got stirred up and hollered and women shamed themselves with shaking and dancing up the aisles.

That kind of excitement always seemed more sacrilegious than worshipful. I believe the Lord speaks to us in still moments, when we're alone. I guess I'm a Baptist through and through. It's what's in you that counts, not how loud you holler, what kind of show you put on.

I must admit I was surprised when Ben started going to the meetings. He wanted me to come along. We had no differences in those early days. Like most new-marrieds we was afraid to disagree, afraid the world would bust up and go to flinders if we was to argue. So I went to a meeting over at Crossroads, and to one near the head of the river where Blue Ridge Church is now. I was so embarrassed at both places I walked out and set in the wagon till it was over.

I said to Ben, "I'm not going back to no such carryings-on. It's wrong for Christian people to holler and dance around like that. And the jabbering in tongues is something of the Devil. If the Lord has something to say to us he'll just say it so's we can understand. The Johnses are known for their crazy ways and goings-on and drinking, but they never held with no such foolishness as that."

It was the war that done it to Ben. Ruint his nerves. There in the camp they had singings and gospel meetings where the boys would shout and holler in tongues. It was the only thing that got them through their misery, he said. That's where he learned the habit, because he was not a loud and emotional man otherwise.

"Ben, I ain't going to another one," I said. But he just ignored me, and kept attending the revivals when they was in season. And he would come back some nights rushed up something terrible when he got in bed, with all the heat of the summer and the service still in him. That was alright, that was a wife's right and duty. But I felt bad about what caused it.

I tried to set an example for the younguns. After breakfast

at sunup Ben and me and Joe and Locke and the two girls would take our hoes from the toolshed beside the crib and go down the trail under the apple trees. We started work before the sun had burned away the river fog. Everybody tried to keep up with Ben, who could weed and sweep fresh dirt around each stalk in the same motion. He took a step and give the next plant two strokes, a step and two strokes, never breaking stride. When one of the children fell behind we all helped out, for it was easier to work together, talking and competing. We could chop out two or three acres a day, working six abreast, except Ben who was always a little ahead. Sometimes we sung hymns as we worked. The Johnses always did have a gift for music. Other times I started the younguns quoting scripture by saying the first two or three words of a verse and letting whoever remembered the rest complete it. Ginny was always the best at quoting.

"For God so loved . . ."

There would not be a pause in our hoeing.

"For God so loved the world," Ginny would say, "That He gave His only begotten son, that whosoever believeth on Him should not perish, but have everlasting life."

When she finished the sentence Ginny paused in her work and looked at me for approval.

"For God sent not His son . . ."

"For God sent not His son into the world to condemn the world; but that the world through Him might be saved." Florrie said the verse without emphasis, and without looking up, as though she was willing to play the game, but not interested in it anymore. She liked to laugh at her sister's enthusiasms, and sometimes said mocking things like, "Why close your eyes so tight when you're praying, like you wanted to be blind?"

Joe tried to quote scripture, but he stuttered so bad Locke and Florrie would help him out. Locke could get Joe's goat anytime by asking him a quick question, then prodding him to answer while Joe's face turned red and he stomped his foot, struggling to speak.

I tried to set the right example when the children asked about the bushwhackers, and about the war.

"Why don't you sue them now for taking all your corn?" Florrie said.

"Christian people have to forgive and forget," I said.

"But they never had to pay," Locke said.

"Don't you hate the Yankees, Pa?" Locke said.

"It was a foolish war," Ben said.

"But what if we had won?" Ginny said.

"Then we would have lost also," Ben said, and kept on hoeing.

They brought the railroad up the mountain ten years later. They built it up from Spartanburg, right up through Tryon and Saluda. They put the depot right near Crossroads, and dug out cuts through the ridge that looked like landslides. They built trestles tall as trees that walked across the creeks, and when they finished the depot at Hendersonville they had a big ceremony and said the new age of prosperity was here. Now markets was in reach, and tourists would come in on the train.

But the railroad killed our nearest market, which was the drovers' stands over on the Buncombe Pike. Many's the time we sold them corn, over at the Davis Place near the South Carolina line, for the stockpens where they kept the cattle, hogs, sheep, even turkeys, drove along the Pike every fall across the mountains from Tennessee and Kentucky down to Augusta or Charleston. The Davises stored thousands of bushels in their big cribs and sold them to the drovers for a fat profit. And some corn they put through their distillery and sold to the thirsty drovers in their tavern. I've even sold them jellies and molasses, potatoes and honey for their business.

But every fall Ben would load up his wagon with hams and walnuts, honey and ginseng, yellowroot and hides, to haul down the mountain to Augusta. I'd help him fix up the load, and he'd be gone a week, camping in the fields and pine groves on the way. He took his gun and avoided the stands for drovers. Everybody knowed about old man Fairfield who worked on the statehouse at Columbia. After writing home he'd be there in two weeks, he started out with his pay and was never heard from again.

Ben brought back books from Augusta. One year he brung a dictionary near the size of a chopping block, the kind with little shelves cut in the side so you would know which letter to open it at. He could look up any word in the big Webster's and tell where it come from. And he got a thick history book of the world that told about Ninevah and the nations of the Bible, and I don't know what all else. I would watch him reading there by the fire in winter, hour after hour, and think how much I wanted him out of the house while I did my ironing.

It was never the same between us after he went to those revival meetings. I done my duty as a wife and I forgave him for attending those heathen services, but I couldn't forget. I was too afraid of that intoxication that was worse than any liquor. It didn't make sense to me completely, but it was the way I felt.

On rainy afternoons he'd go up in the attic and read his books, and I'd think of the harness in the shed that needed patching, or the peas that was to pick and shell on the back porch. Not that Pa or my brothers was ever any better. What, after all, do you expect of a man?

After Joe and Locke was big enough to pull fodder and drive up the cows, Ben left things more than ever to me to direct them. I told him he should have been some kind of schoolteacher, or a preacher, since he just wanted to sit and read, or argue with Hiram about politics. I took care of his old folks until they was dead, and that burden he let fall mostly on me, who was only their married kin.

When I was just a little girl I didn't care nothing about

men, and told myself I'd never marry. They was always eating and just farting on the porch, and was such drunken fools. And then it happened just like that, like something happening to somebody else, and I found myself the married one who had to do the work and bear the babies, and wash the diapers on a Monday.

Ben helped me out with the washing some. He'd carry water from the spring and build a fire under the pot. But I'm the one that did the troubling in the pot and rubbed the clothes on that old washboard on the coldest days, even after he did get in the pumplogs that brung water into the yard.

I tell you what's the truth, there ain't much men and women has in common except the sex thing. Just enough to keep the human race a-going, I say. Otherwise we live in differences. I mean it seems strange to me, stranger than I can say, to find I'm living with a man near fifteen years and still don't understand him at all.

I tell you marriage is what's overrated. It's a long road of making do, and you can't even say it's a mistake, not having traveled any other way. They's times I'd give anything to be a girl again. They's times I've wished I was dead. That won't be necessary in a few hours. My lungs have been weak since I had bronchitis after Locke was borned. And every year I've had chest colds, even smothering, from dust in fall, from mold and damp in winter and spring, from smoke in the house all year, and the cold of hanging out clothes in January.

The holiness preacher come by to pray with me on Sunday and I told him not to waste no time on me. That I was a Hardshell Baptist and I knowed where I was going. None of this being baptized and then falling from grace foolishness. But he prayed anyway in that trembly voice of his, calling me his sister. And I just laid there and watched the light from the window fall on his loose black coat.

Ben won't hardly come by. He was always shy of me

when I got sick, staying out of the house, keeping to the fields and out in the barn. Just slipping in at dinner to ask if I needed anything, while Florrie or Ginny did all the taking care. Men don't know how to do when things get serious.

When I had the first fever, when they put the poultice of salve on my chest to draw the corruption out, I dreamed that Ben come and got in bed and hovered over me. It was like we was flying and instead of him pressing down on me I was pressing up on him, and we was going higher and higher in the sky, and further over the mountains, till you couldn't see nothing of home but a little smoke. And he said, "I'm not going to let you go." And I knowed then it was time. He would not let me fall, and we went higher and higher toward the sun.

But it was later, when I had another dream, I knowed I would die. Florrie brought in the hot irons and wrapped them in towels at my feet. And they put on another quilt because I was shaking, and they gave me a tablespoon of whiskey just like Pa used to. I drifted off, except I didn't seem to be asleep. I seen Pa in his buggy with his doctor's bag beside him, and he wasn't drunk. He was waiting for me to get in the buggy and go somewhere. He had the strangest expression on his face, like they was something he could say but he wasn't talking. Whoever knowed a Johns not to talk? I started to get in the buggy but saw Pa had no hands. He couldn't hold the reins and had no say over where he went. I woke up later sweating, but that dream was real as a toothache.

When Florrie and Ginny changed the sheets all wet I told them to tell Ben not to bury me up on the hill where the Peace cemetery was. I hate that place, where they put Mother and Father Peace, in the woods up on the hill where the crows blurted all around. I would be put in the Baptist ground out near Upward where my folks is.

When I had the chance I talked to all the younguns. I told Florrie not to get married too early. She's too crazy about boys, and about love things. She takes after the Hamiltons that way I'm afraid, and I won't be around to warn her. Not that she would listen anyway. She's got that curiosity, that itch, and only God can stop her.

Now Joe won't say much ever. He just looks on and thinks I'm hard against the holiness things. He loves me, but it can't show, and he blames me for his stammer. He reads and tries to argue, and stutters, and the girls ignore him. And he talks to hisself while he's out chopping wood or cutting tops. Carrying on conversations, making up sermons. He wants to preach, and I doubt that any congregation will ever give him its call.

Ginny is her daddy's girl all over again, down to reading the religious tracts and every newspaper, down to looking in the dictionary for every word that mystifies her. She's never learned to keep herself, and it's too late to teach her. She takes things by spells, studying on something for days, with no thought of other things, talking only about that subject, and then goes on to some other fascination. Whether she ever gets a boy I doubt, being inattentive to men. Men like to be fussed over, and she thinks her own thoughts. But then I never thought I'd make a marriage either.

The next time Ben comes into the room there's something I want to say. But it is too late. I only wheeze and rattle, can't make words. He bends over and says, "Mother, is there anything you want?"

I want to say men and women are so different it's hard to believe they are the same race at all. Him and me has not been perfect mates. If it hadn't been the holiness, it would have been something else. But being almost strangers we still brought comfort to one another at times. Was our mistake in not talking, or talking too much? It was through each other we seen what our limitations was, and the differences made things a little clearer. But he can't hear a thing. He bends down and says, "You'll be alright." And I can tell how scared he is.

It is little Locke that spends the most time with me. He

brings me water, what I can swallow, and puts a cool cloth on my forehead. He asks me where it hurts. He's a doctor for sure, feeling at home with the sick. I must have mumbled for he asks me what I see, and I can't tell him a thing about the great distance closing in like comfort, so instead I just point up and can't see if he notices or not.

DEATH CROWN

I had no sooner walked into the room, maybe into the house, than I saw what the truth was. It was like a smell in the air, or a sound you can't really hear but know is there. It was a feeling in that old house and it hit me as soon as I stepped through the door. I didn't even pay much attention to Myrtle or to Annie where they set by the fire. I must have spoke to them but I don't remember it. It wasn't Myrt and Annie I was concerned with anyway. They didn't seem to realize what was happening though it was taking place right in their own house. And they was just setting there hunched up by the fire.

"Harold," I said soon as we walked in, "you might as well go on back home. I'm staying here to the end." And I don't know what he did after that. He must have stood around the fire with his hat in his hands talking to Myrt and Annie as he always did about the weather and about their cow and about Eisenhower and the terrible people running the government. But I didn't notice. And I guess he eventually walked back down the hill to that little pickup and drove home by hisself. I don't know. I had other things on my mind.

We had come out on a drive to the old place to see how Alice was. It was just a hunch I had, to see how she was doing. It was one of those cold clear days in November, the first real cold day we'd had. The leaves was finally all gone, after about a week of rain, except a yellow one hanging here and there on a branch willow. But it looked like winter and the country had been scrubbed and polished by the rain. It was cold enough so the hemlocks got that black look they have in freezing weather. The ground in the yard was beginning to freeze.

When I stepped through the door into Alice's room the first thing I saw was the ball of white light on her pillow. It looked like the sunlight from the window had poured itself into a little cloud. There was a crack in the blind and the light had found its way right to the pillow and just seemed to hover there. It looked like a puff of breath had stayed and caught fire.

But it was only Alice's hair. She had the purest white hair you ever saw. As she got older it got whiter, not yellow and tired the way some old people's hair gets. It had a snowy look that almost startled with its whiteness.

I couldn't see her face at first. You could smell the change in the room, but it wasn't anything you could describe. Myrt and Annie had kept her clean and it wasn't anything like a bad smell, and it wasn't just the smell of camphor and the old wood smell of the house. The house had been there so long, it had its own scent of leather and smoke and coffee mixed with must in the attic. And sometimes I thought I could still smell the smoke of Great-grandpa's pipe, though he had been dead for twenty years.

This smell was different from them all. It was something in the air like the heat of a hot electric wire, or the feeling there's just been a loud noise which disturbed the elements but wasn't heard by humans. I expected to hear a rustling, or see a curtain move, but the air was absolutely still, even when wind outside pressed the house and shook it a little.

Her hair was so bright you couldn't see Annie's face at first. But when I bent closer I saw a new expression there. It was not a look of pain so much as struggle. The look confirmed the feeling I'd had. I'd seen that look before on Grandma and on Aunt Mary's face before they passed away.

So I just got a chair out of the corner. It had a blanket and a hot water bottle and a pile of papers on it, but I set all that aside and brought the chair close to the bed. If I was going to stay I might as well make myself comfortable. I was wearing my Sunday clothes with my old gray coat. We'd come over after church and I had on earrings and a necklace. But it didn't matter because I wasn't thinking of myself.

I pulled the chair right up to the bed and took Alice's hand. Even though it was under the covers it was a little cold. I held her hand in both of mine and said, "Alice, you know who this is?"

Her head rolled on the pillow and she opened her eyes and looked at me. But she had that wild look, the way she sometimes did. Most of the time she had the mind of a child and was sweet as a little girl. But sometimes she'd get this look in her eyes like she was going to hurt somebody or run away, or no telling what. And then she would quiet down and be herself again. It would scare you to see that look on such a little woman with all that white hair.

She looked at me and then she closed her eyes again. I couldn't tell if she knowed me or not. When she was having a bad spell it was like she didn't know anybody.

"Alice," I said, squeezing her hand. "I've come to stay with you; I'm not going to leave you."

And I could feel her hand squeeze back. It was just a faint squeeze, but I could feel it for sure. She never opened her eyes, but I could tell she knowed who I was.

"I'll be here if you want me," I said.

The sun had moved a little bit off her hair, and I couldn't see her face well. But the shaft of light was still on the pillow, blinding me a little. My eyes would have to get adjusted to the dark.

Ever since I was a little girl I was Alice's favorite in the family. We just naturally enjoyed each other. They never let her go to church or to school, and most kids was afraid of her. I remember once Mama brought me over there for Sunday dinner and I took my doll. It was a new doll, a china doll, with long blonde hair, and I carried it everywhere with me. Alice seen me holding it as we stood around on the porch before dinner and she pulled me into her room and showed me her doll. It didn't even strike me as strange that this old woman, who was really Mama's aunt and whose hair was already getting white, was playing with dolls. I thought, she doesn't have any children but she has dolls instead.

Her doll was just a rag doll, and it was kind of wore out and dirty. But she held it in her arms the way I held my new doll.

"My baby," she said, and rocked it. She had a laugh I liked. We talked about the dolls till dinner time, when they brought her a tray from the kitchen and I had to go set at the table.

And every time I went over to Grandma's house I'd see her and we'd play hopscotch or run in the meadow below the spring.

Her job was to carry water for the family. She loved to carry water, bucket after bucket, up the hill from the spring. She felt useful doing it, and would sometimes empty a bucket off the back porch just so she could go back to refill it.

"I've carried six buckets," she'd say and smile, though I don't think she could count and would just choose a number she had heard.

And when Myrt was doing the washing Alice carried buckets to fill the washpot, and to fill the tub where the washboard was.

But soon as I come over she'd want to play, and set her buckets down on the trail and run to the meadow. We'd run and laugh so hard we'd fall down and roll in the grass. Then Myrt would find us and tell her to quit footercootering and bring the water on up to the house where they was about to boil some corn. That's the word Myrtle always used, "footer-cootering." I never heard anybody else use it. And I'd help her carry a bucket, though looking back I wish I'd helped her more.

"She's been going down since Wednesday," Myrt said, when I went back to the fire to warm my hands. "We called the doctor and he come out and listened to her heart, but he didn't know hardly what to do. He said if we brought her to the hospital he could run some tests."

"Did he give her anything?"

"He give her some pills, but I don't think they do no good. And there's no way we could get her to the hospital. I think she'd die before she'd go. She ain't left this place in seventy years."

Myrt was right about that. And besides, it was too late for the hospital to do any good.

I told Annie to start a fire in the cookstove and heat a kettle of water. I was going to wash Alice off. I thought she might feel better if she was cleaned up a little.

"No, no, I'm going to freeze," she said when I pulled back the bedcovers a little. She held onto the quilts right over her throat.

"Now Alice, I'm not gonna hurt you. I'll just wash a little bit at a time and dry you off. You'll feel better."

She had that wide, wild look in her eyes again. I put my hand on her forehead to calm her down.

"You're gonna be all right," I said. "This is Ellen. You remember Ellen."

She rolled her eyes and come back to herself a little. "How's Evie?" she said.

"Evie's fine," I said.

My mama, her niece, had been dead for twenty years, but I didn't want to upset her. Time had stopped for her long ago.

"I'm going to wash you a little," I said. "And then you'll feel better."

I pulled back the bedclothes a little at a time and washed her feet and ankles and then her legs and upper body. It was pitiful to see how thin she was, just a skeleton with skin, like she hadn't eat anything in months, which she hadn't. I was careful not to drip any water on the sheets. And when I finished I tucked her in again. I was going to empty the pan off the back porch.

"I'll be back," I said, and patted her shoulder.

"I can't breathe," she said. "They ain't no air in here."

"They's plenty of air," I said. But there was terror in her eyes. She fought back at the quilts I had tucked around her.

"Open the window," she said.

"You can't open a window," I said. "It's winter outside."

She tore the quilts almost off the bed and rassled to get up.

"You can't get up, Alice," I said. "You're too weak."

"Open a window," she said.

"All right, stay in bed, and I'll open a window."

I wrapped the quilts back around her and raised the window a crack. Wind cut through even that and chilled the room. It was getting late in the afternoon by then and the sun had moved away from the window. Wind rattled the sash and stirred the papers on the night table. I closed it down to the finest crack, as the counterweights knocked in the walls.

"Open the window," Alice said. "I can't breathe."

I reopened it so she could hear the whistle in the slot. The room was already cool, but it got colder quickly with the fresh air. You could smell the air off the pasture and the sour of the new-fallen leaves in ditches. I got a blanket and put it around my shoulders, and moved my chair far as I could from the window but where I'd still be able to reach Alice.

But the wind seemed to make her feel better. She begun to breathe more regular and she closed her eyes. I thought she was going to sleep. But then she opened them again, to make sure I was still there.

"Alice, are you hungry?" I said, because it was getting on toward suppertime and I could smell cooking in the other end of the house.

"Would you like some soup?" I said. "Smells like Myrt's cooking some hog sausage."

I thought she was gonna nod her head yes, but no sooner had I asked than she closed her eyes and just seemed to go to sleep. She must have been tired from the struggle to breathe. Her breath was now regular. I eased the window down so as not to disturb her.

While Alice was sleeping I wondered what my duty was. Was she a Christian? Was she ready to die? She never had been to church since she was a little girl. Had she ever in her mind reached the age of accountability, as the preachers say? Was she responsible for herself?

My daddy, who was a preacher, used to argue with the deacons about who would be saved. "Ain't nobody going to heaven that's not been baptized," one said.

"But how about the Indians that died here before the white men came and brought the Word?"

"They will die in their sins," Carl Evans said.

"And how about all the people in China that never heard of Jesus?" Daddy said.

"I've heard they will be give a second chance," another deacon said.

"You must be born again," Charles Whitby said.

"And how about the little babies that die before the age of accountability?" Daddy said.

"You must be washed in the blood," Carl Evans said.

But Daddy said later they was just ignorant. It didn't make sense to condemn people that never had a chance to believe. What kind of God would do a thing like that? All the little children that had died early would be in heaven. And Alice in her mind was still a little child.

It put my mind to rest to think about Alice as a little girl, even though her hair was white and her face wrinkled. As it got dark in the room you couldn't see nothing but her hair, which seemed to glow against the pillow. It was like a shiny little cloud that just floated there.

"Do you want some supper?" Myrt said, and light shot from the opened door on Alice's face.

"She's resting now," I said.

"Poor thing, she needs some rest," Myrt said. "The last three nights she kept us awake with her raving. You'd think she had a demon in her the way she carries on."

"She's sleeping now."

"Annie's cooked up some sausage and taters," Myrt said. "You better come eat if you're going to stay with her."

"I can't leave her," I said. "Not now."

Myrt brought me a plate of sausage and potatoes and a glass of iced tea. I lit the lamp on the night table by the bed hoping it wouldn't wake Alice up. In the shadows from the lamp the room looked bigger than it had before. The shadows pulled at the light, drawing it away from the shiny chimney.

It seemed strange to be eating in the room there with Alice, but I went ahead anyway. The belly don't know any shame or any rules except its own. Annie's sausage was hot and filling.

Alice shifted in her sleep and I wondered if she was awake and keeping her eyes closed. Maybe the smell of the sausage woke her up. But her breathing continued regular and I put the empty plate on the night table and leaned closer. The fuzz on her chin sparkled in the light. But her skin was still very fair.

Mama told me that when Alice was a teenager she was the prettiest girl in the valley. Her hair was blond and her skin perfect and glowing. Boys would come by on Sunday afternoons just to sit by the fire and look at her. They pretended to be visiting her brother or be courting her sisters. If she was feeling good, she would sit in her corner and smile. If she was upset, she'd run off to her room and slam the door. Nobody seemed offended by her doings.

One boy, Otho Jarvis, was struck on her more than the rest. He come every Sunday for a year, and had dinner and stayed to talk to the family. One time he took Great-grandpa aside and asked if he could marry Alice.

"She ain't no woman to marry," Great-grandpa said.

"Mr. Jackson, my intentions are honorable," Otho said.

"But you see what she is. In her mind she's just a child, less than a child."

"But she's a woman also. I'll marry her and take care of her, just like she is, and be kind to her."

But Great-grandpa wouldn't agree to it. He said it wouldn't be fair to nobody. That Alice in her childish mind wouldn't be able to take care of children and look after them and raise them. And it wouldn't even be fair to Otho when he got older, trying to look after a place, and the children, *and* Alice. So Great-grandpa put a stop to it. And one by one the other children married and left home and Alice stayed with the old people, carrying water from the spring and playing with her doll. But later Grandma took her in after she heired the old place and that's why Mama growed up with Alice in the house.

The wind picked up again, after it was dark, and rattled the window sash. You could feel the air seeping in through cracks of the old house. The lamp flame fluttered a little in its chimney. I pulled the blanket tight about my shoulders and wondered if it was going to snow. If the wind died down it was certainly going to come a hard freeze. I must have dozed a little.

"Open the window," Alice said. She was awake, and her eyes rolled in terror.

"I can't breathe," she said.

"It's cold out there," I said. "Hear the wind?"

She fought at the covers and was working to get up.

"I'll open the window just a crack," I said. I raised the window just enough so you could feel the cold air slicing through the room but things didn't blow around.

She relaxed again, and lowered her head on the pillow. Her hair had been flattened behind and stood straight up. Her eyes wandered around the room.

"Where's Mama?" she said.

"Mama's alright," I said. "She's in the next room." There didn't seem to be any point in telling her that Great-grandma had been dead thirty-five years.

"Everything's just fine," I said. I looked at my watch. It was almost ten.

"Would you like some coffee, Ellen?" It was Annie at the door. "I just made a fresh pot," she said.

"I'll have a cup," I said. "And maybe Alice will have some too."

Alice was looking toward the door. She had always loved coffee, and the smell of the fresh pot was strong through the open door.

"Bring me two cups and I'll try to feed her some," I said.

Annie returned with two steaming mugs, and took the supper plate away.

"Here's some coffee for you," I said to Alice, blowing on the cup to cool it off.

She was too low in the bed to even sip from the full mug. She seemed lost among the quilts except for the luminous hair.

"I'll have to pull you up," I said, and put my hands under her arms. It's always astonishing to find how hard it is to move someone. Leaning over her I had no way to get any leverage.

"Can you push with your feet?" I said, but she didn't seem to understand me. "Push against the end of the bed," I said.

But I don't think she even understood me. Bracing myself against the bedpost I dragged her up and put a pillow behind her back. I blowed on the coffee again and held the mug to her lips.

"It's hot," I said, but she didn't listen. She took a sip, a big sip, and then spit and shook her head.

"You scalded me," she said, and glared.

"I told you it was hot, to go slow," I said. But she shook her head like a two-year-old.

"Too hot," she said, and looked at me with that wild look.

"We'll just take it slow," I said.

She shook her head and slapped at the cup. "No," she said, and knocked half the coffee down her shoulder and on the pillow.

"Ey, ey, ey," she screamed.

I put the mug down on the night table and tried to sponge up the coffee with a kleenex.

"It's OK, it's OK," I said, and put my left hand on her forehead as I tried to soak up and wipe away most of the coffee. The skin on her shoulder was not even red, so I doubt that she was burned much.

"You hate me," she said, and turned her face away.

"That's the way she treats us all the time," Myrt said from the doorway. "Here's a towel."

I lifted her head and put the dry towel on the pillow, and held her hand. Gradually the crazy look in her eyes went away, and she closed her eyelids. With my left hand I eased the chair closer and set down.

The way her head sunk into the towel on the pillow reminded me of the old story of the death crown. Oldtimers used to say that when a really good person, say a preacher that's saved lots of souls or a woman that's helped her neighbors and raised a lot of kids, is sick for a long time before they die, the feathers in the pillow will knit themselves into a crown that fits the person's head. The crown won't be found till after they are dead of course, but it's a certain sign of another crown in heaven, my Daddy used to say. I've never seen one myself but the oldtimers say they're woven so tight they never come apart and they shine like gold even though they're so light they might just as well be a ring of light.

Alice's head sunk into the pillow like it was the heaviest part about her. Her body was so thin it hardly showed through the quilts. You could look at the bed in the lamplight and imagine there was no body in it at all, only the head at the top and the flying white hair. It looked like her body had evaporated and gone, and left her head there with the fear in her eyes. That was the opposite of what happened when she was a little girl, when her mind had gone and left her in a beautiful, healthy body.

My Mama said Alice was the beautifullest little girl you ever saw. She had been told by Grandma how fair and blond Alice was, with blue eyes and a sweet smile. Until she had what the oldtimers called "the white swelling." I don't know what doctors these days would call it, but back then they named it the awful "white swelling."

What happened was the kids at school, or maybe it was at church on homecoming day, was playing wild horses and cowboys. And one big old boy, Mama said he was a Jones, was wearing these heavy brogans, and he made like he was a wild mustang and kicked her. He didn't mean to actually kick her, but he did, in the shin. And she was just this little girl with her skin all fair and delicate. Where he kicked her it took the white swelling and the whole leg got inflamed.

The place itself swelled up white and she had a fever so high and long it ruint her mind. Her development stopped right there, in the pain of the fever, and never started again.

But the funny thing was her body seemed to get over it. Her leg was swelled up all them months, and they put hot compresses on it day and night, and soaked it in all kinds of things, and put on salves and plasters. And by grannies a piece of bone that had been broke where she was kicked worked its way out through the skin, a splinter off the leg bone. And the place, after about a year, healed up so she could walk again. She limped a little. She always did have a slight limp if you watched her. But she could get around and carry water. And they thought she would be OK, except her mind didn't grow no more. It seemed to go back after the fever to two or three years old, and it stayed there.

I remember bringing Harold over to meet my folks. I was so proud 'cause I was getting married and getting away from home, finally. I was tired of looking after the little kids and

Mama was failing even then so most of the work had fell on me.

Harold had this old truck he used for logging. It had a rough bed and all the men he worked with cutting timber up in the Flat Woods rode on it every morning bouncing up the creek road. I don't see how their behinds stood it in the cold. But they laughed and carried on like a bunch of drunk schoolboys. You could hear them banging and hollering miles away.

Anyway, Harold drove me over to see the folks and I was proud he was such a big strong feller. He was kind of quiet around strangers and women, but you could see Myrt and Annie liked him. And Grandma was alive then and he give her a five dollar bill. Everybody was smiling and Harold stood by the fire with his hands in his pockets. Myrt was making coffee to go with the coconut cake. And Alice comes in with two buckets of water.

She smiled when she saw me. I always brung her something, a dress for her doll, a piece of candy, a little vanity set. She set the water down and come to me smiling.

"Alice, I want you to meet Harold," I said, taking her by the arm. "Me and him is to be married."

And this look come over her face, come over gradually like a stain spreading in cloth, and her lip went crooked and she started to cry.

"Alice, Harold is a nice feller," I said. But she turned and run to her room, leaving the water buckets there on the floor. I had explained to Harold about Alice, but it embarrassed me something terrible for him to see her do that, the first time he visited them.

Alice seemed to be having a bad dream. She said, "No, no," and lifted her arm, knocking away the covers. I put her arm back under the quilt and told her everything was alright.

She was calm for a few seconds, then opened her eyes and

rolled them around, and she jerked back like she had seen the devil or a snake.

"What's wrong, Alice?" I said, putting my hand on her shoulder. She was small as a child, but could push harder than you would think.

"Oh god, no, no," she hollered and tried to raise up. I bent over her.

"What's wrong Alice?"

"He's coming to get me," she said.

"Ain't nobody coming to get you," I said.

Her eyes looked like she had seen hell itself, but they was looking nowhere in particular.

"Alice, it's me, Ellen, and nobody's going to hurt you," I said again.

"Oh lord, he's coming. Oh lord, it hurts," she hollered. There was nothing I could do to stop her but try to hold her down on the bed. Myrt and Annie had come to the door in their nightgowns and asked if they was anything they could do.

"You got any sleeping pills?" I said.

"We ain't got a thing but aspirin," Myrt said.

"Well, bring me that," I said.

They brought me a bottle of aspirins but I couldn't turn loose her shoulder to give her any.

"Bring me a glass of water," I said.

Annie come back with water in a teacup.

"You'll have to put one in her mouth and give her a drink while I hold her," I said.

But Alice kept hollering that something was coming to get her. When Myrt tried to drop an aspirin in her mouth she spit it out, and when Annie held the cup of water to her lips a little spilled on her chin, but none got in her mouth.

"We'll have to forget it," I said. I held her down until she started to get tired. I was getting tired too, and my arms was trembling a little. When she finally quieted down Myrt and Annie started back to bed.

"I hate it you have to do this," Myrt said.

"I don't know what we'd a done without you here," Annie said.

I looked at my watch in the lamplight. It was two-thirty. Almost everybody dies between midnight and six in the morning, Mama used to say. Alice had another three or four hours to go if she was to make it to another day.

She had wore herself out and was still with exhaustion. But she had that terrible look on her face, like she was anguished and scared, like she was crazy as people said she was. People will rumor anything. But she never was sick in her mind really, like they told it on her. She was just simple, child-like. People will spread around the worst things they can think of.

But because she was afflicted the family would never take her nowheres, not to school or church singings, or the Fourth of July picnics. Somebody would always have to stay with her, though she begged in her innocence to be carried along. She wanted to go places bad as a little kid does that sees everybody else dressed up and ready to leave. She cried and begged, and they still left her at the house like they was ashamed for anybody to see her. Mama had to go stay with her a lot when she was young, and Grandma before her.

That was how come Grandma and Grandpa got the place, because they agreed to take care of Alice. When Great-grandma died she left them the house and most of the land for taking care of her and Alice too. That was the way they did things back yonder, leave the place to whoever took care of the old people. Usually it was the youngest that stayed home and done it.

Grandma always hoped Alice would stay in her room when visitors come. That's why the front door was always closed since I was a little girl, 'cause Alice lived in the front room. I was the only one that went in to see her when we come to visit on Sundays. She'd show me her doll, and talk about play-parties she'd been to, infares and dances. But she made it all up, the way a kid will do.

I remember one time we come over at Christmas in the A-model truck. That was before I was married. And we carried up a whole sack of presents to the house to put under Grandma's tree. That little room just seemed flooded with presents. I was afraid the house would catch fire there was so much papers scattered around when we started unwrapping. Names would be called out, and they was oos and ahs and squeals of delight, and "You shouldn't have" and "How did you know what I wanted?" I had brought a little box of candy, just a little box of peppermint sticks, for Alice. And I stood up to take it to her room. She never did eat with the family or join in much by the fireplace.

"I'm giving this to Alice," I said.

"Oh the shame," Mama said. "I forgot to bring her a thing." And I could see Mama was hurt to think she had forgot Alice at Christmas. But that was the way things turned out most of the time.

I must have been sleeping because when I looked at my watch it was four thirty-eight. The lamp was still burning, but the room seemed different. It was real still, inside the house and out. It was like something had been there and just gone. Alice was sleeping, but there was a kind of a catch in her breath, and a faint gurgling in her throat. I didn't know if it meant anything or not. Her face was relaxed, though it still showed the lines of the earlier struggle.

There was that smell in the house again, the odor I had caught when I first walked in the day before. It was a peculiar old-house smell, akin to the scent of coffee soaked into the wood for a hundred years, along with smoke from the fire-place, and mothballs in the big wardrobe, old wool and yellow newspapers. But I couldn't describe the scent itself; it was of age, and dust in rugs. Added to the kerosene smell of the lamp was that other smell, like some electric spark, a warm radio, though there was no radio in the house.

I looked around for Alice's doll, but couldn't see it anywhere. It must be under the bedcovers, I thought. She would never have lost it or thrown it away.

In the still every pop and creak of the house sounded like growing pains. I thought of a ship out at sea, the way they say it will groan and creak as the wood gives with the waves.

The skin on Alice's forehead gleamed almost as white as her hair. It was smoother than most old people's skin, and I thought she was lucky in a way to have never growed up, in the times she had lived through. When she was a girl the trains hadn't even come into the mountains, and she lived through the world wars with never a worry about them. Now people flew everyplace, and they talked about going to the moon. She had lived through the Depression and didn't know a thing about it while she carried water every day up the hill and set under the pines above the meadow, or sipped coffee in her room. I hated it that her mind was troubled now.

There was a longer gurgle in her throat and her breath come in little jumps and then stopped. I was going to run to get Myrt and Annie, but realized there was nothing any of us could do. Alice's mouth fell open and her head turned sideways a little. Her eyes was closed and there was a long sigh of air coming out of her chest.

It was so still I kept waiting for her to breathe again. But she didn't. "Alice," I said, but she didn't respond. Her face started to relax until it was completely placid. I know people like to talk about how somebody smiles or sees angels or kinfolks that have already passed on when they die, but it was nothing like that. She was dead and her face seemed plain and untroubled. It was a beautiful death.

CARETAKERS

I hated to do the parlor most of all. I would put that off until the end of the morning, except there would be more guests there then, sitting around reading the newspapers Mr. Swain brought from town. And I would have to move among them with my broom and dustpan, trying not to get in their way but reaching all the spaces between carpets and under lamp tables. That was the part I really dreaded, working through the middle of the big room where everybody could see me as I bent over to brush the sweepings into the pan. Sarah had been born almost two months ago, and I was losing the extra weight I had put on, but my face got red from bending over, and from being watched by the fancy guests lounging on the sofas and in the easy chairs.

"It's important you get the job done by noon," Mrs. Swain said. "Never mind the guests. In the afternoon you can work in the back doing the wash, and cleaning our apartment."

Even if there was nobody in the parlor I would still have hated it. The room was bigger than many houses, and there was too much furniture to reach under and work around. And there were lamps and cords and ashtrays, and cigarette butts on the carpets. It was the carpets I hated most. If the floor was covered with one big carpet I could have hoovered it easily. But there were dozens of smaller carpets, in the spaces between sofas and armchairs, coffee tables, in front of the table where newspapers and magazines were piled, even in front of the fireplace. Once a week I vacuumed all the rugs, but every day the edges had to be lifted and the dust hidden there whisked out to be swept up.

I dreaded most having to sweep near Mr. Fuller's chair. He spent the whole summer at the Mountain Manor and he sat every morning reading all the newspapers, some in a foreign language. I was sure he drank around the clock, for I could smell booze when I was near him, though he wore a powerful cologne, and there were bottles in his room.

"Oh, it's you again," he said in his strange accent.

"I'll just be a second," I said.

"Don't mind me," he said. "I'm just an old man."

Once he had reached over and patted me on the behind as I worked near him. I quickly stepped away, and I had not told Mrs. Swain or my husband, Roy. But I kept my distance as I worked around Mr. Fuller's chair, and I never turned my back on him again.

"It's a great day," Mr. Fuller said. "A great day." He tapped his finger on the front page of the paper.

"Yes, it's a good day, Mr. Fuller," I said, quickly finishing the edges of the carpet in front of him.

"A good day is what you say in greeting," he said. "No, this is a great day."

While I was fixing breakfast for Roy that morning and warming the bottle for little Sarah, I heard on the radio that the war was over. It meant things would no longer be rationed and my brothers would be coming home. It meant that building supplies would be available again, and that the loan might come through to build a house on the land my daddy had deeded us. Me and Roy would no longer have to work as caretakers for the Mountain Manor.

"It's a great day," I said to Mr. Fuller, and gathered up my cloths and brushes and pan.

As I passed the kitchen I heard Mrs. Swain talking to the maid about serving lunch. Laura was the only maid The Manor had now, and she served as waitress at breakfast and lunch.

"Don't bring in the cake until I ring," Mrs. Swain was saying. "Then you carry it in immediately, for Mr. Swain is going to give a little speech and we can't keep him waiting and all the guests sitting and wondering what comes next."

I hoped I could slip by the door without Mrs. Swain seeing me, for every time she talked to me she assigned yet another job. When I came home from the hospital everything was behind, and I was still trying to catch up.

"Hello Willa," Mrs. Swain called after me.

I had walked past the kitchen door, but stopped, and backed up slowly. I didn't want to seem too willing to do another task.

"Willa, it was so cool last night we had a little fire in our fireplace," Mrs. Swain said. "We burned up a few papers and I want you to clean out the ashes when you tidy up the apartment."

"Yes ma'am."

"The guests love this cool weather," Mrs. Swain said. "It's why they come to the mountains. Sweater weather they call it."

Mrs. Swain had been a fashion model in Miami before she married Mr. Swain. She still carried herself at times as though she was modeling her clothes.

"How's the darling baby?"

"She's sleeping this morning, I hope."

"What a good baby, that you can leave that way. Mine were never that good I assure you."

I had no choice but to leave the baby by herself. Sometimes Roy stayed with Sarah in the morning while I cleaned the parlor and guest rooms. But most days he had too much to do in the yard. Even on rainy days he worked in the shed repairing equipment, sharpening shears, painting flower-boxes, refinishing rocking chairs. We had to leave Sarah in her bassinet for more than an hour at a time, looking in on her when we could.

"Sarah is a jewel," Mrs. Swain said.

"She'll be hungry now," I said.

"Don't forget the fireplace in our apartment," Mrs. Swain called after me.

The Mountain Manor smelled old. Even though it had been repainted at the beginning of the war the rooms still had the scent of age, of must and pipe smoke, of old wood and dinners long eaten. I noticed the smell most when I went into the room above the kitchen where the brooms and vacuum cleaner, polishing cloths and fresh linens were kept. The furniture oil and laundry detergent covered up the old smells a little, but I hated the mixture of dust and mildew under the odor of peeling paint, and wet soap.

"The Mountain Manor is the second oldest building in the county, after the King House," Mrs. Swain liked to tell the guests, showing them the hand-carved railings, the wide yellow pine floorboards.

"The place ain't fit for nothing but tearing down," Roy liked to say, after he had tried one more time to fit the ancient shutters on their pins or rehang a door so it would close in damp weather.

"The Mountain Manor was built by local craftsmen under the supervision of Mrs. Baring herself, and Mr. Proctor from Charleston," Mrs. Swain said to the visitors. "Notice the carvings on the mantel."

I took off my apron and put the broom and dustpan in the corner of the little room. It had been a maid's room at one time, before the caretaker's house was added. There wasn't enough shelves for all the soap boxes and bottles of polishes and blueing.

"The Mountain Manor had its own chair shop and cabinet makers," Mrs. Swain would say. "They made something known as the Flat Rock Chair. Here is an example."

Roy had repaired some of the old chairs so many times

there was hardly a piece in some of them that had not been replaced, and then sanded and stained and varnished to look old.

When I hung up the apron I knocked over a box of washing powders, spilling a little pile of blue dust. But I didn't sweep it up. Mrs. Swain did not inspect the cleaning room more than once a week and she might not even see the spill. On second thought I flattened the little pile with my foot and swept it mainly into the dark corner. In the dim light you'd have to look close to see it there at all.

I hurried down the stairs. I wanted to get back to the cottage before Mrs. Swain could tell me to do anything else.

Sarah was awake and screaming when I came through the door. Roy was already there trying to quiet her, but men don't have a way with babies, especially little babies. He was bouncing her up and down the way you might a two-year-old.

"That won't do no good," I said.

"Well what in thunder will?" Roy said. He still had his tobacco in and needed to spit. He handed Sarah to me.

I held the crying baby to my chest with one hand and got the bottle from the icebox. "There now, there now," I said, but I knew Sarah would not stop until the bottle was in her mouth.

"Did you call the bank?" I said to Roy.

"When would I get the time?" he said, putting on water for his coffee.

"This is the day we're supposed to call."

"They'll be out in the street celebrating," Roy said.

"Somebody's at least got to answer the phone."

"They'll give all their loans to returning soldiers," Roy said. "Without you're a veteran they won't give you a cent."

"If you won't call I will," I said. "Soon's I get the Swains' apartment done."

"It won't do no good," Roy said.

"Here, you give her this," I said and handed both Sarah and the warmed bottle to him. As soon as the nipple was in her mouth she stopped crying.

"Yeah she's a sugarfoot, she's a sugarfoot," Roy sang as the baby ate.

"We won't never get out of caretaking if we don't go now," I said. "Prices will shoot up when all the soldiers come back."

"Little sugarfoot, little sugarfoot," Roy sang. Roy never joined in the hymns at church, but he sang to Sarah. And he used to sing to little Ginger when we had the dog at the Maybanks place.

"Soon as we get the loan I'll give the Swains our notice," I said. I emptied a can of pork and beans into the saucepan and stirred it.

"We'll never get out of caretaking," Roy said.

"We won't never if we don't call the bank."

When Roy agreed to come to the Mountain Manor as caretaker the Swains said they only wanted me to work part-time helping Mrs. Swain with the housekeeping. "Lend a hand from time to time" was the phrase they used. That was the first year of the war, and it seemed that every week a new task was added to my duties. First it was the washing, then the ironing, then the dusting and sweeping. The windows needed cleaning, and their apartment.

"It's the war," Mrs. Swain said. "Help is impossible to get. We've got to pitch in and make do."

But our salary never went up, no matter how much extra I did. We got the cottage and a hundred a month. Sometimes Mrs. Swain let me take home leftovers from the kitchen, things the cook didn't grab for herself. And at Christmas Mr. Swain sent us a crate of oranges from Florida where the Swains lived in winter after the Manor was closed.

Once a task was added to my job it was never taken away.

Besides making the beds and cleaning the rooms, I even set the table sometimes when the maid was sick. I was responsible for the flower garden and for the flower vases, which had to be changed every day. Mrs. Swain made me wash the walls twice each summer to keep down mildew. When I was pregnant with Sarah I had to carry the mop and bucket up the stairs, and carry the heavy wash out to the line.

"Could you just give me a hand with this?" Mrs. Swain would say, and I always did, and that new job would become part of my responsibilities.

With the war ending something was bound to change. I hoped the main change was that we could leave the Mountain Manor and build our own house over on the creek. Part of the trap of caretaking is that you don't have anywhere else to live.

It had been two weeks since me and Roy had driven into town to talk to the man at the bank. Roy had kept the Chevrolet roadster running throughout the war by taking special care of his tires and saving his ration stamps for gasoline and oil. The car was a rosy chocolate brown, but he had to put a black door on the right side after he was hit by a truck in the parking lot of the feedstore. The thing I had always liked most about the car was that, besides the big round headlights, it had two lower foglights. The rich yellow lights and shiny chromium made the little car look expensive.

We drove into town and carried little Sarah right into the bank. One of the tellers opened a door in the fence that divided the middle of the bank and led us back to Mr. Fitzstephan's desk. Mr. Fitzstephan was the vice-president.

"I'm sure you folks know how hard it is to get building materials," the banker said after we sat down.

"The war's almost over," I said. I shifted Sarah from my left arm to my right arm.

"I can see she's going to want a home," Mr. Fitzstephan said, pointing to Sarah. "She's going to want a sandbox in the sideyard and a room where she can put her dollhouse. And a parlor where her boyfriend can wait for her to come down."

"We just need a little house," I said.

"Even a little house may be expensive after the war," Mr. Fitzstephan said. "The price of materials will shoot up when rationing stops. Houses will never be cheap again."

"Roy's going to build most of the house himself," I said. "He can do most everything but the wiring."

"Your collateral would be the land?" Mr. Fitzstephan said.

"Daddy's deeding me fourteen acres," I said.

Mr. Fitzstephan sat back in his chair and put his hands together on the desk. "I'll have to do some figuring and some looking into," he said. "But you call us in two weeks. We should know by then."

I did not know why it seemed that Mr. Fitzstephan was doing us a big favor. It was the bank's business to sell loans and me and Roy always paid our debts. The tone of the interview was like the bank was going to give us something, if we could prove we were responsible people.

After we left the bank I took Sarah to the picture studio. The studio had advertised that for three dollars they would do a portrait of a baby and make three prints. That would be one for me, one for my mama, and one for Mrs. Swain.

"I just have to have a picture of that baby," Mrs. Swain said every day after we brought Sarah home from the hospital. "It makes life worth living to have a baby in the house, doesn't it?"

I was worried about telling the Swains we were going to leave. I don't know why it made me nervous. After all, soldiers would be coming back, looking for work, and women would be laid off from the factories and available for house-keeping. I had been doing twice as much work for the Swains as they said I would when they hired Roy. But anything I could do to be friendly seemed worthwhile, so I had planned from the first to give one of the pictures to the Swains.

"She's a glamor girl," Mr. Reeves the photographer said. "She's going to be a model or an actress."

He seemed to know exactly what he was doing as he arranged the cushions on the carpeted platform.

"You'll have to sit behind and hold her up," he said. "I've got to get the face in the light."

I crouched on the floor behind the platform and cushions and held Sarah up almost in a sitting position, my hands concealed by the blankets. The platform reminded me somehow of an altar on which sacrifices were made, but I couldn't see how to follow the thought through.

Sarah began crying as soon as the bright lights were turned on her.

"She'll stop in a minute. It's just the surprise," I apologized.

But again Mr. Reeves seemed to know exactly what to do. He turned off all the lights except one, and Sarah continued crying. With the end of the rubber cord in his hand he stepped forward and shook a rattle in Sarah's face. She stopped crying for just an instant and the camera flash went off. Then she began screaming.

"That was perfect," Mr. Reeves said.

"Are you sure you got her not crying?"

"It was perfect. Like I said, the girl is going to be a natural model."

The pictures came in the mail a week later, and, just like Mr. Reeves had assured me, they were perfect. He had caught Sarah at just the instant when she had looked with curiosity, and even delight, at the rattle in front of her. She appeared to be listening.

"A darling picture like that makes you feel good for days," Mrs. Swain said. "And you'll have it the rest of your life to remember these first weeks. There is no time like the first few weeks."

After lunch I put Sarah to bed and returned to the Manor to tidy up the Swains' apartment. The Swains' baby blue

Cadillac was parked near the guest entrance. They always left it there during the tourist season, where it could be seen from the highway, and by all who drove into the parking lot. There was a hitching rail with rings on it where visitors on horseback had tied their horses a century ago, and a mounting block where ladies could easily hoist themselves into the saddle.

The Cadillac had glittering wire wheels instead of hubcaps, almost like carriage wheels, and new white tires with deep treads. Because they kept soldiers from time to time the Swains got extra ration stamps for gasoline and new tires. In winter they traveled around Florida and the South distributing brochures about The Mountain Manor.

"The Mountain Manor was built by the Barings to house the overflow of their guests from the Low Country," Mrs. Swain liked to tell her customers. "The Barings presided over the social life of old Flat Rock, and they knew once their friends from Charleston experienced the cool mountain summers they would return and build their own estates here. The Manor was first more a private guest house, and then was taken over and operated as a fine inn by Mrs. Baring's nephew. I like to preserve its tradition of privacy and friendliness."

The Swains were in no way related to the old Flat Rock families. They had bought the Manor as a bargain during the Depression, and had renovated most of the building in the past ten years. But they liked to talk as though they were part of the old Flat Rock summer colony, and had been friends with the founders, the Kings and Lowndeses, the Memmingers and Fishers and Barings. They liked to give the impression that by staying at the Mountain Manor tourists could, for a few days, belong to the old order.

Mrs. L'Heureux, the old lady from New Orleans who had arrived in a long car driven by a chauffeur, stood in the parking lot calling her little dog. It was the kind of terrier that looked covered with hoarfrost. The day before I had had to give it a bath and Mrs. L'Heureux had tipped me a dime.

"Come here Rudy, come here Rudy," Mrs. L'Heureux was

saying. She wore a lavender suit with a huge corsage, but swayed unsteadily on her feet. The little dog came up close to her, then barked and backed away, circling.

"Come here Rudy, come here Rudy," Mrs. L'Heureux said.

"Would you like me to help you?" I said. Mrs. Swain said we must always be helpful to guests.

"Oh that would be lovely," Mrs. L'Heureux said. "Rudy has been very naughty."

I got behind the little terrier and walked toward Mrs. L'Heureux. The dog barked and snapped in defiance as he advanced toward his owner, then stopped and backed almost to my feet, then dashed sideways. I put my foot out to stop him, and when he turned in the other direction I scooped the tiny dog up in my left hand. The terrier barked as though he was being tortured.

"You've been such a naughty boy," Mrs. L'Heureux said, taking the dog from me and cuddling him to her bosom. "Such a naughty boy."

From the scent on my hands I could tell Rudy had been rolling himself in carrion, probably in the dead snake Roy had killed in the rose garden and thrown under the back hedge. Dogs love rotten things like we love perfume, and he had covered himself with the stink.

Mrs. L'Heureux took a lacy handkerchief from her pocket and wiped Rudy's nose. "He's gone out and caught himself a cold," she said.

I headed for the washroom to scrub my hands before going up to clean the Swains' apartment.

It made me more tense to clean the owners' apartment than any of the guest rooms except the parlor. Mrs. Swain was so particular she'd made me come back more than once and dust a bookcase and scrub the bathroom sink. It made me nervous to work among the Swains' things. Their phonograph records were left lying around and had to be put back in their cases. There were many bottles of perfume and cologne in the bathroom that could be easily broken. The magazines scattered around their bedroom weren't like any magazines I had ever seen. Some were in foreign languages, and they had high-fashion pictures of both men and women, some with the models only half dressed. I liked to glance at those magazines as I straightened them up, but I was afraid one of the Swains would come in suddenly and catch me looking.

I took the ash bucket from the storeroom, and brought up fresh towels and washcloths. The rooms in the afternoon always smelled like Mr. Swain's pipe smoke and the bath powders Mrs. Swain used in the morning. The afternoon sun had warmed the rooms and I opened two of the windows to freshen the air. Mr. Swain had several bottles of whiskey on the sideboard, as well as crystal decanters and soda bottles. My job was to line all the bottles up in a row.

The bathroom was a mess. It looked as though all the bottles of bath oil and soap and shampoo and lotion had been left open. Gray water stood in the tub and chunks of foam stuck to the enamel at the water line. The bath mat was wet and curled up. Talcum powder had been spilled on the floor. The sink was in even worse shape. Mr. Swain must have cut himself shaving for there were blood-stained tissues on the counter and on the floor. The blood-stopping pencil was lying on the rim of the basin and the brush was still in the shaving cup. Mascara had been smeared on the sink also.

At a glance I saw the mirror had been spotted by spray from a toothbrush, and splattered with shaving cream. And the toilet would have to be cleaned. There was a brown streak in the bowl, and lint was stuck to the dampness around the rim.

I decided to leave the bathroom till last, after I cleaned the living room and bedroom and kitchen. To punish myself for avoiding the bathroom till last, I would clean the fireplace first. Since I was a girl I had been getting down on my knees and raking the ashes out of fireplaces. You had to be careful not to stir up the bitter dust, and make sure there were no live coals to catch other trash on fire. It was harder to do the Swains' fireplace because the hearth was tiny and I couldn't get ashes on the polished floor. I had to scoop the ashes carefully into the bucket without spilling any.

Sometimes the Swains had a fire on cool summer evenings to warm their rooms, and to burn papers. It looked as though they had started to burn magazines this morning or last night, but left them before all the sheets got consumed. I thought they might have tried to burn some of those odd but stylish magazines. I crouched to the fireplace and shoveled out the ashes, looking at each piece of scorched paper. There were leaves of notebook paper and corners of pages from magazines with parts of bodies, feet and elbows, the hem of a robe, the edge of a mink coat. I hated the smell of the ashes, and worked slowly to keep from raising any dust. One of the pieces of paper was thicker than the rest. It was a corner of cardboard, and stamped on the edge it said "Reeves Photography Studio." I blew ashes off the paper and saw the fringe of a baby blanket and a bootee. The bootee looked familiar. It was the portrait of Sarah I had given to Mrs. Swain.

I looked at the piece several seconds, then set it aside on the hearth. Very deliberately and carefully I finished cleaning the fireplace, sweeping the floor until the bricks were shiny.

After I set the bucket of ashes beside the door I washed my hands at the kitchen sink and swept the living room. I dusted and straightened all the magazines and records, and arranged the whiskey bottles on the sideboard. The used glasses I carried to the kitchen.

Two days worth of dirty dishes were piled on the counter beside the sink. I ran warm water into the basin and shook in a sprinkle of detergent. As I worked in the warm water the tightness in my throat began to ease. I rinsed and wiped each dish and put it shining in the cupboard. The clock above the stove told me it was two-thirty. The bank would close at three. After quickly sorting the silverware into its drawer and sweeping the kitchen, I carried the bag of trash to the door beside the bucket of ashes.

The telephone was on a little stand near the sideboard. It was a private line and didn't go through the Manor switchboard. Talking on the phone always made me nervous, and Mrs. Swain might come in any moment and catch me using the private phone.

I picked up the receiver, and when the operator answered I asked for the bank number.

"I want to talk with Mr. Fitzstephan," I said when the secretary answered.

"And who may I say is calling?"

"This is Willa . . . this is Mrs. Roy Whitmire," I said. "We applied for a building loan."

"Just a moment," the secretary said. It always amazed me how sure of themselves people in business in town could sound. It was like they understood how everything worked and they were in charge of it. I could hear people talking in the background. Mr. Fitzstephan might have already gone home for the day. People were always joking about "banker's hours."

"Hello Mrs. Whitmire," a man said.

"I'm sorry to be bothering you, Mr. Fitzstephan, but we were wondering about the loan we applied for."

"This was the building loan?"

"Yes."

"Just let me check our records. The board met this past Wednesday."

I could hear people talking in the background. I wondered if they were talking about Roy and me. Were they making up an excuse not to give us the loan?

"I'm sorry about the noise here," Mr. Fitzstephan said. "We're having a little celebration on the street, and it's spilling into the bank."

I could hear car horns honking over the phone.

"I have very good news for you Mrs. Whitmire," he went on. "Your application has been approved."

"Are you sure?"

"I'm very sure," Mr. Whitmire laughed. "A check will be issued to you any day you come in."

After I hung up the phone I did not remember at first where I was. And then I recalled the bathroom had not been cleaned. I forced myself to gather up the brushes and cleaners to complete the job. I had to put my hand into the dirty bath water to pull the plug, and as soon as the gray water had swirled out I attacked the grime and suds on the enamel. I scrubbed the tub until it shone, and wiped the faucet and knobs. After dumping in a large amount of cleanser I brushed the bowl and then flushed it. Last I picked up the bathmat and wet towels, wiped the lavatory dry and washed the mirror. After placing the fresh towels and washcloths on the racks I took the laundry, the bucket of ashes, and the trash bag downstairs.

Mrs. Swain was coming out of the parlor just as I reached the ground floor. She had on her riding breeches and probably was going for a ride with one of the guests.

"Oh Willa," she said. "I noticed there's a good deal of ironing to be done. Could you get to that this afternoon?"

"Yes ma'am," I said automatically. Mrs. Swain hurried toward the back door.

"There's something I have to tell you," I called after her.

"Yes, what is it?" Mrs. Swain stopped in the doorway.

"Roy and me are giving notice," I said. "We're going back to the creek to build a house."

"Are you sure?" Mrs. Swain said, smiling faintly. "Houses are more expensive to build, and jobs are going to be impossible to find. Once you leave we'll hire another caretaker and there'll be no coming back."

"We won't be coming back," I said. The words came out more stiffly than I had intended.

"Then I wish you luck," Mrs. Swain said, and swung out the door into the sunlight.

I carried the bucket out to the ash barrel, and I took the trash to the cans behind the kitchen. As I started to the laundry room with the wet towels and bathmat, it occurred to me I needn't tell Roy the good news immediately as I had intended. I would keep the news all to myself for a while, and wait until he thought to ask if I had called the bank.

"It's a great day," I heard Mr. Fuller saying in the parlor to someone. "It's a great day."

As I crossed the parking lot I saw Mrs. L'Heureux holding the little terrier beside the big touring car. "Rudy needs a toddy," the old woman said, putting the silver flask to the dog's lips. "Rudy just needs a little toddy."

Frog Level

I thought I saw Fielding's truck in the parking lot of the new Biltmore Mall when I drove in. But how could I be sure? There must be a hundred red 4x4's with oversize tires in Western North Carolina. I drove past it looking for a space. It was opening day and the lot was full to the very edges. I finally parked out near the end where they were still working. Bulldozers and earthmovers were tearing up the red soil and leveling more acres. And the paving crew seemed to be spreading its black cookie batter right over the clay and pressing it flat as soon as the ground was graded.

For months I had been passing the site where the mall was being built. The paper said it would be the biggest mall in this end of the state, and it looked like they were tearing up a square mile. The parking lot alone was big as downtown Asheville. Now that it was mostly finished and having the opening I saw how impressive it was: a chain of buildings that looked like cathedrals and palaces, with Roman windows and gables, glass roofs and solar panels on top.

When I stepped through the entrance into the air conditioning, through the balloons and ribbons and girls giving away free Pepsis, I saw what a palace it truly was, with marble floors and columns, pink walls and skylights above palm trees and fountains. To think we'd ever have such a place right here in the mountains.

I thought I would buy something nice to celebrate.

And then I saw him. Fielding walks with a swagger you could recognize anywhere. He always had that walk, but now with his fat belly and wide western belt and cowboy boots it's even worse. I'd told him that swagger really makes him look countrified, but he didn't care.

"Hell, I am country," he said.

He had on the plaid shirt I'd bought him for his birthday, the one with western pockets and pearl buttons. And he had on his green cap that said "Lessing's Nursery" on the front. He didn't used to wear a cap, until he got his bald spot.

At first I didn't realize there was a woman walking alongside of him. Or I didn't think the woman with bleached blond hair and leopard-spot tight pants was with him, until she took his arm and pointed toward a boutique where the mannequins had purple punk hair and purple evening gowns.

I was so stunned I stopped right there and somebody ran into me, spilling my Pepsi. I'd had my suspicions about Fielding for years, but I never thought he'd bring one of his women out to the Mall in broad daylight. He thought I was working all day that Saturday. He didn't know I'd gotten off at noon to come to the grand opening, though I must have told him. Nobody ever said Fielding was burdened with too many brains.

At first I thought I might just leave, go to my car and get out of there. But it burned me up that he could come out there on Saturday afternoon with a woman where anybody from back home could see him. Who did he think he was? Some of my friends from the plant, or from the church, might see him.

I threw my cup into the nearest marble trash can and took off after them. I wanted to see who the woman was. There was a terrible crowd, and I kept bumping into people. But somehow Fielding must have felt me coming, or seen my reflection in a store window. For even though I lost him temporarily among all the people, when I did find him again he turned and looked at me. And he took that woman's hand

and started hurrying away. She glanced back at me once and then they ran.

I don't know how they got out of there that fast. There was a stream of people moving in front of me, down the main gallery, and by the time I worked my way through them Fielding was nowhere in sight. I figured he must have headed for the main entrance and I ran there, past the girls in shorts handing out Pepsis and cookies and balloons. I must have bumped into a dozen people, but I didn't pay them any mind. I was too mad to care about politeness.

And when I got to the parking lot he was gone. They must have split up, or were hiding among the ocean of cars. It was hard to see in the bright sunlight, with so many windshields reflecting. I ran toward where I remembered his truck being, shading my eyes. I didn't have time to fish my sunglasses out of my purse.

Sure enough, just as I got to the end of the second row of cars, under one of the big light poles, I saw the red 4x4 squeal out into the driveway toward the exit. From a distance it looked like Fielding was by himself. By the time I got to my car he was already at the traffic light and turning right on red.

My car was blistering hot, but I got started up and drove down the periphery road, out to the lights, fast as I could. There were cars coming on the West Asheville Parkway, and I had to wait for an opening. Finally I pulled out anyway and let the cars behind me hit their brakes. The drivers honked at me, but what did I care?

There were two ways Fielding could go down the expressway. He could drive on into Asheville, risking the lights and the buildup of traffic. Or he could get on the interstate and try to outrun me. And on the interstate he could choose to go either north or south. I gambled that he would have turned south, back toward home, at the first ramp, and not taken the second toward Knoxville. But by the time I merged onto the interstate headed south, he was long gone.

I-26 runs along the edge of the Biltmore Estate. You can't

see the big house from the highway, but you can see the vineyards and pastures. There was no exit until the road to the airport, after the four lanes swung down across the French Broad and then up again along the bluffs. I passed every car on the road. My hands shook on the wheel I was so mad. It was the kind of anger where you have to do something. I just wanted to hit Fielding in the face with my fists. I wanted to ram into him with my bumper. In all the years I had suspected him I had never caught him with another woman. He had left me at home so many nights and I had laid awake in the trailer, and cried, while he was out coonhunting or with his buddies down at the Copper Worm. I had done our income taxes and insurance forms at night while he was off gallivanting. When we used to go see Mama on Sundays, before she died, and he left early, I made excuses for him. And I told people at church he had to work on Sunday mornings.

I wondered if he had turned off and gone to the airport. But that wouldn't have done him any good since you can't just run onto a plane without a ticket. You can't take out a few bills and pay the stewardesses the way you might the conductor on a train. I would have to gamble that he had not turned off to hide in the parking lot of the airport.

There was a rest area two or three miles beyond the airport exit and I slowed down as I approached it. But there was no red 4x4 in the slots in front of the bathrooms and water fountain so I speeded up again. But just as I was passing I saw his truck wedged between two semi rigs in the truck parking area. He must have felt clever, hiding so close to the highway.

I hit my brakes and swung around the "Do Not Enter" sign at the exit from the rest area. Two cars were coming out to merge with the traffic, and both swerved to miss me. They honked and one driver shook his fist out the window and said something. But I didn't hear. I swung over onto the shoulder and into the parking lot. A semi was coming right at me, the bonnet over his cab swept back like a second forehead, both pipes spewing smoke. He hit his big horn and airbrakes, and

I whipped around him.

The truck horn must have alerted Fielding because he was already backing out of the space when I got even with him. I cut him off, and he was hemmed in between the big trailers. The motors of both trucks were running, and the place was blue with exhaust. I got out and ran toward Fielding, wondering if I could get to him in the truck. If he locked me out I'd have to stand there in the truck smoke yelling at him, or find a rock and break his windows. The parking lot smelled like hot tar, and candy wrappers were stuck to the bleedings on the pavement. I didn't care if Fielding tried to hit me, because I could hit him back, out here in the open, in daylight where everybody could see. I was almost as strong as he was, though not as fat.

But just when I got to his window, and tried to open the door, he threw the 4x4 in gear and ran straight up over the curb onto the grass. The cleated tires tore up the turf, and he knocked a picnic table out of the way, and drove on among the other tables where families sat around coolers drinking lemonade and eating potato chips from bags. He swerved to miss a little girl who was trying to feed Fritos to a squirrel. And further on he almost hit a woman walking her poodle on a leash. Because he swept so close the woman screamed at him. He jumped a cement-lined ditch and bounced back into the exit road. I ran back to my car, but by the time I'd turned around and barely missed a stationwagon leaving the parking lot, the red 4x4 had already blended into the heavy weekend traffic. I passed a car on the entry ramp and swung over into the fast lane in front of a Greyhound bus, but Fielding was nowhere in sight.

As I wove in and out of traffic, slowing when I saw a cop, speeding up when the patrol car was out of sight, I realized my hands were no longer shaking. I was sweaty and calm with anger, and more determined than ever to catch him. He had humiliated me for fifteen years, and this was the end of it. I had nothing to lose. I felt the relief of the end already. It had been a hard summer.

Where they had put in a new culvert under the highway I saw the sack fences placed to hold back erosion. The red mud had dried to orange plaster against the burlap. Those sack filters reminded me of Mr. Black, Big Shot Black.

Only the week before, after I got home from work and before I went to my class at Blue Ridge Community College, I drove over to Druid Hills to look at the property. It was the land owned by my great-grandpa and it had come down in the family to be divided up now that Aunt Livia had finally died. Somehow I got stuck with executing the will, maybe because I had looked after Aunt Livia when she lived at the old house and then at the nursing home for so many years. She hated me for putting her in the rest home and she cussed me for having her power of attorney. But Mama had looked after her before, and I saw no way out of it. I had to put up with her, and I had to sell the land once she was dead.

You never saw such a mess as where the cornfields had all grown up in brairs and honeysuckle vines and young pines. The pasture was just a pine thicket and even the old road out to the house was almost grown closed. The yard in front of the old house was a tidal wave of briars reaching over the box-woods and up to the eaves. The house where Aunt Livia and Grandma had lived so many years after Grandpa died was falling down. The porch had collapsed, and the fireplace where we had sat so many Christmases was full of soot and dirt blown out into the room.

I wanted Fielding to go over there with me to see about the place. But he was nowhere to be found. I was afraid that even if we had a prospective buyer the place was too grown up to be seen. And neither Fielding nor nobody else would help me clear it up. All the family members just wanted their money and kept complaining that I hadn't sold the place yet, that I was doing nothing, or that I hoped to keep the place for myself.

So I had to go see how bad things were, into that grown-up place full of snakes and hornet nests. I couldn't even get the car more than a hundred yards into the driveway, for a week of heavy rains and high wind had knocked a lot of pine trees across what was left of the little road.

Back on the county road I had seen the bulldozed entrance and a sign that said Black Construction Company was building a new housing development on the hill, but I didn't think anything about it. There were developments going up all over the county, and Black was one of the biggest contractors in the area. He had arrived from Connecticut only five or six years before, and already he had built hundreds of houses in the outlying creek valleys beyond the city limits. And he had offered to buy our family land, but at such a low price I laughed at the lawyer who made the offer. These developers are all skinflints. They take family land and sell it for millions. I hated what they had done to the county, bulldozing and cutting roads and shelves out of the mountains. That's one reason I was taking the class in ecology and land use at the community college. I wondered what could be done right here in our own county to stop pollution and landfills and overdevelopment. There wasn't a creek left that wasn't full of mud and tin cans.

First thing I noticed, as I got out to walk the rest of the way up to the old house, was the red mud over everything. It was like somebody had painted the floor of the woods with red silt. Mud had built up in cushions in the ruts of the road, and puddles looked like orange glue drying. It was like stepping in red grease. The whole place had been flooded. You could see the dried silt on trees and saplings a few inches above the ground. It looked like some dam had busted above and released its water down the hillside.

The yard in front of the house looked like somebody had poured tons of mud over the boxwoods. Mud had spilled into the toolshed, covering up the plows and rusty hoes. A lot of the briars had been flattened by the sand. Everything seemed colored with the silt. The spring below the house was buried in mud, and rhododendrons had been broken down by the rush of water.

My feet sinking into the silt, I followed the path of the wash up the little hollow, fighting my way through the brush and tangles of vines. The mud was like jelly and so deep you could hear it slurp and sigh when you stepped in it. By the time I got to the boundary I knew where it was all coming from.

At the edge of the woods you could see the whole hill had been bulldozed off, all the way to the top, except for a tree here or there by a house place. There must have been a dozen houses going up, scattered around the ridge, with roads cut everywhere and great piles of red dirt high as revival tents lined with erosion. Gullies had washed across the roads, sending down the sheet of mud that spread through the woods and covered the land.

And there was a pickup truck that said "Black Construction Co." on its door. Standing beside the truck, in khakis and a hard hat, was Mr. Black himself, talking to two of his men. I crawled through the fence and slogged through the mud right up to him.

"Hello," he said, surprised to see a woman coming out of the muddy woods. I'd seen his picture in the paper a lot of times.

"I'm Rachel Lessing," I said. "And we own the property below here."

"Pleased to meet you," he said.

"You're going to have to clean it up," I said. I always like to get to the point, especially when there's trouble to deal with.

"Clean up what?" he said, sounding Yankee and superior. That really burned me up, because we were standing in the sticky mess.

"All the mud that washed down on our property," I said.

"Mrs. Lessing," he said, his face getting red. "A cloudburst is an act of God, and nobody is responsible."

"Clearing off this hill to wash away is not an act of God," I said. "And you took no environmental precautions. You set up no barriers or erosion filters."

I was using language learned in my class at the community college. It sounded good.

"We are not responsible," he said. "And your land is undeveloped anyway."

"Your mud buried our spring," I said. "That spring has been used by my family for a hundred and fifty years."

He got so mad he stomped his foot in the mud. He turned around and wouldn't face me. He wasn't used to mountain people who would stand up to him.

"God damn it," he said finally. "You people don't want your county developed. You want to keep it in corn patches and moonshine stills."

"You'll clean it up one way or another," I said, and walked away.

But it wasn't me that indicted Black Construction Company. Somebody else, somebody that lived over in Druid Hills, called the State Environmental Agency, and they put a suit on him. He had to bulldoze out the yard of the old place and carry the mud away, and he had to throw up barriers and burlap fences at the lower edge of his development. Those sack dams looked like something to catch fish, but all you saw washed up against them was mud and a few sticks and leaves.

Before you get to Hendersonville on the interstate there's a truck weighing station where the highway patrol usually sits. I didn't think I would get past them without being stopped. I slowed down to maybe seventy-five or eighty, but no cop came out of the weighing area. Maybe the tourist traffic was too heavy for them to want to chase anybody. Both lanes were bumper to bumper closer to town, and it got impossible to cut in and out. I wished I had bought a new car, say a Thunderbird, instead of driving the old Maverick.

"She don't even bother to cash her checks," Fielding liked to tell people. "She just lets them pile up in a box until they almost expire."

Somehow just having the checks makes me feel better. Once they are deposited in the bank it feels like the money is gone. Even though I can draw it out there's nothing tangible but a bankbook.

I came over the hill just in time to see the red 4x4 sneaking off at the Hendersonville exit. Wasn't that just like him, hoping I'd think he'd gone on home? I was in the left lane, passing a truck, but I slowed down and cut in behind the semi. Three or four cars behind honked, but I didn't care. Let them sit in their air conditioning and take offense. My life was falling apart and politeness was no longer a concern. I halfway missed the exit ramp and knocked over a couple of reflector poles, but swerved over into the lane. A red light had stopped Fielding at the entrance to Four Seasons Boulevard. He must have watched me approaching in his rearview mirror, for he peeled out, even before the light changed, and ran along the shoulder to avoid hitting the traffic on Route 64.

I saw what he was going to do. The entrance to the Wal-Mart shopping center was just ahead. If he turned there he could go out to the retirement condominiums and rest homes around Highland Manor Lake, or duck into the huge parking lot at the shopping center, before I got close enough to see which way he had gone. I thought of driving on the median to get around the stopped traffic. But there was steel fence along the outside lane. I had no choice but to wait until the light changed and work my way over into the right turning lane. The heat from the pavement and the exhaust from the idling cars seemed to tie the air in crazy knots. The air was boiling in dirty fits, just the way I was.

Once I got off the boulevard I had to make up my mind quick. If I turned into the parking lot he could already be out by the new lake and choosing any of several small county roads. If I drove toward the condominiums, he could be sitting in the parking lot, and easily get back to the boulevard.

Without making a conscious decision I swerved into the parking lot and banged over the speed breaks, nearly hitting an old woman shopper coming out of Wal-Mart who didn't look. These Florida people think they have the right of way everywhere.

I drove all the way past the Western Auto store, the flower shop, and Lil' Critter pet shop. And there Fielding sat in a handicapped parking space. If you want to know how dumb Fielding can be, just consider that: parking in the most conspicuous place in the whole center. Of course he was hoping I'd drive on out to the lake.

I pulled in behind him to cut him off, and he was hemmed in, with cars on three sides and the bars for holding shopping carts on his right. You could see him hesitate for a moment, his big belly up against the steering wheel, before revving the motor and driving into the railings. Fielding never could stand to think about something too long. He had to move. He used up his circuits quickly and was in danger of overloading his switches if he had to think.

The bars must have been only screwed into the pavement for he knocked them over with his bumper and pushed the row of carts out into the driveway. The carts made an awful scraping and banging racket as they tore apart in two sections and he crashed through. Everybody in front of the stores and in the parking lot was looking at him. He left the bent carts rolling away on their own and laid rubber along the edge of the lot toward the second entrance by the Taco Bell. By the time I had backed up and eased around the bent railings, he was already pulling into the traffic toward town.

I suppose every wife wonders from time to time why she ever married her husband. And some wives probably wonder every day why they stay married. But I remember all to clearly what attracted me to Fielding. It was his Jeep. I was in my third year of high school, but every afternoon and every weekend, and all during summer break and Christmas break and Easter break, I had to work in Daddy's fruit stand at Frog Level, on Highway 25. That's what people called the stretch down in the pit of the valley, along the creek where the sun never shone. It's all buried under the interstate now and the creek runs through a culvert into Lake Summit. But then it was a place every tourist knew, driving up from South Carolina into the mountains and back.

Along a mile of highway there must have been nine or ten fruit stands. They all had porches facing the highway and stood on stilts in back over the creek. The valley was that narrow. And while we sold some fruit, some apples and peaches and pears in season, and cider and mountain honey, and little jars of jelly and preserves, it was the bedspreads and trinkets we made the most money on. Clotheslines stretched on either side of the stand held tacky-looking counterpanes and throw rugs on a sunny day. Daddy got them from a mill in Georgia, but he said to tourists they were made by mountain women.

And we sold gee-haw whimmy diddles and slingshots and Hill Billy billfolds. Under the counter Daddy had several boxes of firecrackers and cherry bombs, which were illegal in North Carolina. And he sold liquor too. He kept it in fruit jars in the minnow tank out back in the creek. The county was dry then, and he sold mostly to local people he knew. And sometimes he sold to South Carolina people who had stopped before and wanted a drink for their trip to the mountains. Chestnut Springs had been closed down by the Greenville Watershed and it was hard to get a pint along the highway.

That's why Fielding started coming by the stand every week in his Jeep. He and his daddy made liquor up on the mountain, and he brought a case or two for Daddy and stayed to talk to me. And he started giving me rides in his Jeep. I'd slip away with him and we'd drive out of the dank, mud-smelling clutter of Frog Level, up to the top of the Blue Ridge, and up one of the mountain roads, into the sweet wind and sunshine on the summit. I don't think I've ever felt happier than that, to get away from the fruit stand and my little brothers and sisters for a few minutes or hours.

Daddy cussed and threatened when I came back, and put me to work again, but it was worth it.

"You want to go out with some bootlegger?" he said. "Is that what I raised you for, to marry trash?"

"It's what Mama did," I said.

Daddy slapped me then. He was sensitive about how Mama had married beneath her, had grown up in Druid Hills and then lived in Frog Level. But I didn't care. The next time Fielding came with his Jeep I rode with him again, up on Mount Olivet.

Before we married Fielding promised me he'd quit making liquor with his daddy. And he did for a while. But you know how men are. They'll tell a woman anything until they have her. It wasn't long after we were married and I started working at the battery plant before I noticed Fielding sometimes had big sacks of sugar in his truck. He was selling shrubbery then, digging it in the mountains and peddling it in Greenville and Spartanburg. He liked to drive all the way up to Cashiers Valley to get purple rhododendron to sell to the flatlanders. I think all along he was selling whiskey while he drove around with loads of white pines and hemlocks, until the state and then the county voted wet. After that the 70s came and marijuana replaced liquor as the best money crop.

I've regretted almost every day of my marriage but I don't wonder why I did it. All I have to do is think about Frog Level, and the smell of exhaust along the highway in summer, and the way Mama had to slave there. I'd have done anything to get out of Frog Level.

Fielding had just come back from Vietnam and he was the most exciting person I'd ever met. The big boys in high school wouldn't pay any attention to me, because I was from Frog Level, and I was too shy to flirt and socialize like the other girls did. I was good at school work but I didn't fit in. I was first in my class in shorthand, and I won every spelling bee in grammar school. And when the postmistress was sick I filled in for her because I wrote a good hand and kept neat records. But I got married, and nobody in my family had ever gone to college anyway. How many times I've wished I'd gone to N.C. State and studied agriculture or forestry, agronomy, soil mechanics. That's why I jumped at the chance when I read in the paper that Blue Ridge Community College was offering the course in ecology and land use, erosion control.

The town was bumper to bumper, as it always is in August. They were getting ready to have the Apple Festival Parade, with floats blocking the streets and bands milling on sidewalks in their hot uniforms. Majorettes showed their long tanned legs as they leaned on cars talking to boyfriends. The Cadillacs from Florida, the BMWs and Mercedeses of tourists, were gridlocked with the pickups and local hotrods. The streets shivered in the afternoon heat.

I thought I saw the red 4x4 turning south onto Church Street, but I couldn't be sure. It took me eight or ten minutes to get there, and by then Fielding was several blocks down toward the south end. I thought I could see him near First Avenue as we came over the hill by the Methodist Church. But it could have been any red car. The police were getting ready to close off Main Street for the floats, and were putting up yellow sawhorses on the avenues. There was a lot of honking and cars backed up through changing streetlights. People were coming into town with their kids and crossing the street at any old place. Booths selling cotton candy and ice cream and cider were set up on corners, and the lines of customers spilled out into the street. I wished I had a bulldozer to knock aside all the cars in front, or a tank to blow away every obstacle between me and Fielding. Then I would blast *him* away.

When I finally got through town I headed south, just

assuming that was the way Fielding had gone. And by the time I got to Flat Rock, honking and passing everything, I saw him about a mile ahead, in the stretch along King Creek.

They've built a golf course and condominiums and rich-man's houses along King Creek, spreading Flat Rock right to the edge of the mountains. The driveway entrances have stone pillars and signs that say "Country Manor Estates" and "Honeysuckle Hollow." But after you get to Dead Man's Curve and start up the ridge, you're in regular country again.

Somehow I just knew where Fielding was going. I knew he wasn't going back to the trailer, and I knew he wasn't going to his daddy's place. If he'd been heading for South Carolina he wouldn't have taken the old road through Flat Rock.

When we were courting he used to drive me in the Jeep up the dirt road to Ann Mountain and along the old CCC road to Helen Gap. From the Gap you can look way over to the west, beyond the winding river valley, to the ridges rising one behind the other in upper South Carolina.

I hadn't been on the old CCC road in fifteen years and wondered if it was still open, or if some developer had fixed it up for access. If the road was rough Fielding could certainly leave me behind with the 4x4. My hope was the old road had been closed completely.

I turned off on the Ann Mountain Road and sure enough there was still dust hanging in the air. I spun on the gravel and tried to accelerate, but only banged and slid on the wash-board. There was a line of campers from one of the summer camps walking down the mountain, holding handkerchiefs over their noses from Fielding's dust. They hollered at me as I spun by, "Where's the fire?" and "Don't let him get away."

"This country has been taken over by foreigners," I said.

I was getting close to Fielding because the dust was so heavy I could hardly see the road in places. I almost ran over the shoulder a couple of times. The dust was filling the car, and I rolled the windows up. I was riding the surge of anger still, and if I had to sweat it didn't matter. I was going to catch

Fielding and make him look me in the face. I was going to make him answer me for once. I wanted to hit him in the eyes and on the nose.

Twice I met pickups loaded with hampers of polebeans coming out of the dust. Both times we almost collided and the drivers gave me mean looks. They had been picking beans all day and were covered with sweat for my dust to stick to. They could just get out of my way.

The road had not been scraped all summer and the rains of June and July had left washes across the tracks. Rocks had rolled down in places from the high banks. A rotten tree had fallen across the road and been broken and crushed by the traffic. My car chugged and coughed. The air filter was probably getting choked with dust. I hoped I didn't run out of gas, but I didn't have time to look down at the fuel gauge.

The road runs out the ridge for several miles after you get to the top, past fields and pastures, and the TV broadcasting tower. You can see for miles on both sides, but I didn't have time to look, even if I could have seen through the tunnel of dust Fielding was pulling behind him. My great-grandpa had lived up here, before he moved to Druid Hills. Mama had shown me the place, out in somebody's pasture, but I'd forgotten where it was.

The CCC road turns off to the left, beyond a bunch of new houses built in the Swiss chalet style by summer people. They had paved the road in front of their property for about half a mile to keep down the dust. I could see Fielding just ahead then, and speeded up. I honked at him, four angry honks. If we'd had kids I don't know what I'd have let him get away with. But we didn't have children, and for once I would do what I felt like.

He turned off and I slowed down just enough to make it into the side road, slamming into some dogwood bushes and probably scratching my paint, before getting back on the tracks. To my surprise there were houses built along the CCC road. A sign said "Black Construction Company," and for a mile they had cleared off the top of the mountain. The trees had been bulldozed down and pushed into great heaps. It looked entirely different up there, the road running out in the open instead of under black oaks. What used to seem mysterious and romantic about the road was now ugly. The piles of dirt graded out for house places were crimped with erosion. The road had been widened but not smoothed. In the old days Fielding's Jeep had bucked like a wild horse through there, and it was still almost as rough where the bulldozers had cut deep ruts and the rain had washed holes. I would never be able to keep up with Fielding all the way to the top and then on to the Brevard Road.

I was within a hundred yards of Fielding when the new graded road gave out, at the end of the clear-cut slope, and we bounced and banged on the rocks and ruts of the old road. The middle of the road scraped the bottom of my car. There was no dust now, except for the exhaust that came out of the tail of the 4x4 as Fielding revved it in four-wheel drive.

At the turn, in a place called the Sand Gap, where a logging road goes off toward South Carolina, a Volvo was parked, and further in the woods there was a camper. A man and a woman stood by the car and seemed surprised to see us. It was plain what couples like that met up here for, with a camper.

Fielding had already started up the steep switchback. My car sounded like it was going to stall, and I rammed down the gas pedal all the way.

The first thing you notice, when you get off a maintained road, is the unevenness of the ruts. One track will be washed out, and the other filled up with rocks and sand. My little car felt like it was going to stretch apart. The springs and shocks and metal frame wrenched like cold rubber and the car bounced and jerked over little huckleberry bushes that grew right out in the road.

Fielding was gaining distance. He was at least two hundred yards ahead. There were laurel bushes hanging right over the road and you couldn't see in places more than thirty feet. The air was cooler up there, and I rolled down my window. But a limb whipped in and stung me on the cheek, so I rolled the window up again, most of the way.

The red of the 4x4 flashed in and out of sight. Nobody but hunters and loggers had used the road for years. A big rock hit the bottom of the car and ground and groaned against metal as I went over it. I hoped the transmission wasn't broken. Another big rock, maybe a foot high, lay in the road and I had to back up and drive on the shoulder, knocking down bushes and a little maple. I hated to think what my paint job was going to look like.

The road out to Helen Gap runs right on top of the ridge. Through the trees you can see the sky all around. You feel like you're up in thin cool air, close to heaven. Going up there with Fielding when I was a girl I felt the clutter and smells of Frog Level and the valley all drop away. The air was vivid and everything was in focus at that elevation.

But I saw Fielding was going to beat me. There was no way my Maverick could follow the 4x4 up to the top and over. At some point there would be an obstacle, a washout or a boulder, that I could not go around. It came even sooner than I expected. I rounded a curve and saw the 4x4 rear up, as though it was standing on its hind wheels, and then drop as the back reared up. The red vehicle bounced and went on.

In a few more seconds I saw what Fielding had climbed over. It was a black oak log a foot thick, that lay straight across the road. And just before the log the left rut had washed out into a little gully, making the log even higher. Fielding was lucky to have gotten over it even in the four-wheel drive. There was nothing to do but stop and watch the 4x4 climb on up the ridge. I expected Fielding to stop and look back at me, gloating, but he just went on, bouncing and jerking over boulders, until he was out of sight beyond the rhododendrons. I had to back my car almost half a mile before finding a spot level enough and open enough to turn around in.

It was late afternoon before I got back to the trailer. I don't remember how I drove down the mountain because I was so mad. I must have made the turns and hit the brakes, but all I saw in my mind was what I would do to Fielding if I could. The way the 4x4 had climbed up the mountain reminded me how crude he was. He could go where I couldn't because he was so big and rough. He had gotten away with everything all his life because he was so crude. Images of how repulsive he was kept flying at me as I drove, of the way he picked his teeth and sucked on the toothpick after he'd eaten so much at Quincy's hot bar that his belly stuck out inches over his western belt. The way he wanted to roll you over when you were dreaming so comfortably and he wasn't even that interested, just couldn't sleep. He didn't like to take showers even in hot weather when he had sweated all day. For years I'd carried out all the garbage and burned it behind the trailer. He never touched it. But the thing that kept coming back to my mind, that made me so mad I couldn't think anymore, was the light lavender dress I had bought for Easter three years ago, before Mama died. I hung it in the closet for Sunday, and I was going to take Mama to church. She had to get around with a walker, and couldn't go by herself. The fishing season opened, the trout season, on Saturday. Fielding kept his fishing waders in the back of the closet and when he came in to get them he must have knocked the dress off the hanger onto the floor. And when he brought the muddy waders back he just threw them in the closet. When I went to get my dress next morning there it was, all crumpled up and dirty under those filthy waders. Even with a wet cloth and iron I couldn't get the stains off the silk and had to wear my old yellow dress. The worst thing was Fielding didn't care at all. He just sat in front of the TV with a Budweiser when I showed him the dress. "It looks like a whore's dress anyway," he said.

The trailer sat in a field adjoining Fielding's daddy's place. I didn't know what I would do when I drove up. But soon as I put my hand on the shaky screen door and felt it rattle on its hinges I saw what I wanted to do. The screen door had rattled loose for years and Fielding wouldn't fix it. I jerked down on the frame and the hinge screws flew out of the wall. I slammed the door back and kicked the glass out of the panels.

The release of the kicking and tearing took over like a tidal wave. I don't know what-all I did then, though I remember throwing pans out of cupboards and dumping corn meal in the sink. For years I had hated the trailer. I poured molasses in the toilet and broke glasses. I turned the bed over and cut the mattress. Fielding wasted all his money, so we had never made a down payment on a house. I hated the plastic furniture and the cheap paneling. I emptied the garbage bucket on the couch, and threw the television out into the yard. I got my clothes out of the closet and poured honey over everything of Fielding's until the honey ran out.

What a pathetic gesture it all was. Looking back it seems silly and pitiful. Men don't think women will commit violence. It's clear from the way they act they think women will put up with anything, that we have no choice but to give in. And the reason they think that is it's mostly true. But that one time in my life I was not at myself. Fielding told everybody I had destroyed his property, for no reason, and all his relatives and most of the neighbors sided with him. He showed them the trailer, and the broken dishes, and the shotgun I'd chopped up with an ax. He was lucky, for in my mind it was him I was hitting all the time.

I got my clothes, my iron, and a radio Mama had given me, and loaded up my car with some books and the stereo. I didn't know where to go. I didn't have any close friends. Suddenly it occurred to me I wanted to go where nobody knew me. I wanted to go to a motel and think about things. I could get an apartment later. I had all the checks I had saved for years.

While I was driving back down the washed-out driveway, and down the river valley, past Fielding's daddy's place, and the new brick church, and the new trailer park below the graveyard, I kept thinking of Fielding's stories of his service in Vietnam. He had been on a team that drove out from the base to rescue survivors of airplane and helicopter wrecks. Sometimes they drove for miles out in the jungle to find crashes. Most of the bodies would be dead, killed by the crash or fire, or by the VC. Sometimes a chopper would still be burning as they pulled out survivors.

I had to stop at the filling station before the ramp to the interstate for gas. It had been started by a cousin of mine as a simple fruit stand, after Frog Level was covered over by the new highway. And over the years he had added gas pumps and milk and beer coolers, local produce, groceries, potted flowers, and even a few clothes and fishing tackle, guns and ammunition. The place was now called the Rocky Creek Mall. I hoped I wouldn't see him, but he came out himself to pump the gas.

"Where you moving to, Rachel?" he said, looking at my loaded car.

"Haven't decided yet." He could tell from my tone of voice I didn't want to answer any more questions. "She looked mad and mean," he would tell people later. I didn't care, much.

Once I got out on the highway heading toward town I thought of a specific incident Fielding had told me about. When he was on the rescue unit at Da Nang a fighter bomber went down just short of the runway. But the plane didn't explode immediately and they headed out in the ambulance, into the trees at the edge of the base.

"But I didn't hurry none," Fielding said. "I knew those fuel tanks would go any second, and I didn't want to be standing inside that wreck. The sergeant kept yelling, 'Get the stretcher, get the stretcher.' But I pretended one of the poles was caught under something and I had trouble getting it free. And when we was running toward the crash I fell down and made like I'd sprained my ankle and had to crawl. 'Grab the stretcher,' the sergeant said to the other boy named Griffith. 'Grab the stretcher from that son of a bitch'."

"Griffith and the sergeant run ahead and started pulling one of the pilots from the cockpit. I laid on the ground watching them trying to get the body free of its harness and the crushed fuselage, when the whole air turned to fire. I got my eyebrows and half my hair singed off, and the blast knocked me back a few feet toward the ambulance. I was the only one left from that squad."

Good old Fielding, I thought as I turned into the motel parking lot. I should have listened to your stories more closely, back when I had the chance.

CRACKLIN' BREAD

"Leave a margin at the edge of the field," I say to Everett. "That way you'll have access when you come to dig the shrubbery."

"You'd waste half the field with access," he says.

"Save a lot of back-breaking to bring the digger into every corner."

But he's young, and not as worried about breaking backs as I am. And he can do whatever he wants to. It's his ground now, more or less.

"A margin will help protect the field from wash," I say, thinking of the turf as a protecting band around the plowed ground. But that's only half true, and I don't expect him to listen.

"Shrubbery don't cause wash," he says, and goes on with his loading.

What I don't bother to say is that a margin gives cover to bobwhites and other nesting birds, as well as rabbits and spiders that eat insects. I heard a feller on the radio the other day talking about diversity for the health of acreage. Ecological insurance he called it. But hell, even my pa said you don't want to starve your land with just one thing, and he never even went to school. But Everett's in no mood to listen anymore, not that he ever listened much.

"Times is changed," he'll say, if I make a suggestion.

He threw the county agent off the place once when the

poor feller suggested he might use some of the land for chickens.

"The highest prices are paid for incubator eggs," Moody, the agent, said.

"You got Mama and Daddy started on the chicken business forty years ago," Everett said. "Only you didn't tell them about coccidiosis. Did you?"

And I try to butt in and say that loss was nobody's fault. Coccidiosis could strike anybody's hens. But Everett slams the door of the pickup and drives off, leaving us old guys to talk about the weather.

"I don't want no college farmer wasting my time," Everett says the next day, as me and Ronnie and Sylvia are helping him bag whitepines and load them on the truck.

"Might be they could help," Sylvia says. "You never know."

"How would you know?" Everett says.

"They've studied a lot of things. They might could help."

Everett unwraps a stick of gum and rolls it up before sticking it in his mouth.

"Wish you had married one of those college farmers?" he says, and pushes Sylvia.

"Oh Everett," she says.

He pushes her hard.

"Don't hit her, Daddy," Ronnie says.

"Hit her again and I'll hit you with the shovel," I say.

Everett scowls, and says "Ahh," before throwing down the burlap and getting in the pickup. After he drives away, slinging gravel and mud behind him, Sylvia says, "He just ain't happy anymore." A fog of exhaust hangs in the air when he is gone.

The strange thing was that Mildred and me worried Everett didn't have any get up and go when he was young. He'd hang out at the store with his buddies and waste his money on fishing rods and hot rods. He had no ambition, and no interest in saving any money, or in farming, or the future.

But that all changed when he come back from the army. I noticed he was different, but I didn't know what it meant. Soldiering will change a man, any man. I'd seen it back in the war. He said very little about the jungle and his time in service, and for a while he spent most of his days over at Weaverville with a buddy of his from the army. And when he did talk to us it was always about them college boys that stayed home and got ahead while he was crawling around booby traps.

"They was crawling all over girls while I was crawling in the mud," he'd say, and laugh.

"What a way to talk," Mildred would say. She said we had to help him get over the shock.

"You can still go to college," she said. "It's not too late, and Uncle Sam will pay."

"I got no interest in college," he said.

That much hadn't changed about him at least. My generation didn't have no chance for education, with the Depression and all. Mostly we couldn't take advantage of the GI Bill after the war since we hadn't been to high school in the first place. But this generation has had education handed to them on a silver spoon, you might say.

But then Everett changed again when he got on at Tektron. First thing we knowed he was working overtime for time and a half pay, and double time on Sundays. He did twelve hours a day for eighty days in a row once without a break. And he started a savings account, and bought bonds and CDs. And then Mildred and me was pleased he started going out with Sylvia again. But it didn't seem like the same Everett.

Then after they was married we bought the trailer and put it on the hill behind the old house. And we gave the old house to Everett and Sylvia. They insulated a couple of rooms downstairs and moved in just about the time Ronnie was born. Most couples then was buying new houses, with big mortgages, or renting apartments in town. But not Everett. They lived in those two rooms in the cold months and saved their money, with a coal heater in the old fireplace, and Ronnie's crib right there in the living room.

I'm here to tell you he got interested in farming about that time. It was gradual, him putting in an acre of beans one year, an acre of bell pepper the next, working at night and on weekends. It was the first concern he had ever showed with growing things.

"It's in the blood," I said to him as we stretched wire for the beans. "We Thompsons have scratched this ground for nigh two hundred years."

"No, there's money in this ground," he said. "I always thought it was just dirt."

We used to grow a little shrubbery on the side, even back in the Depression, to sell to nurseries and contractors in Greenville and Asheville. But it was the boom of the '60s that really turned the mountains into one big shrub farm. As the suburbs of Atlanta and Charlotte expanded, and one office building after another went up on the beltways, landscaping firms couldn't keep up with the demand for dogwoods and whitepines, juniper and hemlock, even maple.

I saw early the advantage we had here in the hills. Northern trees like balsam and spruce would grow here, as well as the other evergreens. A gardener could put them in at the lower elevations, and they would do well for three or four years, sometimes even permanently. So this gave us a resource to exploit, like the ginseng my grandpa once went after in the coves and far-back ridgelines.

It never occurred to me to quit farming and put all the land in shrubbery. I never thought of not planting corn and some vegetable crop, and grazing a few cattle, and keeping hogs and chickens. But every year Everett set out another acre in pines or maples, covering up the farm land.

"Pretty soon they won't be space for corn," I said.

"So much the better," Everett said. "Even your damn county agent will tell you how hard corn is on soil. It's near bad as cotton."

"We've got to have corn to feed the stock, and for meal."

"So you can have cracklin' bread," he said, and laughed.

It's a joke he likes to bring up from time to time, how much I liked cracklin' bread. Back when he was growing up we still killed hogs in the fall, and soon as Mildred rendered out the lard and had cracklins left she made us some cracklin' bread, which is really just crisp cracklins put in batter and cooked into the cake. You wouldn't believe how good a flavor them golden cracklins give the bread. We had it every year right after hog killing, until the cracklins was used up.

Of course Mildred hasn't rendered any lard for years, and we don't even keep hogs anymore. The doctor says lard is bad for you. But every time Everett wants to poke fun he brings up cracklin' bread. I don't know why he thinks it's so funny. Must be he got teased about it in the army, or at high school. Or maybe it's because only oldtimers have heard of it. It's one of the things he's ashamed of, like going barefoot, and going to church, and praying at dinner.

Now I never was all that religious myself and I've done a little drinking in my time, in my younger days. But I wasn't ashamed of sacred things, and of showing my feelings either. I think it was the war that took the fun all out of Everett. And I always liked to make money same as the next man, but even after the Depression I never thought of money as the main thing.

In fact I never was able to communicate to Everett that the only real wisdom is in the work itself. If there is any truth at all it can't be explained in so many words, no matter how much education a man's got. It's the work itself, the action and the knowledge of the work. And my pa was able to teach me that without telling me, but I don't think I ever communicated it to Everett. You can't explain it, and you probably wouldn't even want to, except by showing it.

You've never heard me talk much about the romance of living on the land, and the significance of family, the way those newspaper writers who never held a plow or smelled horse farts will. It's the work of doing something right that counts, that allows a man to sleep at night. I'll admit being on my own with the sun and weather gives me pleasure too. But I wouldn't make any fuss over it.

"Afraid you won't have any more cracklin' bread?" Everett said again, and laughed.

But I was too happy he was working back on the place to take offense.

"Let's put all the bottom land in hemlocks," he said. "Hemlocks like water. And we can put a seedbed right there by the river, and put in a pump to sprinkle it."

Because he had kept the job at Tektron he poured money into the operation, building a plastic greenhouse, and buying a loader for lifting the balled and burlapped trees.

"Anybody can't make money these days is a fool," he said.

It kept Sylvia and me busy just mowing the fields he'd set out in summer, getting stung by jackets buried in the rows, swatted by limbs as we passed on the little tractors. Before I had the attack I'd put in a full day, and Everett joined us soon as he got home from the plant. He put up a floodlight by the greenhouse and we worked far into the night. Sylvia would bring us coffee and subs from the Seven-Eleven down on the highway, or Mildred would come down to the field with a box of fried chicken.

"Early bird gets the worm," he said. "Late bird gets it twice."

Ronnie carried water to the seedlings as we put them in the ground.

"Daddy bought me a squirrel rifle," Ronnie said. "He's

gone take me hunting some time."

But Everett never did take him hunting that fall. The .22 was a Remington bolt-action with a scope, the kind of rifle any boy would dream of owning. He took it out behind the house and practiced shooting at Coke cans. And he brought it to the field where we were working and shot at rabbits as they came out of the brush along the river.

"Don't aim toward the river," I said. "Somebody might be fishing there."

He put a Pepsi can on a post of the old pasture fence and shot at it several times. Then he leaned the rifle against the pickup and went off to play with sticks by the seedbed. I thought of a kid who had been given a bicycle too big for him, shiny and with lots of gears but too high for him to peddle easily.

"I'll take you hunting on Saturday," I said.

On Saturday afternoon we still had pines to dig for an order Everett had to fill from Spartanburg.

"I promised Ronnie I'd go hunting," I said.

Everett didn't answer. He was ripping burlap to put around the balls of dirt.

"He ain't had a chance to use his rifle," I said.

Everett never said a thing as I put down the shovel and left him and Sylvia to get the order dug and loaded. But he succeeded in making me feel awkward and guilty as I washed my hands and got my gun and some shells from the closet. My gunrack never looked right hanging in the trailer so I leave it in the closet.

"You're silly," I said to myself as me and Ronnie walked through the grown-up pasture to the hickories. Feeling guilty for squirrel hunting once in the fall. Why, when I was a boy I went almost every day in October and even as Everett was growing up we'd take off all of Saturday to hunt, walking back to the Flat Woods or up on Mount Olivet. We'd carry a sandwich and thermos and a candy bar and stay in the woods all day. And every fall we'd use up several boxes of ammunition, but have squirrel pie maybe a dozen times.

It was not the best weather for squirrel hunting. There was a bright sun, and a light breeze from the northwest fanning the gold hickories. Ideal hunting weather is overcast and still. The damp woods magnify the sound of a squirrel, and when it's quiet they're not afraid to come out. In wind you can't really hear or see them well, and they're too nervous to travel much. With leaves moving, a hawk could circle and dive on them and they'd never spot it.

But it was the time I told him we'd go hunting, and I slipped into the hickory woods hoping we'd be lucky.

"You go in first," I said. "That way if we see a squirrel it's your shot."

The hickories was brown and gold and the sunlight made them glow. The woods seemed gilded, and in the breeze the leaves moved like a million butterflies. Leaves was flying loose and rocking to the ground. It was a wonderful fall day, but impossible for squirrel hunting.

"Let's try to get in the lee of the hill," I said, "out of the wind, where we can hear them."

It wasn't much of a wind, but it was enough to shake the high branches. We found a place just slightly above two big hickories, and sat down in the leaves and fallen nuts.

"Where are they?" Ronnie said.

"Always point your gun away from yourself and other people," I said. "You wait for them to come out."

We sat in the leaves for a few minutes, but the mood was wrong for hunting. It was like I was in a hurry to get it over with, to give Ronnie a chance to kill a squirrel, and then get back to loading the pines. You can't enjoy a hunt in that state of mind. You've got to give time to the looking and waiting, to going further in the woods, listening for their bark and chatter. I caught myself looking at my watch, and thinking how many more pines I could have loaded, and how much later tonight we'd have to work to make up for this lost time.

Used to I could give whole days, even weeks, to hunting

in the fall after the crops was in. We had no money but that didn't seem to bother me. Mildred would fix an early breakfast in the dark house and I'd be off on the ridge by daylight. And there was no hurry. I'd take as long as it took to get some game.

"How much longer, Papaw?"

"Shhhh."

I scanned the canopy and saw a squirrel come out of a forks on the bigger hickory. It ran out a limb, rippling its tail, and back, as though confused by the wind. I pointed to it, and Ronnie raised his rifle.

"Wait till it's in the clear," I said.

He squeezed the trigger but the safety was still on.

"No hurry. Take your time," I said.

The squirrel spiraled up the trunk a few feet. It must have seen or heard us. Ronnie ran to the side and fired twice at the vanishing tail. We ran all the way around the tree, but the squirrel was gone.

"Dang blast," Ronnie said.

"Put your safety back on," I said. We didn't see another squirrel that afternoon.

"Let's plow up the pasture and set it," Everett says.

"In whitepines?"

"Whitepines or dogwoods."

"Dogwoods like shade. They like to grow under other trees," I said.

"It's too dry for hemlocks up there. We can put out maples."

"It'll wash away."

"Not once the grass takes under the trees and we can start mowing. It's not like you're going to graze cows there anymore."

Everett turns the pasture with the big diesel. He plows the hill all the way up to the hickories, like they did in the old days, growing corn on the mountaintops and under cliffs. But they didn't know better then.

"How long will it take for all the topsoil to be carted off in balls?" I say to Everett. "Pretty soon all our humus will be in people's yards in Spartanburg and Columbia."

"It'll take years," he says. "Longer than your lifetime."

"But not longer than yours or Ronnie's," I say.

"Don't worry about it," he says. "We can grow more topsoil. Besides, we're being well paid."

I want to say, how does he expect to build back the soil as long as he's selling it off in chunks with whitepines and hemlocks? But it doesn't seem worth the effort. He will oppose a point just because I make it. I did the same to my pa. Clearly he's worried the shrubbery boom won't last, and he's trying to make the most of it. We can worry about the soil later. Or at least he can.

Everett won't talk much about his money. I know he's putting a lot of it in his new house out beside the old one. But even that's a small skimption compared to what he must have made at Tektron and with the shrubbery in the past few years.

"Here's your topsoil," he says, and shows me a sheaf of bank certificates, when he comes back from town. They're green, and look like oversized money.

"Won't do you much good if the bank folds," I say.

"There you go again, still living in the Depression," he says. "Keep your money in a coffee can behind the spring house?"

Of course he can't understand why I never used a bank again. My pa lost eight hundred dollars when the bank failed. He worked twenty years to put that in, and in one day it was gone into somebody else's pocket. I was only fifteen at the time, but I swore I'd never trust a bank again.

"The Federal government insures every penny," he says.

"And what if the Federal government goes bust?"

"It can't. The government will just raise taxes."

"Then why is the Federal government itself in so much debt?"

But he's like a horse that's got his head, and there's no reining him in. Besides the pickup and the loader and the big truck, he's got two tractors, a bushhog, three mowers, an irrigation pump, two lawn tractors, a stationwagon, and the Lincoln Continental. Then there's the new house.

When he brought the bulldozers in and carved a shelf in the hillside beside the old house I said, "What do you have in mind, a mansion?"

"You just wait and see," he said.

"We always wanted plenty of room," Sylvia said.

And when the Jones boys, who are doing the contracting, poured the footing I believed her. You never saw such a foundation unless it was for a school or hospital.

"Part is the garage. There'll be room for three cars," Sylvia said, a faint note of embarrassment in her voice.

She showed me and Mildred a picture the architect had sold them with the plans. It was to be a brick house, with wings on either side, and three stories tall in the middle. The front had white columns going all the way up, I guess twenty or thirty feet."

"You sure that's big enough?" I said.

"Come on Dad, Everett's earned it," Sylvia said.

"You can't expect us to hunker down in that old house forever," Everett said. "Even you and Mama moved out of it."

"I'm not trying to hold you back," I said. "I like to see you prosper."

"But you don't want me to show it."

"I just wonder how you can heat such a house and keep it up, if the shrubbery business goes."

"If the shrubbery fails us, I'll open a trailer park in the bottom."

"He's just kidding, Dad," Sylvia says.

"No, a trailer park's a good steady income," Everett says.

I don't answer that. I have to get out of there. There's something scary about all the plans.

"The world's moving on," Everett calls after me. "It's not going to wait on us. There'll be no more poke sallet and cracklin' bread."

When me and Everett quarrel we never shout. I've never been a shouter. I don't want to get worked up and lose my head. I'd rather keep some control of myself even if I'm shaking mad. It's one thing that makes us mountain folk look quiet to outsiders. We don't like to get in mouth-to-mouth hollering matches. I'll stalk out and slam a door; I'll try to make some hurtful comment. But I was never one to stand hollering fury in somebody's face.

Then, there's always a first time, as they say.

Mildred, when we was first married, had a herb garden out behind the house. It was adjoining the regular garden, and beside the shrubbery beds, and the asparagus beds. Even when we moved up here in the trailer I kept the garden area mowed, and Mildred gathered the parsley and dill, her sage and mint the same as always. And I kept the asparagus weeded.

I see Everett plowing there, right through the old garden and the asparagus, and I run down the hill. He's already turned over half the herbs and when he comes back he'll finish them. The thought that crosses my mind is how will we explain it to Mildred.

"Hey," I say, and flag him down.

He leaves the diesel whining and I have to talk over the roar and the exhaust.

"What will your mama say?" I point to the turned herb beds.

"It's got to be done," he says.

"Who says it does?"

"I say it does."

I'm suddenly so mad I'm shaking, and my breath comes short. To think that my son would talk back like that on my own land. I try to holler above my weakness.

"We never planted this close to the house."

"The old house is going down soon as the new one is finished."

This is the first time I've realized the old one will go. I was born in it, and it's stood here all my life, though it's been added to and renovated. Great-grandpappy built it when he came back from the Confederate army.

"Who give you permission?" I shout.

"I don't need permission." He puts the tractor in neutral and leans down to holler in my face. "It's my land."

"Not yet, it's not," I holler back.

I want to grab him by the collar and throw him on the ground. I want to hit him up the side of his face.

"You get down from there and we'll settle this," I say.

"You're a dry-balled old man and you don't know it yet," he screams.

I reach up for him. I don't know if I am going to hit him. I just know this has been building ever since he come back from the army, and I want to finish it.

"Get down here you little shithead," I holler.

I reach up to pull him off the tractor seat and he swings. I take his fist right on my cheek bone, and it knocks me backwards. I slam against the big tire, and remember thinking, this is what it's come to, fighting your own flesh and blood. And I feel the ground hit my lungs from the back. But after that it blurs.

They say the tractor somehow slipped back in gear and jerked forward, over my left ankle. If Everett had hit me less hard I would have fallen closer and the tire would have rolled right over my middle and killed me. I remember the smell of exhaust and dirt as everything went black.

When I wake up in the hospital they have my leg in a cast, all tied up. But I can't feel a thing.

"You'll be alright," Mildred says. She stands there with her handkerchief in her sleeve. "You'll be alright."

When I get a wit or two about me I say, "I can't feel it down there."

"They say you've had a stroke on that side," Mildred says.

"A stroke?" The word comes out a little sideways.

And then I start to feel the pain. It isn't in my leg exactly, but all down my side, and all over.

"That's the damaged nerves," the doctor says when he comes in. "They'll hurt you for a while. I'll prescribe a painkiller."

At first I hesitate to take the pills, but the pain gets worse, and later that night I tell Mildred to pour me a cup of water. Sylvia and Everett come in as I start to feel better.

Everett doesn't say anything. He just stands there by the bed while the women do the talking. He's like me in that way.

"He's already feeling better," Mildred says.

"He better take care and come home soon," Sylvia says. "There's a lot of work to be done." She puts a little pot of flowers on the stand. "We have an order for a thousand maples," she says, "from Warrens, in Atlanta."

"I'll put in a herb garden close to the trailer," Everett says. "We'll get seeds at the organic place up in town."

"No use to," Mildred says. "I'm too old to take care of them."

When Mildred and me was first married, just before the war, I remodeled the house. Pa was still living then, and I could see he didn't cotton to so much fixing up and changing around. He was good about it, but he didn't want to be bothered. After working in the fields all day I'd eat supper and then hammer away, removing the partition between the kitchen and dining room as Mildred and the county extension worker had suggested. And I sheetrocked all the rooms downstairs, hammering and spackling till past midnight while Pa tried to sleep upstairs. Several nights he got up and came down to make coffee. He'd set there in the kitchen watching me. I was too young to care how irritated he was by all the changes around him. The house was still technically his. He'd sip his coffee and say, "I see hammer tracks on that piece up there," and point. And I was actually angry that he was picking flaws with my work, and not helping me.

"I see it," I'd say. What the young don't know they wouldn't believe.

With the war coming I saw materials would get scarce, so I did it all quick, even borrowing money from Pa. We had got electricity three or four years before, and I piped water from the spring down into the house, and put in a sink for Mildred. I tore out the old cabinet that had been there fifty years. It still had burn marks on it from the fire Grandma had started in the kitchen with bacon grease.

"You don't have to do everything at once," Pa commented. But I had a head of steam. I even worked on Sunday once, in the afternoon at least, sawing palings for the picket fence out behind the house. I painted the whole house in ivory, and trimmed it in offwhite, and I made a kind of trellis over the gate for Mildred's roses to run on. It was all a little garden for Everett to play in when he come along.

As Everett half lifts me and half pulls me out of the car, I see the little building beside the trailer. It's not been painted, but the roof is on, and it sits on a cement slab poured in the hillside.

"Who done that?" I say, straining to stand on my one good leg.

"That's a jacuzzi, Dad," Sylvia says. Mildred giggles by the door of the trailer.

"Ah shucks," I say.

With Sylvia on one side and Everett on the other I hobble up the steps and inside.

"Who's going to use that thing?" I say as they ease me down into the big chair in front of the TV.

"You are, Dad. Everett has put it in for you."

"Shoot," I say. I still have the pain in my side, but it has eased off slightly in the weeks I was in the hospital. Or maybe they have made a better match between the pills and my particular pain. With some physical therapy they say I'll be able to navigate a little with the walker. Maybe even walk a little eventually.

"I have enough trouble just getting to the bathroom," I say.

"The physical therapist says it will do you good. The rush of the water will soothe and strengthen your leg."

"That'll be the day," I say.

I don't even look out the window at the little building for two or three days, as I try to adjust to being home and being an invalid. Ain't nothing the same when you can't walk. It's simple to say, but a lot harder to live with around the clock, day after day. You forget about it, and then in the middle of the night you want to take a leak and can't do it without waking somebody. You realize it's mail time, and that you can't go to the box. Just moving your chair a foot to keep in the morning sun is an operation.

Ronnie comes by on Saturday with his trunks and says, "Papaw, let's try it out."

"Too old to try anything," I say.

"I'll help you," he says.

"Go ahead," Mildred says, "Everett built it for you."

"Ah shucks," I say.

"I can't try it unless you try it," Ronnie says. "That's Daddy's rule."

"You can't deprive him of it," Mildred says.

To humor them I let them put the trunks on me and drape me in the terry robe. Anything is better than the boredom of just setting. They lead me out to the little shed a step at a time.

I'm disgusted at myself for going along, but it's too late. Inside the little building it smells like new plumbing. There's a big tub and a pump and heater, and a bench. Ronnie turns the thing on. I watch the water churn and the tub fill.

"Oh," I say, as Ronnie eases me down into the warm water. I should have taken an extra pill before trying any such stuff as this. But the doctor has warned me to stick to his sacred schedule.

The push of the water hurts like the physical therapist walking my leg. I'm not sure I can stand it. I'm going to demand they lift me out, but I see Ronnie is enjoying himself, leaning back with his head on the rim of the tub. I'll suffer it just a few minutes, to give him a chance to use it all. Mildred stands above, as though afraid we might drown.

"You should come in," I say.

"I will one of these days," she says.

And then I begin to feel the lift of the water, the roll and lift of the current. I haven't felt this light in years.

"Shucks," I say.

"How does it feel?" Mildred says, sitting down on the bench.

But I don't answer. I close my eyes and the stream rubs and licks around me. This is something I dreamed about as a kid, a warm creek pool where the current caresses and nusses you. A pool where you get down in it level with the horizon all the way out to the edge of the earth. The warmth goes through my leg in green and purple waves and eases all the way up my side and into my shoulders. The water washes away age and pain for a minute or two, drawing them away from my nerves.

"How do you like it, Papaw?" Ronnie says, his face glowing.

"Ah shucks," I say.

The Bullnoser

"He thinks he's shit on a stick, but he's really just a fart on a splinter," Carlie said. It was a cottonmill saying she had been repeating for years. She especially liked to say it about T.J.

T.J. was walking back down the hill to his pickup. He had brought her another case of Budweiser, a bottle of pills, and a carton of Winstons.

"He's hoping I will drink myself to death and then he won't never have to pay me," Carlie said as she tore open the carton.

"Whyn't you get the law after him in the first place?" I said.

Carlie lit a cigarette, and pulled a can out of the box of beer.

"Give me one of them," I said.

"Get your own beer you lazy pup."

I helped myself to a can and popped the top. The beer tasted a little bit like aluminum, but it was cold, and mighty good on a humid day. It was a taste I craved when we didn't have no money.

"Whyn't you get the law after T.J. in the first place?" I said again. This was a conversation we had at least once a week. I knew all the answers already, but we couldn't resist going through the motions, especially when we had beer. When Carlie was on her pills she liked to listen to rock and roll on the radio and laugh and sometimes dance. She danced by herself in the dark room with a cigarette in her mouth. She circled round and inhaled and laughed. And she didn't want the light on. She didn't want to see the mess on the floor and on all the chairs. She just wanted to turn in circles and smoke and think about when she was a girl working in the cottonmill and had a boyfriend named Grover. That was way before she met Daddy and moved up here to the farm.

"On Saturday nights we'd go dancing at the Teenage Canteen," she'd say. "That was just before he went overseas." Sometimes she'd say Grover was killed in the war and never did come back, and sometimes she'd say he returned and married somebody else. It was hard to know what the truth was in her stories because she made up so much. In fact, I don't think there ever was a Grover. I think that was just a figleaf of her imagination.

But when Carlie drank beer she liked most to talk about how terrible T.J. had done us, and was still doing her.

"Why'd you agree to sell him the place in the first place?" I said.

"'Cause your Daddy, bless his poor little dried-up soul in hell, borrowed five thousand dollars from T.J. and I couldn't afford to pay it back."

I noticed a speck of dirt on top of my can. "I wonder where T.J. gets such dirty cans," I said.

"Probably at the Salvation Army," Carlie said, and laughed. She laughed so hard she bent over in her chair and the ash from her cigarette fell in the floor.

"The world is my ashtray," she said in falsetto.

"This floor ought to be swept," I said.

"You're a big strong feller, sweep it yourself," Carlie said. "'Stead of sitting around on your fat ass drinking my beer."

"T.J.'s beer."

"It's payment on what he still owes me."

I wiped the top of the can with my sleeve. For some reason I like the top of a can to be dry when I'm drinking from it.

"Why'd Daddy owe him five thousand dollars?" I said.

"'Cause your daddy didn't have a mite of sense and he had cancer and couldn't work. The truth was he never did work much. And I was too sick after you was born to go back to the cottonmill."

"So he just borrowed?"

"He borrowed against the place. He was going to inherit this big place. Everybody said Riley's place was the finest place on the creek."

"Give me a cigarette," I said.

She pulled the carton out of my reach. "Get your own cigarettes," she said. "Besides, smoking is bad for you."

"And it's not bad for you?"

"Don't do as I do, do as I say do." She laughed, but the laugh turned into a cough. I took a cigarette from the pack and lit it.

"Next time T.J. comes tell him you'll sue him," I said.

"And he'll say we got to move out."

"We can move out if he'll pay us the rest of the mortgage."

T.J. had built a trailer park on the pasture hill, cutting out level places almost to the top of the ridge. The ridge was called Riley's Knob after my grandpa, who kept it clear and grazed cattle on the very top.

"How much does he still owe us?" I said.

"He claims he don't owe us nothing, that we done used it all up in rent for this old house and in the beer and little bits of groceries he brings."

"People say he paid you years ago and you drunk it all up."

"That's a damn lie."

"He tells people he lets you live here out of the goodness of his heart."

"People are dog puke," Carlie said, and opened another can.

"Ain't it about lunch time?" I said.

"No, it's almost time for 'Tucson Days'." That was a soap

151

opera that came on in the middle of the day which she had been watching for several months. It was all about people in a retirement community and their families and people who work at the center. There was always somebody dying of cancer, or some old guy who turned out to have a second, younger family in Phoenix. And then there was somebody with AIDS, and somebody impotent, and a young nurse who was trying to marry an old guy for his money, except the young nurse is really a lesbian.

"Maybe I'll get my gun and go talk to T.J.," I said.

"You ain't gone talk to nobody," Carlie said. "You want to talk to somebody go talk to somebody about a job."

It was a point that always came up in our conversations, that I had lost my job. And she knew as well as I did it was impossible to get another one. When I worked in the cottonmill they put me to lifting boxes in the stockroom and I hurt my side. Their crooked doctor wouldn't give me disability and when I stayed out a few days for my side to heal they fired me. Because they fired me no other company would give me a job. All these plants work together against poor people.

Carlie turned the TV on and sat about a yard away from the screen. She kept her lighter in her right hand and a can in the left.

"Ain't you going to fix no lunch?" I said.

"Get out of here," she said below her breath.

You always feel stuffy when you've been drinking in the daytime and go out into the sun. It's like the light presses against you and pushes you around. And you don't feel like doing anything either. Even while the beer makes you feel lighter, it pulls you down inside. That's why Carlie likes her pills in the morning, and sometimes even when she's drinking.

I'd grabbed a pack of cigarettes on my way out of the dark house and I lit one, bending over to get out of the bright light and the breeze. The smoke tasted good. It was the only thing interesting out there in the yard.

The pickup still sat where I had jacked it up the week before. "I'll let you have my old pickup," T.J. said. But he'd just use it as another excuse not to pay us the rest of the mortgage. You don't get nothing from T.J. for nothing. The bearings were gone in the left front wheel, but I couldn't afford another set. I could squirt some grease in and drive it to the store if I had to, but the front end shimmied like sixty and I was afraid it would ruin something else. I had to wait till I got some money from T.J., or from working for the rich people down on the lake. They'd come after me sometimes to help fix a railing on a deck, or dig out a ditch along their driveway. But my back had been killing me again, ever since I wrenched it crawling under the truck to get the bearings out.

"You get that damn truck fixed so we can go to town," Carlie said.

There wasn't a thing to do but walk down to the mailbox to see if a letter had come from the unemployment office. I applied for compensation but they said I couldn't draw anything unless I could prove I was laid off in good standing. They said I'd have to contest the mill's claim I was fired. I filled out another form for them. I said I was as hard a worker as the next man, except when my back was acting up. It was their crooked doctor that wouldn't give me disability.

So they said they would have a hearing about it, and I've been waiting ever since, and have not drawed a cent from the government.

Used to, Grandpa kept the yard mowed clean in front of the house. But after the lawnmower broke down and wouldn't start I couldn't keep up with all the weeds. And then Carlie throwed out her old washing machine in the side yard, and the rusty barbecue grill and about five hundred cans, and it was such a mess you couldn't hardly walk out of the house without stepping on glass or a snake. And the weeds had already growed up around the truck like it had been parked there all summer.

When I was a kid Grandpa kept the driveway neat as a golf course. But T.J. had covered up the old drive and made a road to his trailer park. He was always bringing in trucks and building more spaces for trailers. I could hear a bullnoser somewhere up there grading, way on back of the Knob.

I took T.J.'s road across the little creek and up the hill to the mailbox. Grandpa had a little bridge there, and it was the perfect place for a kid to play, where the mowed grass came right down to the water and you could watch minnows shoot around the pools. I waded there and made little dams, and fished with a stalk of grass. I could slip through the edge of the pasture when the bull was penned up. Grandpa would take me over to the orchard on the bank below the road and peel an apple or pear with his knife and let me eat it. It looked like a little park in there, the way he kept the place, the gate and apple trees, the little bridge over the branch, the box-woods along the driveway. Carlie sold all the boxwoods right after Daddy died to help pay for the funeral, she said. If she had known what T.J. was going to do, she would have sold off everything else too.

When I was a kid, one time I went by the barn and pulled all the railings out of the gap. I liked to slide the poles back and forth in their slots and drop the ends on the ground. But they were too heavy for me to lift back into their holders so when I saw the mailman stop, I left them down and ran to the mailbox.

When the bull got back to that end of the pasture he walked out, just stepped right through the bars. And he was a mean bull too. Everybody was afraid of him. Grandpa kept him to breed people's cows, and he made some money for he charged three dollars a time. People were always driving their heifers down when they were spreeing, and bawling along the road. And the bull would hear them and bawl back, and then come running from whatever part of the pasture he was in. People usually brought their cows down late in the day, after they had stopped work in the fields and when they knew Grandpa would be around the barn, milking or watering the stock.

But when the bull got out it took half the people in the valley half the night to find him. I knew I'd done something bad, but Grandpa said nothing. He lit his old barn lantern and went out looking. Carlie smacked me across the mouth with the flat of her hand so my lip cracked.

"You'll get somebody killed with that bull and we'll all go to jail," she said.

I followed Grandpa and didn't go back to the house. The men hollered and ran along the fence at Fairfield's place, where the bull had run trying to get in with the cows. Grandpa couldn't hear too well and the men talked about him like he wasn't there.

"Riley's too old to keep a bull," they said.

"And Riley's boy has fouled his nest," they said.

"Now he's got cottonmill trash in on him," another said.

"Got to keep your breeding stock up, otherwise a family will run to ruin in two generations."

Grandpa walked along with his lantern not saying a thing. They followed the bull along the fence up into the holler and cornered him among the poplars. Grandpa snapped a chain to the ring in his nose and they put a halter over his head.

"You want us to lead him back?" they said.

"Much obliged," Grandpa said. "I can handle him."

I walked in front of Grandpa carrying the lantern.

Where the old driveway wound through the apple trees up to the mailbox, T.J. had bullnosed a new road for the trailer park and put in a culvert over the branch. It was all raw dirt. Grass wouldn't seem to grow on anything T.J. made.

"This place is all clay," he said. "I don't see how Riley ever growed a weed on it."

But T.J. knew how to grow trailer sites. They were all over the old pasture, all over Riley's Knob to the very top.

There wasn't no mail except a circular and three bills. I threw the circular in the ditch and stuffed the bills in my pocket. Carlie won't hardly ever pay bills until they cut the electricity off, and then she has to ask T.J. for the money. Of course, if T.J. owns the house like he says he does, the bills should come to him.

I saw I was going to have to have it out with T.J. I couldn't count on what Carlie said. She got mixed up, and she'd stretch anything to suit her, depending on who she was talking to.

I tried to remember if T.J.'s truck had gone up the hill after he left the beer, or if he had turned back toward the road. If he was up on the Knob I could catch him and have some things out. But I couldn't recall. I had been too busy arguing with Carlie about the beer to notice where T.J. went.

You could hear the bullnoser up there, working somewhere on the Knob. And there was always trucks going up there, pulling new trailers and carrying loads of this and that. You would have thought he was building a shopping mall up there for all the stuff they hauled up the mountain.

I hadn't been up on the Knob in years. It was a steep climb, and T.J. had cut down all the trees so there was no place to squirrel hunt. And they were always working up there. You could hear the bullnoser going almost every day, and the clank of a well driller, and the shower of gravel being dumped on the road.

I'd just go up there and have a little talk with T.J. There wasn't anything else to do, except go back and watch TV with Carlie. The beer was wearing off and I was starting to sweat.

The old house sat on the only spot of ground that hadn't been bullnosed by T.J. Where the barn and shed stood he had covered up the old boards with dirt and filled in over the culvert. The whole hill behind the barn had been skinned off, with rocks and dirt showing. Where T.J. sowed grass around the trailers it mostly didn't take, and the little bits of shrubbery died. But them people living up there didn't care. They came and went, some working at the cottonmill and some with construction crews. Several trailers had Mexicans in them. They worked in the shrubbery business as diggers and weed cutters. But you almost never saw them. They left before daylight and didn't get back in the rattly pickup until after dark. One time I heard they bought a goat and roasted it for a celebration. But I don't think it was anything voodoo. They just like goat.

My feet kept slipping on the gravel of T.J.'s drive and I was out of breath before I got halfway up the hill. Too many smokes, I thought, and too much beer. Most of the trailers I passed were deserted. Sometimes you could hear the sound of a TV from one, or the buzz of an air conditioner. Pretty little wives sitting around in shorts watching television, I thought. That's what you could have if you worked: a pretty little wife in shorts sitting cool at home when you get off from work. The oil tanks on their stands stood like steel cows behind every trailer, and off on the side of each one a satellite dish tilted like a big white flower. I glanced through a window or two but I couldn't see anybody inside.

Up ahead a little kid was peddling his plastic racer around. It was a low tricycle that was meant to look like a motorcycle. The plastic wheels crunched hollow on the gravel.

"Ruddunn, ruddunn," the kid said, revving his engine. The kid was making so much noise with his throat and with the sound of the wheels on gravel, he couldn't hear a truck coming round the switchback above. It was one of those trucks with sideboards, the kind they use to deliver building supplies. The kid kept peddling out into the road, and the truck didn't slow down, but seemed to be gaining speed.

"Hey," I hollered, and tried to run up the hill. I tried to flag the truck driver, but he just kept coming, like he didn't see the tricycle. The kid was peddling right out into the middle of the road, and at the last second the truck swerved and missed him and then passed me in a cloud of dust. I didn't even get a look at the driver. The name on the truck door said something about "Division" but I didn't have a chance to read it.

"Does your Mama know where you are?" I said to the kid. He didn't seem worried by what had almost happened. I felt like I had been electrocuted, and needed to stand still. The dirty little kid had nothing on but a pair of shorts.

"I'll race you down there," he said, and pointed down the road.

"You better get back in your yard," I said. There was no woman in sight around the trailer, and no car neither.

"Better get out of the road," I said.

"You ain't my daddy," the little boy said, and peddled on down hill. It wasn't clear which trailer he belonged to.

Grandpa used to take me for sled rides on the pasture hill. He'd hitch up the timber sled he used to get wood around the Knob and let me stand on the runners while the horse pulled it up the pasture hill.

"Why don't you use the wagon?" I said to him.

"Because it's too steep here," he said. "A wagon would tip over or run away."

From the Knob you could see all the way down to the river valley, and the lake and cottonmill town. Today all I could see was the superhighway they cut through above the cottonmill. The traffic on it was a steady roar. It was too hazy to see much further.

I heard the bullnoser going around the back of the Knob, and thought that's where T.J. must be working. He must be clearing more woods and cutting out more places for trailers. I'd just go over there and see what he was doing.

The Knob used to be a grassy top where you could sit and look all over the valley. But it had grown up in bushes and briars, right at the summit. The new road T.J. had cut went around to the back, into a kind of holler between Grandpa's land and the Casey ridge. What could T.J. be doing back there? It wasn't even part of the place.

Whatever it was, they had been busy, for the road was packed down and dusty. A few ragweeds drooped in the middle, but they didn't have much of a chance against the traffic and dust. Dead roots stuck out of the bank of the road.

The new road went further into the holler, into the trees. I could hear the bullnoser rev up and then quiet down, screech into reverse, lurching and grinding like a tank. That seemed strange. Why would T.J. be making another trailer place further in the woods when he still had space in the pasture?

You could smell the diesel exhaust in the holler. Kudzu had climbed up the oak trees right to the top and then hung over. I don't know how the kudzu got started because it wasn't there in Grandpa's time. The Caseys brought their bottles and cans and dumped them in the holler. Maybe they had brought a sprig of kudzu or a seed of the stuff with their trash.

T.J.'s pickup was parked right in the road, and then there was another big truck beyond it. "Republic Industries: Carrier Division" was painted on the big truck. It was the kind of truck that had an elevator at the rear, but the bed was empty.

T.J. stood at the edge of the clearing watching the bullnoser work. The whole place had the smell of opened dirt, which always reminds me of mothballs and camphor, and the smoke of hammered rock. There must be some kind of fumes that come up out of the ground. Far above the clearing the kudzu hung from the oak trees in a mournful way.

I couldn't tell what the bullnoser was doing, except there was oil drums and big paint cans on the ground, where they had rolled them off the truck.

You should have seen the look on T.J.'s face when he saw me. Maybe he knew what I'd come to talk to him about.

"You ain't got no business up here," he said. "This is no-trespassing land."

"It ain't even your land, yet," I said, sounding madder than I felt because of the heat and being out of breath.

"Don't start that again," he said. "This wasn't never your

Grandpa's land. This was Casey land and I bought it from them."

"Just like you bought Grandpa's?" I said.

"Let's go talk in the truck," he said. "It's air conditioned."

He practically pushed me toward the truck.

"It's time to settle this," I said, feeling bolder than I ever had before.

"Let's get out of the heat," he said.

T.J.'s pickup was practically new, but the cab was already dusty and piled with bills and invoices, candy wrappers, old coffee cups, a crowbar, and a basketball goal.

"I'm going to put that up for Jerry," he said, pushing the goal to the floor. "When I get time. Just push everything out of the way."

When he started the motor and turned on the air conditioning it was hotter at first, and then the breeze got cold. The sweat made me shiver, and I could see he was hoping to cool off the anger I'd worked up. It's harder to be mad sitting beside somebody than standing up and facing them. I expected him to start in telling me how Carlie had already drunk up half the price of the place, and smoked and borrowed the rest, like he always did. But he didn't.

"Are you hurting for money?" he said. "I knowed you got laid off."

"I'm always hurting for money," I said.

"I could let you have some," he said.

"T.J. it ain't dibs and dabs I'm talking about. This was a big place."

"It's just a rocky mountainside."

"Not when Grandpa had it."

"Your Grandpa killed hisself to make something out of this brush and hardpan."

"You're going to have to pay up," I said.

"Or you'll what?"

"Or I'll go to law."

"If you need a few dollars I can let you have it."

From the cold inside of the truck I could just barely see the bullnoser. But for the first time it occurred to me what the bullnoser was doing. Those oil drums weren't full of fuel. He was covering them up. He was burying the paint cans and barrels.

"What you putting in the ground there, T.J.?" I said.

"Just some trash from the Republic plant." He offered me a cigarette, then put the truck in gear and started backing away. "We can talk better down at the house," he said. "Or better still, we could go down to the highway and get some dinner. How'd you like a hotdog and a Pepsi?"

Nothing T.J. said was what I expected him to say. He didn't get mad and cuss like he usually did. His face was red but he didn't seem mad. He hadn't even claimed the place was paid for a long time ago.

We bounced down the ruts and washes of the road, and the truck whined on the switchbacks as he geared it down. He had a real good air conditioner. It was a funny feeling, looking down on the valley through summer haze from Grandpa's Knob, from a box of chilly air, and winding among the trailers and scraggly bits of shrubbery T.J. had set out.

And then it struck me what the bullnoser was covering up back there, and why T.J. was being so friendly.

"You're burying poisons and chemicals up there," I said. Carlie and me had seen on TV about how it was illegal to put chemicals in the ground. You could be sent to jail for poisoning the water system.

"What you mean?" T.J. said. "I give them permission to put trash from the factory there."

"Them barrels are full of poison," I said. "Now I see."

"You don't see nothing," T.J. said, all his friendliness gone.

"You could be sued."

T.J. was driving faster, banging on the washouts.

"You cottonmill trash will have to get off my land," he said. "Tell Carlie she's got to move."

"We ain't moving," I said. "Not after I tell the law what you're putting up there."

T.J. kept going faster on the switchbacks, sliding on gravel and throwing rocks every which way. I was glad to see the kid on the plastic bike was off the road and waving from the shade of a trailer.

"You tell the law a thing and you're out in the road with your old TV and stinking couch," he said. "And they'll lock Carlie up in the asylum for crazy people and drug addicts."

"And they'll lock you up for poisoning the ground," I said. "Then the place will come back to us."

"Get out," he hollered, and slid to a stop in front of the house.

"You're in trouble," I said and slammed the door. He spun off throwing rocks fifty or sixty feet. The heat felt good after the cold cab.

The screen door scraped on the back porch when I opened it. The bottom of the screen had scratched a curve on the floor boards. I'd meant to fix it for months, but a door is harder to repair than it looks. We'd probably have to replace the whole thing one of these days, because if you unscrew the hinges and put them on again slightly different, the door will rub in other places, and the latch won't click, or one of the corners won't fit into the frame. It has to be a complete job or nothing.

Carlie had tied a piece of cloth over the hole in the screen to keep the flies out. It looked like something put there for a charm to scare the bad spirits away.

"Where the hell you been?" she said.

"I've been around," I said, and pulled the bills out of my back pocket to hand to her. She'd had two or three more beers since I'd left, and maybe another pill from the jar.

It was so dark in the house I could only see her face reflecting the TV light. The air was filled with smoke. She was so wrecked she couldn't tear open the envelopes, and gave it up and threw them on the table.

"You'll have to pay them," she said. "I'm just an old woman."

"You got years left in you," I said.

"Trifling lard ass," she said, and tossed her head, as she does when drunk, like she was a debutante on TV.

"I seen T.J.," I said. I wouldn't tell her about the chemical dump for a while. It was my little secret.

"You get any money from him?"

"I told him he'd have to pay up."

"You lazy-assed chicken," she said. "I'd rather eat shit with a splinter than beg for money." That was another of the cottonmill sayings she liked to bring out when she was drunk. She lit another cigarette, not touching the flame to the tip until the third try.

I decided I wouldn't tell her at all. The oil drums buried across the Knob would be a secret between T.J. and me. He would keep me in beer and cigs and maybe get the pickup fixed. There was no way he could throw us out, and I didn't need to tell Carlie a thing about it.

"Give me one of them beers," I said.

"Get your own beer."

There was a game show on the TV with a laugh track. I hated game shows as much as Carlie loved them. I popped a beer and headed back outside. I hadn't felt so good since I found a twenty dollar bill in the parking lot of the plant before I was laid off. I sat on the porch looking down at the driveway T.J. had put in where the barn was. The cold beer tasted like hope and confidence. I'd have the pickup running again by next week.

When Grandpa was old and couldn't really work anymore he piddled around the barn, mowing a few weeds, watering the horse, sharpening his hoes, and talking to hisself. When I was home on leave from the army he took me down to the shed adjoining the barn where he kept his tools. There was an old table with sacks piled on it, and he showed me one by one where he hid his mowing blade and pliers, his hammer and wirecutters, whetrock and file. He said people stole so bad nowadays you had to keep things hid. He wanted me to know where they were in case he died. The tater digger and ax leaned behind some boards in the corner. The good harness for the horse was behind the table with some sacks piled on it.

Mack

When Mack runs out into the road my heart stops, for the way traffic goes today he wouldn't have a chance if one of these hell-fire drivers comes along, and there are more of them now than ever. He'll dash right out into the center, his blond and pepper hair combed by wind, and wait for me. My heart's liable to stop any time anyway, but I can't stand to see him out there where the traffic goes both directions fifty or sixty miles an hour. There's a law against such speed here, but nobody pays it any mind.

Annie says, "You're going to kill yourself running after that fool dog." One day a car stopped and another almost hit it from behind, and Mack just walked as happy as ever back across to me.

"That dog's a menace, Pop," somebody yelled from the car.

"Come here Mack, come here Mack," I said, and I picked him up and carried him across the pavement. I carry him every time we go for a walk until we're across the road. Luckily he's a miniature.

Even though you wouldn't think it to see him run out into the road, Mack's awfully intelligent. For hundreds of years his kind have herded sheep in Scotland, in the Highlands and on the islands. I've heard one dog can look after a hundred sheep or more. In fact he's the most intelligent dog I've ever seen, but like most smart people he has his weaknesses and blind spots. You know what they say, all geniuses are fools in one way or another. Mack's genius doesn't show unless you know him well. Now that I've come to understand him I see he's smarter than most people. A dog's mind has its own perspective, but once you see it you know it's wise. I learn a lot of things from Mack every day. Every day I watch him deal with the world and see how much humans have to learn.

"He likes that dog more than he likes me," Annie will say to visitors, to the preacher. And I smile, being sociable. I want to get along with neighbors, and be a good sport. Mack has helped teach me that.

"You'll have to put a leash on your dog when you take him for a walk," the dog warden said.

"Certainly I'll get a leash," I said.

And I got one, a bright green nylon leash which I carry in my pocket when we go out. I see somebody coming I take it out and snap it on Mack's collar. But it's not right for a lively animal to be tethered and bound when all he wants is to run over the ground and be free in the air, to race with himself and explore and be out with me.

"We've had a complaint from a neighbor," the dog warden said. "You'll have to keep him up and use the leash."

I know who turned him in, but I won't say nothing to the warden. You have to get along, especially with neighbors, people you have to see every day. Mack has reminded me of that. He doesn't hold a grudge. If somebody yells at him, or if something goes wrong, he's just as hopeful the next day, and ready to be friendly and have fun. Watching him has been an education for me. If only people were half as smart.

Dogs have an advantage being down close to the ground. They see and smell and are in touch with everything. On all fours they don't need to worry about balance, and they're close enough to sniff their shadows.

Now people stand up in the light and put on airs. They're proud and vulnerable, with their bellies showing, and easily knocked down too, I might add. They're defensive and belligerent and feel above everything. They don't want to get their paws in the dew, or follow out a trail of scent. People want to look down their noses and not get in the thick of things and enjoy it. How much better off we would be if people could just innocently sniff each other's behinds when they meet, and not go through the rigamarole of false smiles and irrelevant questions. Everything humans do reeks of pretension and interest, not to say duplicity. A little plain sniffing wouldn't hurt, say at a church social, or a White House diplomatic reception.

When I say such thoughts to Annie she shakes her head. "You're getting senile and silly," she says. "You're just an old man." But she doesn't understand what I'm getting at. Being around Mack has taught me a whole new way of looking at things. Watching him and listening to him I have learned more about my own weaknesses, and the waste of energy I have expended in my eighty-five years.

"You mark my word," Annie says. "That dog will be killed on the highway. And then you'll be a heart-broke old man."

But I take him in my arms when we cross the road, and I'm careful not to put him down until we're well past the shoulder and into the field on the other side. It is my job to look after him, and I mean to do it. Just as he in his own way is looking after me.

Even Annie admits it was a good thing to get Mack. "You've been a lot better since then," she says. "And you don't cry nearly as much."

I used to cry in the morning because there was nowhere to go and nobody to see, and my heart was too weak for me to do anything but walk a little. When your heart goes bad it gets you emotionally. I don't care what anybody says, a bad heart makes you depressed in spite of yourself.

When we went out to the woman's house on Kanuga to get the puppy I saw Mack in the pen immediately, and he saw me. He had the most intelligent eyes of all the litter. I spotted him instantly as the dog I wanted because he had already chosen me. That's the way it really was. As soon as I saw him I knew he had picked me. I ignored Annie's bargaining with the woman.

"He's an old man," she said. "And he has nothing to occupy his time and he needs a dog. But we can't afford a hundred."

"They're purebred collies," the woman said.

"He wants one bad, because he imagines he is in Scotland," Annie said. "But we can't pay more than fifty."

She says I imagine I'm in Scotland because I talk about Scotland a lot. But she knows I know where I am. Women like to needle you, even if they are good women.

The thing about love is that it humbles you. When you care that much about something the love spreads around and rubs off on everything you do. You see things for the first time, and you think how you've wasted so much of your life just getting to that point. But also you feel lucky to have finally been given so much you never expected.

When my heart acts up I get short of breath and have to stop. Once or twice I've actually blacked out and found myself sitting in the yard or along the trail. I don't tell Annie about those times, for she would just drive me to the doctor. Luckily it wasn't along the highway or on a high place when I fell. I'd hate to break a hip or shoulder.

When I carry Mack I can feel his heart knocking against his chest. Did you ever think how much a dog is like a human, their front legs like little arms and hands, their claws like fingers and toes? And the backbones and ribcage are similar to humans', not to mention their sexual parts. Even their eyes and their grin look like people's. Anybody can see we're close related.

A dog is a kind of little human except he has more hair and looks better for it.

But it's the way Mack takes an interest in everything I most admire. Whenever I'm ready for a walk he's already anticipated me. By the time I get out on the porch he's whimpering with excitement and wagging himself end to end, like he's just been told something wonderful is about to happen and he's busting to let you know.

"Let's go for a run, Old Mack," I say. "Have you been a good doggy? Come with Daddy for a run." And when I let him out of the pen he circles my feet jumping up on my knees, yipping. He's too happy to contain himself.

"Are you happy to see me?" He runs through the leaves, stirring them with his paws, and his silky hair flows in the breeze. And my own breath feels stronger when I go with him.

As we approach the edge of the yard I call to him, "Mack come here. Here Mack," and stoop down to gather him in my arms. He licks my face and neck. There are only two or three cars in sight, but they are spaced just far enough apart so I can't hurry across between them. And they are going slow enough so that I know another car will appear before they are all past.

"Hold on, hold on, Mack," I say, as he jumps in my arms. I talk to him the way I used to hear Annie talk to the babies. I can talk to him for hours and not run out of things to say.

A squirrel jumps into a Spanish oak and flows down the trunk nearby. Mack leaps out of my arms to chase it. He has never done that before. I watch him follow the squirrel between the oaks and suddenly, tail throbbing in the breeze, the squirrel darts into the road and Mack follows. I stand empty-armed and can do nothing as the second car hits its brakes and skids to a stop, the bumper a foot away from Mack, while the squirrel hops on across the other lane.

"Asshole," a teenager driving the car shouts at me. "Look after your dog, asshole." He jams in the accelerator and squeals a tire down the road.

"Come here Mack, come here." I bend down to pick him up again. I am shaking and my breath is short. The third car passes and we step onto the pavement. It is only when I am halfway across, right at the yellow line, that I see the blue car coming from the other direction. But this driver does not bear down on me. He slows and lets me finish crossing. Now I am almost out of breath, and stop to rest in the weeds on the other side.

"You stay off the road or you'll be killed," Annie says. "Or at least have sense enough to wear your hearing aid when you go out."

But the hearing aid buzzes and distracts me and I can't enjoy walking with it crackling up against my brain like a broken radio.

The tears come as I rest, holding Mack. He looks up in sympathy, but I can't help it. In recent months I've been crying more, and I don't know why. Sometimes it's just when I feel so bad because I can hardly get around and my breath is so short, and I sit in my chair and cry.

"You're worse than a baby," Annie says, but she pats me on the back. She doesn't know how she sounds when she talks. If she once heard herself she would die of shock.

"Here, take one of your heart pills," she'll say.

But I knock the pills away.

Sometimes in the night I lie awake and cry. I can't sleep with the pain in my chest, and my throat tight. Annie and I used to lie awake for hours talking in the middle of the night. But she sleeps now, except when I wake her up with my coughing. She doesn't like to be waked up.

"You're more trouble than the babies were," she says.

A few yards from the road I put Mack down and start walking. My breath is stronger, but there is a humming in my ears from the anger. I'll have to take it slow if we walk all the way across the field to the branch and back.

There was a time I could walk any amount of distance. When I was seventeen I walked all the way to the Smokies carrying a sixty-pound pack on my back. When I was young, people walked everywhere. Even on dates boys and girls walked to singings and to other churches in the valley and village. And in the war we walked twenty miles a day with all our equipment, a loaded rifle over the shoulder, and complained all the way, and did it again the next day.

When I was young and setting out for a walk my feet seemed weightless, and the soles of my shoes gripped the ground. My strides got longer and surer and I breathed deeper and deeper, drawing the whole rich atmosphere into my lungs and releasing it again. It felt like I was walking right across the horizon. It felt like my head was in the sky and I could see the curve of the globe ahead.

There was a rhythm I would get into, not just a left-right of marching but more of a waltz time as I strode along the trail and beside the creek, one-two-three, one-two-three. It's all a dance that takes you forward. That's what Mack seems to know. It's all a dance along the surface of the earth. I just wish I had realized that more when I was young and could have made more use of it.

I had a dog back then I called Old Boots, but I couldn't let him go with me. If I was fishing he jumped in the river and scared the trout, and if I was hunting he barked at the squirrels. I could never train him. And if I was trapping he left his scent on the trail and around the sets. Old Boots was a happy dog, but I didn't have time to understand a dog when I was young. You have to slow down and pay attention to his pace and moods to learn from him. And my daddy never liked it the way Old Boots wet his fine English boxwoods and burned one side of each. So I gave him away. And I never had another dog of my own until we bought Mack.

Skirting around the edge of the pasture I have to stop again. My breath gets rougher and rougher, and my head feels as though a lake is rising around it. Even as things start dimming out, it's as though I can hear noise from great distances, as you can under water. Even without my hearing aid I catch the roar of cars on the highway a mile away, and birds calling down along the creek, and a jet plane way overhead.

"Just your imagination," Annie says. "You hear things when you're about to pass out."

But I wonder if it's not some sort of compensation. As some senses start to go blank others become more acute, as they say happens with deaf or blind people. It makes me wonder about death, too. If the voices start up as we begin losing consciousness, does that mean we're already in another dimension and are just deaf to it, that daylight and what we think of as consciousness just blot it out, blind us like too bright a light? Could it be, like some preacher once said, the heavenly choirs are singing all around us and we're too distracted by things to listen to them, except when some accident diverts us?

As I stand in the dimness my heart bangs and then flutters, whispers and sighs. That one valve out of sync has its own timing, the doctor said. It's arhythmic, and always has been. But now the other valves are slipping and its aberration is exaggerated. I remember running and running as a boy, through the pine woods, along the pasture, down the steep trail to the creek. Then I would stop and listen to my heart, and the hammering in my ears. I imagined a horse galloping in my chest, its hoofbeats getting farther away.

Mack is running around my feet and jumping up on my pants. Some would say he is questioning. But I think he and I are on the same wavelength. He's knows I'm OK and is saying, wake up, let's go, you're going to be alright. He says, don't sink down into the comfort of the dimness and daydream. He knows there's the soft bed waiting for all of us, soon enough, and there's a temptation not to go on. He's saying, awake, and go forward. There's plenty of time to sleep. There is forever to dream in, to become the elements in their waft and tides.

The noise dies down and the ground stops shaking. Not shaking really but rolling, rippling like it was firm liquid. Mack has already run out ahead, and disturbs a rabbit from its bed. He chases it a few rods, and then gives up. He wants to stay with me. Collies are not dogs of the chase but herd dogs. They keep order and safety, in partnership with people.

I follow him into the branch cove, the glen, it would be called in Scotland. He sweeps around a clump of pine and comes running back to me. I wonder if he misses work. It must be boring not to have a job to do. He and I are both retired, you might say, unless I am his employment, looking after me, and he is mine. I step carefully down the gully side toward the branch. The raw dirt is bright as a flame between the pines, eating into the hill.

"Here Mack," I say. It's time to rest again.

I would like to sit down and rest but if I did it might be hard to stand again. I have a lot better use of myself than most people eighty-five. But sometimes my joints get stiff after walking, and when I try to stand up my head swims as though I'm being carried away in a whirlpool.

So I rest with my feet apart, and Mack lies down in the grass in front of me. He is so at ease on the ground. I watch him lie there, happy to be out of his house and pen and with his best friend. If only I could learn to be that much at home in the world. To feel connected to things you have to slow down. I don't think I've been that wise since I was two or three. It seems I can just recall the feeling of *being down there* close to everything and not worrying about the past or future, of resting on the ground as on a strong wave that carries you forward.

You've heard people say their heart knocked like a hammer on the chest. But if it's a hammer it feels like a hammer of leather, filled with water that squirts out with every blow. Hitting and leaking, hitting and streaming out its load.

I always like the little meadow by the branch, where the maples lean over the stream. But there are no cows now to keep the grass cropped on the bank, and big joe-pye weeds and thistles crowd around the water's edge. I wonder if these are the same kind of thistles that grow in Scotland. I've always meant to look that up, or ask somebody that knows. I need to go back to the house and sit down for a while.

"Here Mack," I say. "Here Mack."

You can tell he's disappointed to be returning to the house so soon. But he doesn't let it show for long. He's like a young woman with an old man who tires tco quickly, but is too gracious to let disappointment show. He bounds back up the trail ahead of me, then looks under a thorn bush where a ground squirrel disappears. He comes trotting back to my feet. Mack is so agile he never gets in the way of my steps. However slow or fast I walk he is always dodging around so I don't stumble on him.

It takes me longer to get back up the hill, and I don't enjoy it as much as the descent. The return journey is like the last few miles of a long hike, when you're just trying to make it home, or when you tire yourself out at lovemaking and just have to finish, sweating and determined.

But Mack is still in good spirits, and I have to call him twice as we approach the highway. Finally he comes back and I almost fall as I bend to grab him. It is the old problem of the blood rushing to my head and my head swimming. But I hold Mack to my chest and he licks my chin until things stop spinning.

There is more traffic now, from both directions, and I'll have to wait for a break.

"You're going to be killed on that road, you and that dog," Annie says.

"You've got to die sometime," I say.

"Just remember I warned you," she says, and laughs.

A delivery truck stops in front of the Seven-Eleven up the highway and traffic backs up behind it while cars in the other direction are passing. It will be my chance to cross if there is a break in traffic in the other lane. Mack whimpers. It always makes him nervous to cross the highway. Dogs are even less suited to the world of traffic than people are.

There is a gap in the other lane, and I start across. But just then a red car whips around the delivery truck and bears down on me. I try to get to the yellow line in the center, as though that ribbon of color is a kind of safety. But my breath deserts me and the air starts to dim. There are horns blaring and cars on all sides of me, but I can't see in what direction to go. If I could just sink down under it and let the traffic go on above my head it would be OK. And the noises I hear, beyond the horns and engines, are the thresh of the river, and a jet plane straight above, and water dripping through rocks in the ground far below. And there is a crisp sound, which is the crackle stars make on a cold clear night.

"Pop, you can cross now." It is the man in the red car, leaning out his window. He motions for me to go ahead.

Mack trembles in my arms, but I hold on tight to him, as though to a life preserver or buoy pulling me toward shore. The traffic is stopped in the other direction also, and all the drivers are watching me. The only horns sounding now are cars just arriving, behind the lines of waiting vehicles.

I take a step, and then another, and another. Soon as I reach the shoulder the cars slowly go by, and it is only after ten or fifteen have passed that someone yells, "Get yourself a wheelchair, pop."

I pace myself as I climb into the yard, and let Mack jump down to run ahead. I hope Annie has not seen the traffic stop for she will say I can't cross the highway again. The time has come to stay in the yard. She knows I can cross the road perfectly well except when my breath is short and the cars are going too fast.

Mack is already feeling better. He runs to the fence beyond the forsythia and races back, inviting me to join him. He is too smart to worry about the little things that distract him. You can see by the way he holds his head when he runs he's ready to enjoy the rest of the day.

THE MOUNTAINS WON'T
REMEMBER US

It took me forty-five years to focus my mind on it clear enough to do something, but once I did get it worked out, what had to be done, I knew I'd see it through—unless I died in the meantime. By that point I had the time, and I even had a little money to see things get done. I've had two marriages, one divorce, and three engagements. And now my children are gone, and the old woman is free to pursue her youth.

I don't know what Troy would say about all this effort to find out about him. First of all he wouldn't believe it. And he wouldn't believe many of the things that have happened since his death, since the war. I'm not sure I believe them, and I've been here all the time to watch them happen. Sometimes I push myself to the window and look out on the lawn they keep so neat and imagine showing him the kinds of airplanes they have now, the kinds of cars, and the houses and condominiums all over the mountains.

But of course you can't really imagine such things. He will always be the boy I last saw in '42 when he shipped out for England. My son Jerry is now ten years older than Troy was then. The last time I touched Troy he was lean and bony. He had lost weight in the Air Corps, from staying up all night working on those airplane engines. And he had took up smoking then, in the service. I remember the difference in the way he smelled, the tobacco scent in his clothes, the smoke in his curly red hair, mingled with the rose hair oil and the aftershave.

Then for almost half a century I didn't really know what happened to him. The telegram that came to his mama and daddy said he was killed in a plane crash, a B-17 that caught fire after takeoff and went down near the vilage of Eye in East Anglia. And that was all anybody would tell us. There was nothing to explain why he was in the airplane over in that part of England. I got out a map of Great Britain and looked, and saw Bedfordshire and Buckinghamshire, where he had been stationed, near the middle of England. It didn't make any sense he'd be flying in that airplane so far away from his home base.

"Maybe he had worked on the motors and they were trying it out," his brother Joseph said. "Them planes come in all shot up and have to be patched and fixed overnight for takeoff the next morning."

"But he was killed in the morning, at 10:46 it says."

But that was the best explanation we had, for forty-five years. I was in no mood to investigate anything in those times. I was just a girl, and the war was on. And I was paralyzed with grief. Looking back now I can see it was mostly grief for myself. I was young and selfish. All I could think of was what I had lost, and what was I going to do. I didn't have any plans, except to marry Troy. I didn't know how to do anything except work in the dimestore. And Daddy was going to give us the nursery.

The grief of those around me wasn't real to me. His papa and mama seemed not to comprehend what had happened. His sister was then pregnant, and I stayed with her for two weeks, and we cried on each other's shoulders, and I helped look after her little girl.

But I was just a girl myself, and thought things must turn out right on their own. I remember thinking it must be going to turn out even better in the end, that there must be something beyond this grief meant especially for me, after all the suffering was over. That's why I acted so silly, thinking only of myself. Like Job I would be given something greater, after it was all over. Nothing will make you a fool like selfishness.

And it was everybody giving me advice. Even Troy's own sister said, "Sharon, the thing for you to do now is go on with your life. You're a young woman with all your life ahead of you. Instead of grieving you've got to go ahead, find another man, marry, raise a family."

It was such kind advice my eyes wet over just listening to her. I knew she was right. And in my heart I thought, I'll get beyond this awful time and live a long and useful life. I had to be brave and get through the shock, and then life would start all over.

"You've got to live to help others," the preacher said. And I knew he was telling the truth. But looking back I can see that I understood, and yet didn't understand a thing.

But Troy's mama didn't say hardly anything. During the whole two weeks I was there on the creek she didn't speak five sentences. She sat in the corner much of the time, and she went through the motions in the kitchen. But it was like she wasn't there. While everybody else was hugging and crying she didn't take much part. Not that she snapped at people, or pushed them away. But it was like she was distracted; she was thinking her own thoughts. If I hadn't been so young and foolish I might have helped her, if anybody could have helped her. I was just there in the way, and everybody was fussing over me, the fiancée, not even the widow. My very claim on the family was tenuous.

We had been engaged since before Troy joined the Air Corps two years before. I would have married him the time he came back on furlough in '42, but he said that wouldn't be fair. It wouldn't be right to leave me alone while he went off to England. So there I was with an engagement ring, and a little shrunken photostatic copy of a letter with half the words blacked out arriving every two weeks. I complained to him about how short and few his letters were. It hurts me to remember that now. Him working all night in the grease and cold to get an airplane ready to fly the next morning, and coming in all tired and finding a letter from me complaining about how little he wrote. I'm ashamed to say I even complained about how few visits I got from his family. Only a spoiled and foolish girl could have said such things. I still blush, here in the nursing home, thinking of him three thousand miles away in the cold and mud of England reading such stuff.

I was relieved at the time there would not be a funeral, because his body was over there, if indeed it was ever found in the burned wreckage. I didn't think I could stand a funeral. But looking back I can see it would have been better for us, if there could have been some kind of service, some ceremony around which to focus our grief. Then once the rites were over, a part of our grief would have been used up, and we could have gone on with things. Everything is a kind of ceremony, even living.

There was a service, five years later, after his mama had died of cancer. They brought the body back across the ocean to the family cemetery. But I was married then, and had two little boys. And Charles my husband wouldn't so much as let me mention Troy. I had to hide any memorabilia I'd kept. It was awful, the way I'd sometimes sneak into the bedroom to look at the one picture I kept under the pillowcases in a drawer. I'd take out that photograph of Troy in uniform, made on his last leave home, in the dim bedroom light, and my eyes would get wet. And when I heard a step in the hall I'd slip it back under the linen. Charles never did find it, for if he had he'd have burned it up.

It hurts me to think of the things he threw away, boxes I had packed off in the attic, and the presents Troy had sent me, like a radio and a pink vanity set. But the thing I feel worst about is the arrowheads.

"I want you to have some of Troy's things," Mrs. Williams

said, when I was about to go home after the two weeks. "It's right you should take some of his things. It's what he would have wanted."

I wish I had protested more. I wish I had been firm. But what did I know, at the age of nineteen? She took me up into the attic of the cold house, in the cold November air, and showed me the boxes he had left when he went off to service. I remember it was warm right there by the chimney, and it smelled like tobacco, for Mr. Williams had hung some leaves to cure from the rafters. Tobacco was rationed in the war, and he had grown some of his own.

Troy was a wonderfully gifted painter. He had two sets of oil paints bought with money from the CCC and the cottonmill. And I took one of the paint sets, a box full of little tubes with the fingerprints still on them. And some brushes that had been washed and cleaned, but were noticeably worn. And there were five or six canvases he'd stacked there by the chimney. A lot of his paintings hung on the walls downstairs. But these he had left stacked in the attic, and they had gathered dust. I remember thinking that if they were just going to collect dust I might as well take them all.

Mrs. Williams opened up some of the boxes, and I saw dozens of arrowheads in each. Troy had sorted them according to size and shape. There were boxes with only black arrowheads, and other boxes with milkquartz arrowheads. In some pillboxes he had put the tiny arrowpoints used for shooting birds, some no bigger than a tooth, so you wondered how the Indians fixed them on arrows. And he had spearheads and tomahawks, pieces of pottery stacked in compartments according to patterns on the clay.

"Mrs. Williams, I don't think I should take any of this," I said.

"He would want you to keep it," she said. "And I don't need it around reminding me of him."

The flint arrowheads gleamed like jewels in the boxes. They were cold when I ran my fingers through them.

"I"ll just take a few," I said.

"Take all you want," Mrs. Williams said.

I'll never forget how dizzy I felt up there in that attic. Maybe it was the heat from the chimney in the dusty air, or the fact that I hadn't eaten much for two weeks. I was so skinny my skirt turned around on me. And the dust made my nose run.

I steadied myself with a hand against the chimney, and sorted through the boxes. In one little box there were only badges, his lifesaving pin, and the medal for perfect attendance at Sunday School. The last had a gold wreath around it for recognition of a second year's attendance, and four bars hanging below it for additional years. And there was his letter for playing basketball at Flat Rock, before I knew him.

In another box were the letters I had written him when he was in training at Biloxi, and then at Tampa. I was doing OK until I saw the bundle of letters bound with a rubber band, and recognized my handwriting on the envelopes.

"I can't stand to look anymore, " I said to Mrs. Williams.

She led me out of the dusty attic and back down the steps into the warm living room. But before I went home I did get those paintings and the boxes of arrowheads I picked out. If I could only have known their fate, I'd had left them up there in the dust.

"Mrs. McGraw, it's time to change your bandages," the nurse says, and gives me her sweet smile. At least she doesn't call me her "girl" like the night nurse does. She wheels me over to the bed and helps as I pull myself out of the chair and onto the mattress. The amputation was done more than two weeks ago, seventeen days to be exact. They cut me off just below the right knee, and I still feel the twitch of my toes and the flex of the ankle now rotting somewhere in a landfill.

At night, when I'm lying still, trying to sleep, I can feel the fever of the phlebitis. But mostly what I feel these days is the itching in the stump. It's like when you've been bee stung and the place itches so bad you want to tear the skin with your fingernails. And when an itch stops on one spot another starts nearby, every itch slightly different in feel and intensity.

"Oh, that's beautiful," the nurse coos. "That's just beautiful." She unwraps the stump. There is very little blood on the bandages anymore. What there is is a kind of yellow stain, made partly by the salve they put around the scabs and partly by the seepage from the scabs as they break in the process of drying. But there are only a few spots of yellow this morning.

"That's just lovely granulation, Mrs. McGraw," she says, rubbing on more of the salve, and unwrapping a fresh bandage.

"Your new foot will be here in a few days, and we'll begin the conditioning and practice walking."

She thinks I just sit in this chair all day and dream of walking again. It's the way I'm supposed to feel, and I don't want to disappoint her. I want to have the right attitude, to show I am a good patient, and appreciate their care. I never could stand ingratitude.

When Annie came by the other day I said, "I wouldn't have minded if the phlebitis had spread. It was good to feel feverish and numb."

"What a thing to say," Annie said. "What a terrible thing to say. You could have gotten blood poisoning."

I would never accuse Annie of being self-righteous, because she is one of my oldest friends. She was the one that introduced me to her brother Troy. We worked together in the dimestore uptown, and I came home with her one weekend. Her brother Troy came after us in his old Plymouth. On Sunday afternoon we took a long walk down to the river, the three of us with Annie's fiancé Muir.

There were two rocks in the shoals there. They were maybe ten feet apart and most of the river gushed between them. Troy took a run and jumped all the way across.

"Come on over," he called from the other side. "Who's

next?" And we just stood there laughing. Even Muir wouldn't try that jump, and he was taller than Troy.

"Come on over and we'll walk down to the store for a Co-cola," Troy called.

But he ran on down to the store and met us at the bridge with four cold drinks.

"You still have a lot of life ahead of you," Annie says. "A lot to live for."

I want to say, that's easy for you to say, with your one husband still alive after all these years. And your children and grandchildren coming to see you.

But of course I don't say such things. It would come out meaner than I intend. Instead I say, "My life ended in 1943, and nothing I've ever done could get it started again. It may be my fault; it may be a failure of character. But it's the truth."

"Sharon, I'm surprised at you. You raised your family. You've lasted forty-seven years since. That's a long life."

"Too long," I say.

"Shame on you," she says. "You should have more faith. I won't listen to such talk."

Annie looks older than I do, but she's still going strong. She's one of those women who grow tougher and stronger the older they get. She never had any more education than I did, yet she worked her way up to managing a clothing store in the mall before she retired. She still has a finger in all kinds of enterprises, from selling Christmas trees from the nursery to raising money for missionaries.

"I envy your confidence and energy," I say. "Maybe I just don't trust the Lord enough."

It is an old matter of contention between us. She has never thought I had enough faith. After Troy's death, when we heard a Thanksgiving prayer on the radio, thanking God for protecting us, I blurted out, "Well he didn't protect Troy, did he?"

And you could see the look of horror on his mama and daddy's faces.

"Sharon, you're not yourself now," Annie said.

But I was myself, and that was exactly the way I felt. I couldn't see anything God had done for me. He had killed the one person in the world I really cared about. I was just a foolish, grief-stricken girl, but I couldn't help the way I saw things.

"You've got to have faith the Lord always knows what He's doing," Annie said. "We can't know what His plan is."

"The Lord sees the Big Picture," Muir said. "He has plans so large and so long in time humans can't grasp them."

I wanted to say that was true, I couldn't grasp them. But I learned to restrain my tongue then and there when religious things were brought up.

Whatever Annie thought of my faith, it was my second marriage she really disapproved of. Charles finally left me after fifteen years of misery. He never could forgive me for having loved Troy before him. It was partly my fault, for I never told him how deeply I had cared for Troy. It didn't seem wise to even talk about Troy so much in those awful days of the war. And everybody said, "Now Sharon, you've got to find another man and fall in love and go ahead with your life. Only that will cure your grief."

And sure enough, within two months of Troy's death, I did meet another boy, a soldier, Charles Fulton. He was entirely different from Troy, and even that seemed for the best. "Forget the past, start over," everybody said. "Don't look back," the preacher said. I met Charles at the Teenage Canteen in town. During the war they entertained soldiers there. I was no longer a teenager, but it was the place young people met. The Canteen was under the street, under the bank building, and had a tile floor where we danced with the soldiers. You went down a long stairway from Main Street to it, like going down to a subway.

I'm sure Troy's family wouldn't have approved of the dances, if they had known. But what could they say. I was on my own now. I had the boxes of arrowheads and the paintings and Troy's letters, and some of his clothes. But there was the rest of my life to face. It was my life, and Troy was not there to help me.

Charles and I danced a couple of numbers. It was hot down in the canteen so he suggested we walk out on the street. It was winter time, but a mild clear night. As we came up the steps he put his arm around me and I felt good for the first time in many weeks. The streets were all dark, blacked out for the war, but we could see by the starlight.

"I'm shipping out on Monday," he said.

"Where to?"

"Wherever they need infantry," he said. I was so relieved he was not in the Air Corps. He wasn't as tall as Troy, and he wasn't as shy. He seemed more normal. I don't think the Williamses are typical people. They are quieter and more serious. And Troy was a talented artist. But I was ready for somebody more ordinary. I had fallen in love with somebody special and look where it had gotten me. That shows you how confused I was, and how disturbed by Troy's death. What woman in her right mind would fall in love with somebody just because he was nothing special?

And Charles was nothing special, believe me. If I had told him that night I was still grieving for somebody who had been killed, and that I hoped to get over it soon, but felt washed out and incapable of love, he would have gone back to his unit and shipped out and I never would have seen him again. But oh no, I was looking ahead, forgetting the past, just like everybody said I should.

When he kissed me in front of the darkened drug store I kissed him back. When he put his hands on me I put my hands on him. I needed arms around me. It was 1944 and the town was blackened for war, and there was no telling how long the man who held me might be alive. Shipping out could mean the Pacific.

"I'm glad I met you," he said.

"Me too," I said.

Charles was from the county too. His folks owned an apple orchard out toward Bear Wallow, but he wasn't sure he wanted to stay there when he came back from the army.

"I'm from Saluda," I said. "My folks run a nursery."

"Not Wilson's nursery?" he said, stepping back.

"Yeah, Wilson's," I said. He laughed.

"We've bought a lot of boxwoods from them."

Before he drove me home that night we were engaged. He was so different from Troy in every way. It was what I needed, I thought. If only I had not pretended, I would have saved myself years of misery. I acted like I was happy and in love because I thought that's how I should act. I knew that if I looked for somebody *like* Troy I would never be satisfied, since you can't replace somebody. Even I knew that. And it wouldn't be fair, always trying to see a man as somebody else.

But the opposite wasn't necessarily true either, that if somebody was different from Troy he would be the one to marry. I was in a hurry. I'd known old maids from the World War who never married because their fiancés were killed in France. I knew I didn't want to be like them, always living for the pictures, puffing themselves up with their martyrdom. Being a professional widow had no appeal to me either, even though that's what I became.

And to be fair to Charles, horrible as he was, it could not have been easy for him to return from the Pacific and marry somebody who was a stranger, and then find out she was still in love with somebody else, somebody dead, somebody he'd never seen.

"What are these?" he said when he found the boxes of arrowheads in the closet.

"They belonged to a friend," I said. "A man who died in the Air Corps."

"A friend?"

"A fiancé."

He stood with his hands on his hips. "Was that before you met me or after?"

187

"Before, of course."

He grabbed up the boxes and charged out of the house. I followed him a ways, back through the shrubbery, but I let him go. He walked to the edge of the creek and emptied each box in the water, flinging the hundreds of flint points and pieces of pottery into the current.

When he came back to the house he threw the boxes into the incinerator.

"I can compete with any live man," he said. "But I can't compete with no dead one."

I was too young and foolish to know what to do. I should have run to him and assured him he was the only man I loved. But I acted like I was paralyzed with anger and fear. I had been taken by the surprise of his fury. But the only thing I really wanted was to be alone again to think about Troy, or to talk with somebody who knew him, either his family or a friend.

There are days early in that first marriage that are burned in my memory like they had been put in a kiln. I wish I *could* forget them. A marriage is mostly a set of habits, and in those awful months Charles and I established all the wrong habits. If on Saturday I ran into Troy's sister Annie in town, he wouldn't speak on the way home. If he caught me brooding in the corner he'd yell, "That won't bring him back."

And I was so angry I never knew what to say. My best hope was to wait this period out, I thought.

I had told Charles the paintings had been done by me, that I had taken art lessons before the war. I had six canvases placed in various rooms around the house. One was a portrait of my Daddy's hound dog Troy had done when we first started going together. It was the least sophisticated of the paintings, done quickly while he was thinking about leaving, and I hung it in the hallway, which was dark most of the time. Another was a picture of an eagle in flight, its wings raised like flames several yards high. That was the painting that showed what Troy was capable of if he'd lived and worked at his art. Another was a scene of the river in moonlight, a trail of reflections cutting across the stream. I said I had made them when I took a class at the community center one summer.

About six months after he had thrown away the arrow-heads, we were having Sunday dinner with his sister Joan and her husband Harold. It had reached that time when the dessert is eaten and everybody is full and just making conversation. We talked about how beautiful the leaves were that fall. It had been the most colorful year any of us could remember.

"That maple by the fence is so red it glows in the dark, I bet," Charles said.

"It's never been this pretty before," Joan said.

"We should take a color picture of it," I said.

"Why don't you paint it?" Joan said.

"I never painted a thing in my life," I said, laughing.

"You have too. Don't be bashful. I've seen all those paintings in your house," Joan said.

"That was a long time ago," I said. "I'm all out of practice."

But I had seen the look on Charles's face. He knew I was telling the truth when I said I'd never painted anything.

On the way home I kept busy with the baby, hoping my surmise was wrong.

Back at the house Charles built a fire in the living room heater. It was cold by late afternoon and I sat by the stove nursing Jerry, who was two months old.

I heard something rip and looked up in time to see Charles slashing the portrait of the eagle with his pocket knife. He sliced the canvas into strips, broke the frame, and threw it into the stove.

"You thought I would never find out," he said. "You put them right under my nose where I'd see them day after day, and thought I'd never figure out who done them."

Again I was stupid with confusion.

"I didn't think it would hurt," I said.

"Well you was wrong," he said. He slashed and burned

the other five paintings I had been given by Troy's mama also. I'll never forget the smell of the paint scorching in the stove. I felt guilty for having taken them and for letting them be destroyed.

On the walls where the paintings had hung were light patches untouched by dust. I left them there for several months without putting anything over them. In their way they were portraits too.

The single most embarrassing moment of my marriage to Charles came within two months of our wedding. Charles had been wounded slightly, and he was discharged early, just before the end of the war. We were married as soon as he came back, in the spring before it was all over. I don't know if it was before or just after he threw away the arrowheads. But things were tense, and we were new to each other. I was trying to make a go of it in my ignorant way.

Charles had brought a bag of chocolate drops home from the store. He knew I liked them especially. And we were sitting in the kitchen eating from the bag. It was late on Saturday afternoon.

This car with a Georgia tag drives up in the yard. It just sits there, with nobody getting out, and we wonder who it is. Then just as Charles gets up to see what's going on, a man in uniform steps out and, leaning on a walking stick, comes to the door. When I see the Air Corps insignia a chill goes through me.

"Don't answer it," I said.

"I'll go to the door in my own house," Charles said.

"Does Sharon Wilson live here?" the man said, leaning on his cane.

"Yes she does."

"Could I speak to her?"

The man in uniform limped into the hallway. I almost ran back into the bedroom, but it was too late for that.

"You're Sharon," the man said. "I recognize you from your picture."

Charles closed the door behind him.

"Why don't you come in and sit down," I said.

"I'm Robert Trammel," he said. "I was Troy's best buddy all the way back to mechanic school at Biloxi. I don't know if he mentioned me or not."

"Oh yes, he mentioned you when he was home on leave."

Charles was still standing in the doorway to the living room.

"I'm Sharon's husband," he said.

Trammel looked around at him and his face reddened. "I didn't know you were married," he said.

"For about two months," I said.

"Troy and me made an agreement," he said. "If he was killed I was to come back and visit his family. And if I was killed he would come back and visit mine in Georgia. But since you're married I guess there's no need to talk."

"I want to hear about him," I said. It came out without my thinking. I would have given anything to be alone with Trammel for just a few minutes to hear about Troy's life in England.

"I never saw him after he went to England," I added.

"You heard what the man said," Charles said. "There's no need to talk now." He was already opening the front door.

Trammel's face got even redder as he strained to get up.

"So long," he said as he limped out of the room.

Charles stared hard at him as he went through the door.

Watching Trammel get back in the car and drive away I was so ashamed of myself I couldn't think. For the first time I really felt ashamed for having gotten engaged so soon after Troy's death. Even though everybody told me it was the thing to do, including Troy's mama and sister, I should have known better. I couldn't blame them, or the preacher, or my own mama and daddy.

"Sharon, it's your life," Daddy said, meaning I had to forget about Troy. He had promised us the nursery after the war. He liked Troy, and he had always wanted a son. He had never had any real help, with just me growing up on the place. And much as a father cares for a daughter and is proud of a daughter, he never really knows what to *do* with a daughter. There was the nursery to take care of, and the woods to hunt in, and the house to keep up. He liked to buy new dresses for me and see me look pretty, but I was useless to him otherwise. Troy was strong, and a worker. He and Troy got along from the first.

When Trammel was gone Charles slammed the door and went out. I was left alone with my punishment. I felt guilty for not taking charge and making Trammel stay in spite of Charles. And I could at least have gotten his address. I could have followed him out to the car and asked a few questions quickly. But no, I was paralyzed as usual when something needed to be done. I felt that big things had happened very quickly, and I had let the chance slip away. For two years of war Trammel had waited to see me. I would never know what kind of dangers he had been in, what missions he had flown, what Troy had told him about me. He and Troy had made a pact to visit each other's family, and I had made it impossible for him to fulfill his commitment.

Charles didn't come back inside all that afternoon. That was one time I would just as soon have had him come in and shout at me. I wanted to have it out. He had no cause to be rude to another veteran, someone who had done him no wrong. Trammel had seen as much action as he had. I had to come out of my paralysis some time.

All through the long afternoon I sat in the living room rehearsing what I would say. But Charles stayed away. That was the first time I realized our marriage really wasn't going to work. Before that I imagined we were going through a period of sorting things out. Once Charles understood that Troy was dead, and once I learned to live with loss *and* expectation for the future, learned to work again, things would improve, I told myself. But Trammel's visit showed me, shocked me, into seeing how hopeless it was to be with

Charles. He was spoiled; maybe he was damaged by the war. He would never get over the idea that I had tricked him into marrying me, by not telling him about Troy. He was not the kind of person who could put things behind him. Even after the two boys were born he never liked me any better.

"Still thinking about him," he'd say, if he caught me daydreaming.

I saw then I would never like him either. There was nothing about him I respected, much less liked. I was just waiting until the boys were a little bigger before divorcing him. As it turned out I didn't have to wait that long.

"Listen girl, are you in pain?" the night nurse says.

"No, I was just thinking." I didn't realize I was crying until she came in and turned on the light.

"Be a good girl and go to sleep."

"I must be getting a cold."

"Do you need something, an antihistamine?"

"No, I'll be OK."

"You been a bad little girl," she says. "You got to get your rest. Tomorrow they come to take your measurements."

"For a casket?"

"No, silly, for your new foot."

The night nurse doesn't seem like a woman. You've met these women I'm sure who act more like men with long hair and dresses. It has more to do with their manner than anything else. It's the way they push, the way they write you off with their aggressiveness. She calls me her girl to keep me in my place. And it's not just a matter of superiority, of nurse over patient. It's more like roughing you up. She doesn't want any trouble from her patients, so she intimidates them first.

When they measure me tomorrow for the artificial leg I'll tell them I don't want to walk. I've walked enough in my life; I've been everywhere I intend to go.

The best thing my feet could ever have done was take me out of my first marriage. I could have walked out with my two boys. Those steps would have been the best steps I ever took.

Charles and I fought for almost ten years. I stayed with him after Trammel's visit, though I knew I would never love him. I told myself I was afraid of him, of what he might do if I left. But that wasn't really true. What I was most afraid of was what I would do on my own. There was a stupid inertia in me. Just when I would work myself up to leave, things would get a little better suddenly and I'd put off my move. Or one of the boys would have measles or mumps, or scarlet fever, and I'd have to wait until that was over. Or I'd wait till spring, or until I got another job, or until I'd saved a few more dollars. Once I told Dad I would move back in with him. But always in the end I found an excuse not to leave.

Then in the middle fifties Charles, who worked at the hardware store in town, started coming home later at night. And he was gone on Saturdays till midnight. And he quit paying any attention to me at all, even though we'd always slept together, even when we were quarreling. It's funny about people, how they can have sex with each other even when they hate each other. It shows how much sex is a habit, or how impersonal sex really can be.

All this sounds like something from a soap opera, except I never did catch Charles with his girl. I knew something was different, but I didn't want to think about it. But there was something changed about him. He looked different, and his clothes seemed different, as though he had changed them all around. And he quit yelling at me, and saying the kind of sarcastic things that had become his way of communicating.

For a while I thought he must have gotten tired of our quarreling. And that was depressing in itself, because I didn't want to make peace with him.

But the strangest thing was, when he actually said one Saturday that he was going into town and wouldn't be back, and when I found out from his sister he had moved into this apartment and was seeing this girl from Brevard, I was furious. I felt betrayed and humiliated, just as though I was in love with him, and even though I had wanted to get rid of him. I didn't want him to get rid of me; that wasn't fair. It was the form of the thing. I was hurt just like our marriage had been successful. Now you explain that to me.

I threw things around the house, and I sulked. And I burned some of the clothes he had left. And the first person I called was Troy's sister Annie.

"It may be the Lord's way of working things out," she said. (Everything to her is the Lord's way, I thought.)

"Why would he do that to me?" I said.

"You'll be relieved, once you get over the shock," she said.

"I knew he was sorry, but I didn't know he was that sorry," I said.

"Men will always fool you," Annie said. "Just when you think you've got them pegged."

The upshot of it all was I took the boys and spent the next weekend with her and her family down on the river. Troy's mama and daddy were dead, but it felt like coming home to be in that old house. I hadn't been there since the Thanksgiving after Troy had died, when the war was still going on. Even though they had fixed it up with sheetrock and a new stove, and some new furniture, it looked old and small to me. I remembered it as a vast house, full of people, but it looked tiny.

"Just make yourself at home," Annie's husband Muir said. "You're practically one of the family."

That weekend I took the boys down to the bottom fields where Troy had found all his arrowheads.

"You have to look close to see them," I said, as we walked along through the corn stubble.

"Do we have to cross all this dirty field?" Will said.

"That's where you find them" I said, "in the dirt. The Indians used to have villages down here."

It's strange how when you do something you may hardly

be aware of it until later. When Troy was alive I paid no attention to his paintings or arrowhead collection. They were there, but I had my mind on him and on myself mostly. When a girl thinks of love she sees herself as the star of a romance with a happy ending. It's a good thing men don't realize they are just accessories to the starring role a woman gives herself. Every girl wants a leading man, but one she can overshadow. Even girls who want to be dominated imagine themselves as the center of the drama, rescued perhaps, even ordered around at times, but always the focus of attention.

When Troy was alive I hardly noticed the world he came from. Even his family was just a part of the swirl, in those quick visits before and during the war. His paintings, his metal work, his search for Indian things were just a part of his interesting personality. I was too young and ignorant myself to appreciate his accomplishments in themselves.

Going back to the farm with Jerry and Will after the divorce it was as though I saw for the first time the valley along the river, the mountains and the stream he had painted in those pictures Charles had burned. We walked across the pasture where he and his brothers had played kickball in the evenings after supper and where he had planned to build our house. He had developed his great physique by running in the pasture and swimming in the creek.

But it wasn't until I took my sons down into the fields to look for arrowheads that I saw how hard he must have worked over the years and how skilled he must have been at finding arrowheads. We searched among the cornstalks and chips of flint, and got our feet dirty, and found only fragments that must have been parts of arrowheads.

"Here's one," Jerry said, and held up a piece of milkquartz.

"That might have been a piece of one," I said. "The Indian who was making arrowheads might have broken it and thrown it away."

I wished the boys had a father to explain things to them.

"Let's go home," Will said. "My eyes are getting tired."

The winter rains had washed under the cornstalks, and left many pebbles and bits of rock standing on columns of dirt. But all the rocks we saw were the wrong shapes, or had been broken.

"He must have found all the good ones," I explained.

"Who was that?"

"Troy, Annie's brother."

"Was he your boyfriend?" Jerry said.

"He was a friend when I was a girl," I said.

"Let's go home," Will said.

It was exactly thirty years later, as I sat with my foot in pain and rotting, needing to be amputated, my second husband dead, that I began to go back over my memories of Troy in detail. I thought of the boxes of arrowheads Charles had thrown away, the paintings he had burned, the letters I had burned before he saw them, and the things Troy had said to me. Sitting late into the night, unable to sleep, numbed a little by the painkillers, I could hear his voice. It was all inside me, waiting to be pulled out. His words are nothing dramatic, but still precious to me.

We are walking down in the fields after Sunday dinner, on my first visit to his house. He shows me the west end of the bottom where he and his brothers had cleared the fields when he was just a boy. There is a tongue of land that goes out into the horseshoe of the river. The ground there is powdery from the silt laid on by centuries of flooding. When he was a kid he liked to hoe corn there because the ground was so soft and cool just below the surface, as though cooled by the river nearby. Deerflies were hiding in the shade trees along the river, and came out in cloudy weather, or when you got close enough to the stream. But they avoided the direct hot sun. Sweatbees were the worst menace, sticking to your sweat and stinging if you touched them.

Troy explained how he and his brothers found arrowheads while working. And then they started returning to the fields on Sunday afternoons to look for more, instead of walking down to the highway to watch the cars pass. They competed to see who could find the biggest and the most perfect points. Joe and Wade, Jr., and Fred would shoulder him aside if they saw a likely stone. But because he was smaller and closer to the ground, and because he worked harder, he began to find more and build up a bigger collection.

The boys in the valley traded arrowheads like marbles. The most valued were the pure black flint ones. But any unusual shape or color was valuable too. Once Troy found a perfect arrowhead of orange quartz which everyone tried to trade him for. But he refused all offers, and made it the center of the collection which he kept in a cigar box under his bed. One day the orange arrowhead was gone, and he never found out who had taken it. His brothers said Scott Morris, a neighbor, must have got it while they were working out in the field.

Once Troy had surpassed them his brothers began to lose interest in the search. More often than not they returned to the highway or the store on Sunday afternoons. Wade, Jr., got a Model-T and they drove it to homecomings and church singings up and down the valley. Troy was left on his own to comb the fields with some of his younger friends, who he taught to spot likely rocks. He often came home to supper with his pockets full of points.

Sitting here in the dark, with no light but my digital clock, I can almost smell those cornfields along the river. There is the sweet scent of corn leaves burned by frost, and drying out in the winter sun. It's strange how things I hardly noticed forty years ago come back so vividly. You wonder if the painkillers make you imagine things. Of course that's one feature of getting old, that things recalled from youth are clearer than recent and present events.

I've been told any major operation speeds up aging. It's the trauma of surgery, the shock of the anesthesia on the body. I feel twenty years older since the amputation, slow and uncertain, and I mix up times and places, I'm afraid. But it's true: things that happened forty-four years ago are as clear in my mind as if they were this morning.

I've been sitting here in the dark remembering the night I saw Troy die. I'd never believed in such things as telepathy. But it had been an awful time. Even reading the paper you could tell how dangerous things were in the fall of 1943. And the worst news they kept out of the papers. They said more than sixty planes had been shot down in one day on the raid to Schweinfurt on October 14. I knew each of those airplanes had ten boys on them.

"Flying coffins," the paper said the Germans called B-17s.

And Troy's letters had got shorter and sadder. He had told me in a letter postmarked from London he wouldn't be able to mention his work. And from then on his letters were just little photostatic copies with many of the lines blacked out. Almost the only thing he could talk about was the weather, and whether he'd got his Christmas package or not. He sometimes talked about how much weight he had lost or gained.

But even so I'd give anything to have one of those little letters on its slick kodak paper. Charles made me burn the last ones when he found them in the trunk. With him watching I fed them into the heater. I still don't know how he missed the photograph of Troy I kept under my linen.

Not that there was anything in the letters except talk of the rain and mud in England. I think he hated the place. Sometimes he mentioned how he wanted to build a house in the pasture, in the meadow above the branch where the big cedar grew. And another time he said he planned to save his money and buy some land. He seemed to have forgotten about Daddy's offer to give us the nursery.

Maybe he hadn't forgotten but was telling me he didn't

want to move in with Mama and Daddy. Surely it was important to him not to hurt Daddy's feelings. I worried about that, and I worried about the shortness of his letters. I wondered if he had met some English girl over there, some-body who was there and could win him away from me. We'd heard how crazy the English girls were about American GIs who had so much more money than the British soldiers.

I worried that his letters seemed cold. Every day I worked at the dimestore and came home to find the mail on the table in the hallway. And most days there was nothing but some ad for war bonds. And when there was a letter it was just a short little thing.

And I'm ashamed to say it; it hurts me to remember that I wrote him how I felt. I told him I thought he had forgotten me. And I complained how his family never came to see me. It's hard to believe how silly I was at the age of nineteen, expecting them to come visit me, hard as his mama and daddy were working, and as much as they had to worry about with all their other boys in service, and with the first grandchild staying with them during the day while Annie worked in the cottonmill. It's a good thing the young don't know how foolish they are, otherwise they'd give up.

But that night in November I was sitting in the dark in my robe. I couldn't sleep, and I sat in my chair by the window, half drowsy and half awake. Though the sky was clear and the moon visible over the mountain, I had the sense it was raining. It was very cloudy and raining steadily. The air was heavy with dampness.

And I saw Troy. He looked so awfully sad. I could see his face through the airplane window. He was looking down at something I couldn't see, as though he was reading or watch-ing. Suddenly he looked startled, and turned his face right toward me. It was like he could see me for that instant, with that horror on his face. He was looking at me, and then the flames reached up past his face and the window. He sank down out of sight. There was a hot explosion and terrible heat, and then another explosion, white this time, almost blue, and other explosions one after the other. But otherwise it was silent. There were no screams, no collison, no crashing sound. Just the explosions on and on, getting smaller, in the awful heat. It was so hot it was like the air itself was burning up and collapsing from inside, closing off space. But I never saw any more of Troy after that startled look, when he saw me.

And after the explosions stopped there was this awful smell of chemicals and metal and flesh. And I could hear the rain again, steady, never slowing, on and on.

Then the rain stopped and I could see the moonlight again above the mountain. There was no sound except a plane going over in the distance, and my face was hot and wet.

It was late the next day that Troy's daddy got the telegram from the army.

After Charles left I still worked at the dimestore, and I had to raise my boys. But they had learned from their father not to respect me. Or maybe it was partly my fault for not being strong enough when they were young. But by the time Jerry and Will were in high school I didn't have a bit of control over them. Charles gave them .22 rifles for their birthdays and they were always out shooting at birds and blasting bottles down by the creek.

They stayed out late and a lot of the time I didn't know where they were. And they quit going to church with me. There wasn't much I could do about that either. And Jerry took up drinking in high school too. Even Charles got onto him about that. I felt like everything I had done was wrong. And there was so much I hadn't done. Maybe I was never meant to have children. I wasn't equipped to raise them. Maybe after Troy's death I was supposed to remain single, I thought.

After the boys joined the army I was completely alone. I saw Annie from time to time, but she was busy with her job and her own children, and didn't really have time for me. We'd get together sometimes for a coffee break when she was uptown, and we laughed about our early days in the dime store, and talked seriously about Troy. But more than ever before I could tell she didn't approve of me. With my divorce, and my boys in court for stealing hubcaps and drunk driving, and selling pills, she had decided I was not what she thought I was.

And then the dimestore fired me. I'd heard they always fired their managers before they could retire and draw their pensions, but I didn't think they'd bother with a salesclerk. After all, my pension would have been so small it was hardly worth worrying about. But sure enough, as I approached my thirty years with the store, things began to get difficult. I stood at the same counters I had managed since before the war, but nothing I did seemed to please the young manager. When I swept up in the evening he would come by and say, "Mrs. Fulton, you left some dust there."

And one day when he handed me my paycheck he said, "You're just not turning over the businesss you used to."

But the most humiliating thing was when he took me off the counter and put me in the stockroom. I knew they wanted pretty young girls at the counters in front, and over the years they had moved me around the store, working gradually back toward household goods. My hair was gray, and I had a few lines in my face, especially after Will's trial for stealing—the judge let him go to join the army—but I was better at sales than ever before. Over the years I had come to know so many people in town and from the country that they often came to me with questions and for help with items in other parts of the store.

The stockroom work was heavy, slicing open boxes, rearranging shipments. There was a boy to do the heavy lifting, but you still had to sort and shift around to count items and confirm invoices. And worst of all it was cold back there. With the door open for unloading trucks, and wind whipping through the dark shelves, I shivered, writing on the clipboard, checking off orders, making sure stock was unpacked for the store.

The draft gave me a touch of arthritis in my elbow. And I had one cold after another from the dust and chill. Maybe I stayed out for a few extra days, dreading to return to that dank place.

"You're not well enough to work here," Wimberley, the manager, said.

"I'll be OK back in the store."

"You're not able to stay on your feet all day and remain alert," he said.

Back in those days if their doctor pronounced you unfit they could fire you, and they didn't have to give you a cent.

In my fifties, gray-haired, divorced, alone, I was out of a job. I had not felt so low since Troy's death. Even quarreling and fighting with Charles had not been as bad. From time to time I called up Annie just to talk. And it was clear she felt sorry for me, but there was little she could do. I drew my little dab of unemployment, having to go into the offices and stores every week asking for jobs, and then appearing at the unemployment office to be interviewed. I had not been unemployed since graduating from high school.

One day I sat on one of the benches uptown, dreading to walk into another office and ask for a job. Everybody knew Wimberley and they knew he had fired me. I was old and had no special skills and I was too shy to be good at door to door sales or management. It was a warm spring day. I was going down to the E.& S. Insurance Co. to ask about a job they advertised in the paper. I didn't really have any office skills except a little typing. I would tell them I would pick up bookkeeping and work as a receptionist. I knew perfectly well that what they wanted was some pretty blond just out of high school who could type eighty words a minute and take shorthand. I just sat there, putting off for a few more minutes the pointless interview.

It was an early spring day, and the trees along the street were just turning green. The robins were back, and recent rains had washed the sky and the street. The sun felt warmer on my back than it had in months, and I just sat there. It was too early in the season for tourists and the sidewalk was quiet, with cars passing from time to time. I knew I had to go to the interview, but I sat there another minute, and then another. It was as though I had taken some drug, a muscle relaxer. I didn't want to move, and I didn't feel drowsy. I just wanted to stay there a while longer in the warm spring sun.

Grass was coming out lush in the crack between the sidewalk and the curb, like a narrow lawn I thought, running all the way down the block. A robin pecked in that little seam of turf. Overhead there were a few white clouds, and an airplane crossed, the Chicago Delta we called it. It moved diagonally across the line of the street.

I can't imagine how I looked sitting there, my pocketbook in my hands, my gray hair uncovered for everybody to see. But it was as though something had clicked off. I had worried as much as I could about solving my problems, about money and loneliness, about getting old and having ungrateful children. It was as though I had exhausted the pressure. It just vanished.

It's hard to express the relief I felt. It wasn't that I felt lighter. I was just *there*, at ease in that instant. There was nothing I had to do. I was in one day of my life, and I could sit on that bench as long as I wanted to. I had years behind me, and I had all the rest of my life ahead, and the interview at the insurance company could wait. People passed me, and some, who knew me from the dimestore, spoke. I don't know what people thought, but I just enjoyed sitting there.

I don't know how much time passed, but finally, when I saw it was getting cooler, I stirred myself. It was too late to get to the appointment. I would call another day and tell them I had a flat tire.

The thing I wanted to do, before the sun went down, was

to go home and start planting the garden. It was the perfect time for dropping potatoes and putting in corn. It must have been my daddy's blood in my veins, but that's what I wanted to do. I stood up, stiff from the long sitting, and walked to the car. I drove back and changed my clothes, and began slicing seed potatoes, two or three eyes to each piece.

"Mrs. McGraw, are you going to take your sleeping pill?" For once the night nurse calls me Mrs. McGraw.

"It will help you," she says. "You need all the rest you can get for the healing."

Medical people like things to run on schedule. That's why they use drugs and pills so much. They want you sleeping on schedule and waking up on schedule. If somebody breaks their routine, they feel they are failing.

But night is the time I think best, and my greatest pleasure is remembering my childhood and my days with Troy just before the war and on his thirty-day furlough in 1942. If I take a sleeping pill I just drop off and have worry dreams all night and end up tired from sleeping the next day anyway. My only way to really extend my life is backwards now. There is so much I want to try to understand. We are so ignorant when we are young and living our lives. I know everybody says, if we could only live our lives over. But that wouldn't work either. You can't be young and receptive to experience, *and* be old and knowledgeable at the same time. It would be inhuman.

But I do enjoy trying to reconstruct, trying to decide what happened to me. And the long night hours when everyone is quiet, except for Mrs. Brown who sometimes screams down the hall, are my best privilege.

"We want you strong enough to wear your new leg," the night nurse says. "You'll be dancing by Christmas."

Annie and I remained friends until my second marriage. That's a story in itself. I know she felt sorry for me and thought I was a weak person. But we always remained friends, talking on the phone, seeing each other in town, till I got married again.

It was the strangest thing. Suddenly when the pressure to get a job vanished and I stayed home and worked in the garden, I got offered a job almost by accident. A friend at church heard about this old couple that needed somebody to stay with them. They were from New York and their name was Burger. They had plenty of money, and they needed somebody to do the cooking and housecleaning. They even had a nurse that came to stay with Mrs. Burger during the day, so there wasn't a whole lot of bedpan and sheet-changing work. They paid a hundred dollars a week plus, of course, room and board. I hated to leave my garden, just when I had got it started in April. But they gave me one day off a week, and I could come home and tend it then. Nobody knew how long the job would last because Mrs. Burger was pretty sick, and Mr. Burger was so old they could either of them go any minute. The money was better than I had been making, and I didn't mind the uncertainty of the arrangement. For New York Yankees the Burgers were pretty nice people. Even if they talked loud I soon saw it didn't mean anything. They were too grateful to have me there to look after them. I could even tell Mr. Burger had a little bit of a crush on me, but that's the way with old men, and it didn't amount to anything.

Bill McGraw worked in the yard for them, and he sometimes drove their big Cadillac into town when they needed to go somewhere. And he got their groceries for them. I had seen Bill when I worked in the dimestore. The first thing I noticed about him was his plaid flannel shirts. He wore these shirts like hunters are supposed to wear. Around the Burger house where everything was so gloomy those shirts were awfully bright. And he had a variety of them too. They weren't just red and black, but also red and blue and black, and red, yellow, and black. And some of his shirts had maroon and even lavender in them, in varieties of plaid. I was always pleased to see him just to look at his shirts.

I knew Bill was married but I'd never met his wife Mabel, though I'd seen her with him in town once or twice. She was a little bitty hunched-over thing. I learned later she was a terrible hypochondriac. Bill never mentioned his wife, at least not at first.

We started going to get the groceries together, and sometimes Mr. Burger came along too. He liked to get out of the house when the nurse was there to look after Mrs. Burger. Bill and I hit it off pretty well from the start. We were about the same age and he had known Charles in high school.

"I always felt sorry for you," he said. "In some ways Charles was a good old boy, but he was never cut out to be no husband."

"That's what I found out," I said.

"'Course he was never right after the war."

"I never knew him before the war."

"Marriages are made in heaven and lived in hell," Mr. Burger said.

"Now Mr. Burger, you don't really mean that," I said.

"I do mean, and I am mean," he said, and we laughed. Mr. Burger was always playing with words. He liked to tell jokes, though many were ones he had told before.

"You know what God said to Moses when he went up on the mountain?" he said.

"No, what?"

"Take two tablets and call me in the morning."

We laughed again.

But we had fun picking out the groceries. Mr. Burger would let us get anything we wanted. When we passed the meat counter he always said, "Know what the butcher did when he backed into the hamburger machine?"

Bill and I smiled.

"He got a little behind in his work."

We picked out cookies and coconut pies and candied dates and fresh pears.

"You can take some of this home," Mr. Burger said to Bill. "I know your wife is often ill."

"She don't feel like cooking much," he said.

I started fixing him plates of meat and vegetables to take home to Mabel, after he had eaten with us.

"She complains about everything," he said. "But I don't notice her leaving much on her plate."

For a while Mrs. Burger was feeling a little better, and Mr. Burger suggested we take her for drives around the country-side. She loved to get out and see the mountains. So every day for a while we drove her out into the county in the big Cadillac. Bill and I sat in front and Mr. and Mrs. Burger in the back and we drove along the back roads way out toward Brevard and down to the Green River Cove. Once we passed my house near Saluda and I showed them my garden.

But for some reason the part of the county Mrs. Burger liked best was the northeast side out toward Big Hungry, Bear Wallow, and Sugar Loaf. That is pretty country, with rolling hills below the mountains, and pastures and little farms in the valleys. Mrs. Burger said it reminded her of Virginia, and of England. I remember one day in August when it was especially clear after a long rain. Everything was so green and bright it sparkled. The ironweeds were blooming down along the branch, and looked like heaps of floating purple.

"The rain has kept things green," Bill said.

You know how it is when you're falling in love and just beginning to realize it. Everything seems a little more vivid, the colors, the light, even the grass and the mountains. And you begin to appreciate other people more. You feel in love with everything. Just going out for a drive is such a delight it's almost painful. But you hardly notice food. Maybe that's why lovers lose weight. The thrill and pain kill your appetite.

What times we had that summer and fall. Mr. and Mrs. Burger sat in the back of the big air-conditioned car and we drove around Fruitland and Edneyville, and down to Chimney Rock. Once we went all the way up to the Parkway and across Pisgah. And once or twice we got caught in thunderstorms. I was on duty and I was supposed to be working, but all I did was help Mrs. Burger in and out of the car.

Sometimes Bill looked at me as we drove along. But we didn't need to say anything. We knew what was happening. And it seemed strange, believe me, to be falling in love in my late fifties. It didn't seem possible. I hadn't felt anything like this since I was nineteen. And there was the painful fact that he was a married man. I felt a little guilty, though I told myself we hadn't done anything wrong. So far we were just friends. I didn't know then how bad his marriage to Mabel had been.

But gradually, as we had coffee in the mornings, or when I helped him rake leaves in the back yard, he told me little by little about his life with Mabel. And I came to see how, even though the details were different, his life had been so much like mine with Charles. They had married during the war, just before he was drafted, and even then she complained of headaches and dizzy spells if the least little thing bothered her. After their first child was born she hardly ever left her bed.

He had taken her to dozens of doctors, and their findings had been vague and contradictory. No two specialists in Asheville or Greenville had agreed on what her trouble was. One diagnosed a defective thyroid gland, and prescribed hormones. Another said she had a heart murmur.

"Whatever it was we never found out for sure," Bill said. "But no matter what happened, if you got mad at her, or asked her to do something, or suggested the house was a mess, she would have them headaches and dizzy spells, and go back to bed for a few more days. I do most of the housework, because it's so much easier just to go ahead and do it myself."

I could tell from the way he talked it was true. He didn't tell it all at once, just a little at a time, in bits and pieces, while talking about other things. Bill was a hard worker, and he liked to have fun. I just found myself in love with him.

The stars are out tonight, but you can't see many of them because of the street lights around the nursing home. You never get to see the sky nowadays like it was when I was a girl. The lights of towns flood out the stars, and the air is so dirty all you see is a general glow even in clear weather, except for a few of the brightest stars. It's like the sky has closed in on us. And most people are inside anyway, watching television, never leaving the air conditioning.

"Oh help me," Mrs. Gibbs down the hall moans. Mrs. Brown died last week, and they put Mrs. Gibbs in her room. She has been calling out like that for the past three nights. She has emphysema and can hardly breathe.

"Oh please God, help me," she calls again. At least I think that's what she's saying. It's garbled by the walls and her breathing tube.

I don't think she's that close to death, or they would have taken her back to the hospital. I talked to her the day she moved in and she told me she would rather die than go back to the breathing machine. But I doubt they'll let her die here. As somebody approaches death they always rush them to the hospital.

"Oh God help me," she moans again.

Someone rushes down the hall rolling a cart or machine. They already have her on oxygen. Maybe they have some kind of pump or fan that will help her breathe, even though she asked for no special measures.

A phone rings at the desk, and a car swings into the parking lot. Its lights come through the window like the flash and flutter from a movie projector, and are turned off. Maybe they called the doctor to come look at Mrs. Gibbs. Another cart rolls by.

"Get the tube, get the tube," someone calls.

"I can't do everything at once," the night nurse says.

"Ain't life a bitch," the orderly sings to himself just outside my door.

There is more wheeling around and slamming of doors.

"Oh God, oh God," Mrs. Gibbs calls. She sounds closer, which means they have the door open, or have her out in the hall. There are more steps running by, squeaking on the floor.

"You'll be fine; everything's fine," the night nurse says.

"Ain't but just a little way now," the orderly says as they pass the door.

A door slams and an engine starts. The ambulance slips away into the night.

"That was close," the night nurse says as they come back down the hall.

"You could 'bout touch them pearly gates," the orderly says.

If Mrs. Gibbs dies tonight they will have somebody else in her room tomorrow. This is retirement country and there is a waiting list to get in here. If Bill hadn't left me his insurance I couldn't afford to stay here after the operation. In the future, if people keep living longer, there will be thousands of nursing homes all over the mountains, full of old women with trembling hands and blue hair, living to be a hundred. After they fit me with the new foot, and I can get around with the walker, I'll have to leave and shuffle around on my own.

It was when Bill brought me the first gift that I knew there was no turning back. I really didn't know how starved I was for attention and affection until I had some. I mean of course I knew, but it wasn't until I tasted again what it means to be loved that I realized how much I had missed. Charles had left me hardened and empty. I felt like a girl again that year in the Burger house.

Bill went off to the drugstore to get Mrs. Burger's medicine while I shopped in the grocery store. Mr. Burger hadn't come along because Mrs. Burger was worse. He and the nurse were watching her.

When I got back into the car with my bags Bill handed me a little package wrapped in silver paper.

"This is for you," he said.

"Why?" I said, and we both laughed.

"Because I want to," he said.

It was a little bottle of emerald-colored cologne. I put it in my pocket as we approached the house. I had not had such a sense of well-being since my days with Troy, before he left for England.

It was a long and bumpy road before we could marry. I'm glad I don't have to go through that again. But I'm also glad to say I wouldn't have missed it for anything. And I'm not ashamed of what I did.

But you would have thought I'd robbed the cradle from the way people acted. Here Bill was, as old as I was, and he'd had this awful marriage for thirty years. I've even heard that when he left her Mabel got better. She got out of bed and started looking after herself. He had just spoiled her all those years by giving in to her complaints.

It took a long time to sort things out, even after we had made up our minds to get married. First, there was Mrs. Burger, who was dying, and we had to look after Mr. Burger all those months. Bill and I drove him down to the funeral home to make arrangements about a month before the end finally came. Mrs. Burger had asked him to. She said she didn't want him to have to worry about all the decisions at once. That's when the funeral parlors really take advantage, selling you the most expensive of everything when you are in a state of shock from a death. We went in with him and watched him pick out a bronze coffin with cream-colored lace and pillow. Bill held my hand in the dim light while nobody was watching.

Mr. Burger bought a plot at the Memorial Park for Mrs.

Burger and himself.

"You two will bring flowers to our graves each year?" he said and winked.

And he wrote out a check for ten thousand dollars, and signed a contract which they had fixed up for him in the office.

"My funeral's paid for," he said as we were driving back. "Now I can afford to die."

"Mr. Burger you shouldn't joke about such things," I said.

"My girl, solemnity won't extend your life a minute, and it won't improve it either," he said.

After Bill told Mabel he was leaving her, and she had started divorce proceedings, he moved to an apartment on Highway 64, not far from the Burgers' house. It was just a tiny place, with a bed that folded out in the living room, and a miniature kitchen. It was a terribly shackly old bed-couch that squeaked. But we had some good times there. It was such a pleasure to get away from the sickness and gloom settling over the Burger house even for an hour or two. And with Bill I realized I'd never enjoyed sex before. I'd done it out of duty and out of habit and for brief pleasure. But Bill taught me to relax and give myself to lovemaking. In all my fifty-five years I had never really let myself go. I know this will sound strange, but sex with Bill was like a conversation, a long talk that goes this way and that, and then back, at least right up to the end. Bill gave you the feeling that anything could happen, and it was all fun, and there was no hurry.

We'd lie there in that creaky bed sometimes for hours afterward watching the light change and evening come on. I would start to say something and Bill would put his finger to my lips. It was as though a single word would have broken the surface and poise of our long moment. For it felt as though time had stopped and we were balanced on the top of a wave before it broke. Finally I had to get up and let Bill drive me back to the house, where nurses and doctors were now coming and going several times a day.

When I tried to explain myself to myself I sounded guilty, but I certainly didn't feel guilty. For one thing, I had married the first time with the good advice of everyone, and had brought disaster on myself. This time I was going to please myself, because my own advice could not be worse than theirs. I was an old woman, and it was my own damn business. For some reason I remembered Trammel and the way he had stalked out when he saw I was married to Charles. There was no way to please everybody. I was lucky to be pleasing myself, finally.

"Look Mrs. McGraw," the therapist says. "I've brought you a leg. Isn't it beautiful?"

She holds up a foot with all kinds of leather and laces on it.

"It looks wicked," I say.

"Aren't you something," she says and laughs.

She takes off the bandages and wraps the stump in fresh gauze and then elastic. "It will get sore at first," she says. "But the skin will grow tough."

I can't really see the end of the stump, but apparently it has healed and the scabs have come off. For weeks it itched like an enormous bee sting. At night I still feel the nerves going down into the foot, sometimes. But that is natural to amputees. Your nerves have a memory of their own.

The therapist laces up the leather tight on my shin. This way I will still be able to bend my knee, though it will be restricted a little by the fitting. She takes my hands and pulls me up. I stand with most of my weight on my left foot. It feels as though my right foot has gone to sleep.

"That's great," she says. "Now ease a little weight onto the right."

I lean slightly on the right knee, and a pain jabs up my leg. I try not to wince, but I do.

"That's beautiful," she says. "It will hurt or tingle. Takes some toughening up to get used to."

I try again, and the pain is the same.

"Maybe it needs to be laced tighter," she says.

I sit back down with her help, sweating and shaking.

"It will take some time," she says. She is like an adult encouraging a child to walk or swim for the first time or to ride a bicycle. That is what I have become, a little child.

"Now try again," she says, standing up.

"I'm tired."

"Of course you're tired. This is hard work, and you have been in bed for five weeks. But we'll do a little more each day. You'll be walking in no time."

When I stand up again and lean on the right leg there is less pain. I can't tell if the artificial foot is laced on so tight the leg is numb, or if the tighter fit absorbs the weight higher up and keeps it off the stump.

"Now take a step," she says.

I do a slight shuffle.

"Very good, now take a real step," she says.

I shuffle again, almost an implied skip or hop.

"Good, good. Now put your weight on the right foot all the way, then the left all the way ahead of it."

I take a short step, and wince.

"Wonderful, wonderful. Now take another, further. Put your right foot all the way ahead." She holds both my hands as though we are in some kind of dance.

Sweat drips into my eyes and my bones wobble as though turning to jelly. I would not have dreamed I could be this weak. I could be a hundred years old. I'm glad nobody but the therapist can see me.

"One more time, honey," she says. "One more time."

The pain is almost unbearable, but I take a longer step. She won't let me sit down again until I do. If she wasn't holding my hands I would fall.

"There, there," she says. "Now we're getting some-

215

where."

She lets me sink down into the chair. I am so weak I feel brittle. If someone shook me I would crumble to little pieces.

"We'll take six steps tomorrow," she says. "We'll double the number of steps every day." She starts to take the leg off, then stops.

"I'll leave it on a while longer," she says. "That way the leg will get used to wearing it." She puts her hand on my shoulder as she leaves, but I am too tired to say any more than "Thanks."

When I was a little girl growing up around the nursery I was lazier than most kids are. I was an only child, and Daddy never made me work much. He did the potting and repotting, the digging and mowing himself. Sometimes Mama helped him, and sometimes I would pretend to help, watering the boxwood cuttings for a few minutes, or carrying sand from the sandpile to mix with peat in the potting soil. But most of the time I played in the shade. I carried my dolls around and talked to them and made play houses under the pine trees.

But once or twice, when the weather or air pressure was right, I just felt like running. It was as though I had been given a second wind. I went skipping over the trails around the fields and down through the juniper and boxwood patches. I ran up on the ridge and down to the creek. I dashed across the porch and through the house and out the backdoor. I hardly touched the ground. I traced the lip of turf along the road bank, and I followed the bottom of the dry ditches halfway up the hillside. There seemed no reason to ever stop. My breath wasn't heavy and I wasn't even sweating. Distance invited me to keep going. There was no place I couldn't run to. I looked up the road to where it crossed the ridge and felt I could run up there and just keep going into the sky. I even remember the smell that day. The honey locusts were blooming, and the new leaves coming out along the creek. Some of the fields had just been plowed and the dirt smelled clean as camphor.

It wasn't till after Bill died and I was drawing Social Security as well as his insurance money that I had time to think a lot about Troy again. My life with Bill had not been perfect, but it had been busy. What young person would believe the love story and lovemaking of two old folks sixty years of age? But it just seemed to happen on its own, the way most things that work do.

In the hard period after Mrs. Burger died and while I was waiting for his divorce from Mabel, I stayed on with Mr. Burger for several months.

"You're not going to desert the sinking ship?" Mr. Burger said.

Bill stayed on to work in the yard too. But things were different. The nurses and doctors were no longer coming and going. Not only was there the worry of the divorce proceedings, and Mabel spreading rumors about us, but Mr. Burger began to change quickly too. It was like the only thing that had been keeping him young and spry was looking after Mrs. Burger. Once she was gone he began to show his age rapidly. You've never seen anything like the change. Just a few examples will tell you what happened. It's like he started giving up and losing control. Always before he had been so careful about the way he dressed. He had this collection of tweed jackets in all colors and sizes of weave, and he wore them, often with a tie, throughout the day. He'd dress himself before breakfast, fresh shaved and smelling of cologne.

But after Mrs. Burger's death he started getting dressed later and later, sometimes wearing his bathrobe all day. I'd find him sitting in the living room with his pants on and no shirt, with the bathrobe over his shoulders. I thought it was just a depression he'd pull out of. But no sir, it didn't get better, and I saw that his mind was affected too.

He had always told jokes, even corny jokes, and slightly smutty jokes. He kept talking and laughing. And you felt like laughing with him. You felt like nothing would get him down. He talked back to newscasters on television in the funniest ways.

"A poll shows that most Americans are still patriotic," Walter Cronkite would say on the evening news.

"Sure, which pole, the flagpole or the tadpole?" he'd say. And he'd go on like that till the news was over. But now he just sat and watched television half the day, sometimes sitting in the dark but not really watching it, his face lit by the screen.

And he did strange things that fall, like using the bathroom and not closing the door, so you could hear him all the way in the living room. And sometimes his robe would fall open and he would expose himself, but he didn't seem to care.

Often he couldn't remember what he was saying, and stopped in mid-sentence. Or he said things that didn't really make any sense. I couldn't tell if he knew they didn't make sense or not.

"Oscillations," he once said to me as we were having supper. "I guess it's all oscillations."

I must have looked at him funny.

"Don't you see, it's all oscillations. Everything in the world is oscillating. Sea, temperature, people."

And then he developed a theory about the moon which never made any sense to me.

"It's all hollow inside," he said. "Don't you see, there's a hole at each end, and it's all hollow inside. But there are people living in there. That's where our ancestors came from, the cities inside the moon."

He had it all worked out in scientific detail, but I can't remember what-all he said. And he got mad if you couldn't understand him, mad enough to pound the table or stalk away.

"Agh, there's nobody to talk to," he'd say.

But the most embarrassing time was when he decided he

218

wanted to marry me. It was an idea that just seemed to occur to him one day. He started taking my hand whenever he saw me. "I've had a special feeling for you since the day you came here," he said.

It came on him like a little boy's crush, the kind where a twelve-year-old falls in love with a schoolteacher. It grew on him until he couldn't help himself. I was scared by the whole thing. At first I didn't tell Bill.

"Sharon, you were sent to me," Mr. Burger said.

"I've enjoyed being here," I said. He took my hand.

"God sent you to me," he said. "This was intended to happen."

I didn't exactly pull away, but I patted his hand and led him to a chair.

"It's the only thing that will make me feel right again," he said.

"You're getting stronger all the time," I said.

That night, in the middle of the night, he came to my room. I heard somebody fumbling around at the door and I turned on my light.

"Sharon, you've got to marry me," he said. "It's what Vera would have wanted. I have a lot of money. We can live in Florida half the year."

"You should go back to bed, Mr. Burger," I said.

"Call me Ralph," he said.

"You shouldn't be up this time of night," I said.

"I can buy you anything you want," he said. "And when I die it will all be yours."

"You're not making sense," I said.

"I'm making perfect sense," he said. "I know when I'm in love."

The next morning he said, "I know what's holding you back. It's Bill, isn't it? He can come along with us, just as he does now."

I couldn't tell if he had forgotten that Bill and I were getting married, or he just didn't care. Mr. Burger's mind was so vague he couldn't think anything through anymore.

"Make an old man happy," he kept saying. I liked him and it was painful to see him go downhill so fast. If I had been unscrupulous I would have married him for his money. But people don't know that. They listen to rumors and don't know that I gave up a fortune to be with Bill. Within another month Mr. Burger had to be put in a nursing home, and the house was put up for sale.

I moved back to my house in Saluda till Bill's divorce was final.

When Bill died of a heart attack it was so sudden I had no time to prepare myself. He had complained of heartburn from time to time, and sometimes of pains, but he always laughed and said it was just indigestion. He had even had a physical not two months before, and they said his heart seemed normal.

"There's a slight enlargement," Dr. Burleigh said. "But that in itself doesn't mean much."

"He has a big heart," I said to people.

"You never know about a heart," the doctor said. "But he looks fine now."

Bill promised to cut down on salt and fatty foods, and that seemed the end of it.

The thing about being married when you're older is the freedom you have. Young people, even if they're very much in love, feel the burden of their futures. Their livings are yet to be made, the children raised. Young people are still trying to find out who they are, and marriage often complicates that process. I remember how closed in I felt when I was young, as though all of time was pressing down on me. And I don't think it was just being married to Charles, though that didn't help. There is so much uncertainty, about paying the bills, and knowing how to act responsible. Looking back it's hard to believe you got through it, but at the time your hope and ignorance help. The young feel so tied down, so restricted by their lack of confidence.

But older people have at least some of these questions answered. Or they know they don't need them answered. Getting married at fifty-six you have a sense of open space ahead. It's like New Year's Day, when the light on the same old yard and floor seems different. You can't know how much time you have, but what you have is free.

Mr. Burger left us each ten thousand dollars in his will, and with that money we started setting out the nursery again. Bill didn't know that much about shrubbery, but we took one step at a time. The demand for boxwoods was gone. Landscapers were now using white pines and maples, hemlock and dogwood. For all the building around Greenville and Anderson, Augusta and Atlanta, they wanted white pines mostly. And since pines grow fast and are easy to seed, they were the perfect money crop.

But we never got into shrubbery in a big way like so many others in the area. We just kept busy, if the truth be known, and after a couple of years had Social Security to supplement our sales. I've never known another man who could enjoy himself the way Bill did. He could just forget his problems and have a good time. He made me see what a worrier I was.

And he was never bothered when I mentioned Troy either. For a long time I didn't, knowing how Charles had reacted. But when I did refer to Troy the first time he said he knew who he was, had played basketball against him when Edneyville played Flat Rock. "He sure knew how to sink them," Bill said.

To show what I mean about Bill enjoying himself, let me give you an example. Social Security checks come every third of the month, unless the third is Sunday or a holiday, in which case they come the day before. Now getting our checks is so exciting for us oldsters that we wait right outside the little post office on the morning of the third until the mail is sorted, and then ask for our checks before the mailman leaves on his route.

It has become a kind of ritual, waiting outside the post office in our cars, talking with the windows rolled down, and driving to town to cash our checks, do some shopping, maybe eat at the cafeteria in the mall. It was a kind of luxury and leisure most of us had never known before. I suppose I felt a little guilty for making the postmistress sort the mail quickly, but it couldn't have been that much trouble. And maybe I felt a little guilty for having that government money to spend. But the truth is we enjoyed it all.

Bill had an even better time than I did. On that Tuesday, the third, he put on his new plaid flannel shirt, the one that had royal blue and yellow and red in it, and his new tweed hat, and we drove to the post office about nine-thirty. That's when the mail truck from town arrives. It had rained the night before, and everything seemed clean and shiny.

"Let's drive up to Grandfather Mountain," Bill said. "Let's cash our checks and eat dinner at the mall, and then drive on to Grandfather Mountain."

"That's a long way," I said.

"The day is young," he said. "And the road is straight."

We pulled up in front of the post office where four or five cars were already parked. Esther Wood's car was right next to us and I smiled at her. She smiled back, and then started motioning. I couldn't figure out what she meant. She pointed at me and looked upset. I rolled my window down.

"What's wrong with Bill?" she said.

"Nothing," I said, "except he's too big for his britches."

"Something's wrong," she said.

I looked over at Bill and there he was slumped back behind the steering wheel, his eyes open, and he was jerking a little. But I think he was dead already. He must have died the instant he turned off the ignition.

"Mrs. McGraw, there's someone to see you," the nurse's aide says. My leg is still sore from practicing with the artificial foot. The therapist shouldn't be here for another hour.

"Well, how are you?" It is Annie standing in the door. This is the first time I've seen her in a long while, though I talked with her on the phone a few times when I was searching for information about Troy.

"Can't complain," I say, and we laugh. It's what her daddy used to say, no matter what the situation, if he had the flu or had just lost half his bean crop, "can't complain." And her mother would say, no matter when you asked the question, "The same old sixes and sevens," which must be a saying that goes back a hundred years.

"Same old sixes and sevens," Annie says. I'm glad to see her. She doesn't look at my leg or even at the wheelchair.

"So when will you get out of here?" The truth is I kind of like it here in the nursing home, with so many people to look after me. But if I tell her that it won't sound right.

"Maybe two or three weeks, soon as I learn to walk on this thing." I point to the artificial foot with all its harness and laces on the table.

"Once you get that on nobody will be able to stop you," she says. "You'll be climbing the mountain."

"I'd settle for a walk to the outhouse," I say. Annie and I always did get to laughing when we talk. It's like a chemical reaction between us.

"I brought you something," she says, and takes an envelope out of her pocketbook. "It's Troy's Social Security number."

I asked her once for the number when I began my search for his records. I knew his serial number, but not his Social Security number.

"It's on his unemployment card," she says, and takes out a little yellow ticket-shaped paper. "When they laid him off at the cottonmill they gave him this to present to the unemployment office."

The little card is dated September 29, 1937, more than fifty years ago.

"Makes you feel old," I say. "To look at that date."

"We are old," she says. "But we haven't done so bad."

Annie has not aged as much as most of our generation. Which is surprising since she never was that strong, and since she raised three children and worked all her life in the dimestore and then managed the clothing store in the mall. But she looks ten years younger than me now. She holds herself straight, and her hair is still blond with some gray mixed in. I wonder if it is because she stayed married to the same man all her life, or because she is religious and always had peace of mind. And then she never did smoke like most people of our generation. Even Troy had taken up smoking in the service, right at the end of his life. We used to laugh at Annie for her talk about whole wheat bread and avoiding chemical additives. Long before it was a fashion she read books about nutrition and we called her a health food nut, but it must have paid off.

"When you get out you can visit us," she says. "Spend a whole weekend or several days."

"You know what I'd really like?" I say. "Is to go down to the river and walk along the rocks of the shoals where we had the picnic with Troy. I'd just like to see the place he jumped across the river again."

"We can go down for a picnic," she says. "It will be warm soon."

"That was the most beautiful place," I say. "I've thought of it a lot of times. Troy enjoyed that visit home."

"They have built houses on the ridge above the shoals," Annie says. "It don't hardly look the same now, though the river itself is the same, except where they built the highway bridge."

"They built houses right there in the woods?"

"Right on the ridge above. It's a good view. And the superhighway cuts across the valley just above the Beegum Hole."

"Then the place doesn't look at all the same?"

"No it doesn't look the same. But it's still pretty."

When the physical therapist comes Annie leaves, but I promise her to come down for a visit when I get out and can get around. She leaves the card with me, for my file on Troy's career in the service.

I can't remember exactly when I started my search to find out what happened to him in the Air Corps. It was after Bill died. I was in shock for days, maybe even weeks, and went through the visits, the funeral with his children and Mabel, like it was all a dream. But when I was by myself again I found the picture of Troy I'd kept all those years. It was still in the dresser drawer, under the pillowcases. I took it out and put it on the table because it gave me something to think about.

In high school they told me I had a good mind for research. I loved to go to the library and look up information and assemble reports. But it was a talent that had never been developed. When I came out of high school there was no money to go to college. Nobody in my family had ever gone to college. I had taken one little course in bookkeeping, and one in typing, but I was lucky to get on at the dimestore.

There was never any decision. It was just a matter of one thing leading to another, you might say. One day I saw this piece in the paper about how you could write off to the National Archives in Washington for personnel records of servicemen. That got me started.

It's curious how frustration will arouse your interest, as though the very difficulty of a job makes it more fascinating. A few weeks after I wrote to Washington this form came back. It listed several possible responses, including one colored with a yellow marker: "Subject cannot be identified without Serial No., date of birth, and date of induction into the service."

If I knew all that I wouldn't have to be looking, I thought. I was tired, and I hadn't used a typewriter in twenty years. They had a long form that needed to be filled out.

For several days I let the form lie on the table, and at least once I almost threw it away. There was no way to find out the serial number and the date Troy joined the Air Corps without calling Annie. I was certain she had saved many of his effects, but we hadn't spoken in fifteen years, except briefly when we met on the street. We never quarreled; it was just clear she didn't approve of my second marriage. She probably didn't even approve of me marrying a divorced man. I know Mabel had spread rumors about me.

With Bill gone I had so much time on my hands. I cleaned the house in the morning and I had a second cup of coffee. There were blackbirds outside, getting at the cherry tree. I ran out on the back porch and hollered at them, but only a few flew away. It was getting to where you couldn't hardly raise cherries, without putting a net over the tree.

Finally I went in and looked up Annie's number and dialed her. She seemed glad to hear my voice, and said she'd look in her bureau drawer for the serial number. We talked a long time, and she found both the number and card that had been sent her parents saying Troy had enlisted in the Army Air Corps, August 23, 1941. I knew it had been about that time, because it was almost time to pick apples when he left, but I had forgotten the exact date.

"The Lord took him and it doesn't matter about the details," Annie said.

"I'm just curious to find out what I can," I said. "Of course there may be nothing to find out."

One of the things she reminded me of was the memorial service they had for Troy when they brought his body back from England in 1948. His mama was dead by then of cancer, and I was married, with two little boys. Of course I didn't attend, with Charles acting the way he did. But I saw a notice of the service in the paper. I had heard that his mama just worried herself so much after he died that she took cancer.

When the coffin was shipped back from England some of the family wanted to open it, but Annie and her daddy decided not to.

"There's no telling what's in that casket," Annie said. "It would destroy Papa if he opened that thing and there was just a bone or two, or a rag of a uniform. When a plane crashes the bodies are always burned. And this was a bomber, maybe loaded with bombs."

So I missed the ceremony when they finally preached his funeral and handed his daddy the flag that draped the coffin. Up at the graveyard on the side of the mountain a line of soldiers fired their rifles over the grave as they lowered the unopened casket into the ground.

I had to miss the service, but I did go up there later, after I was divorced from Charles, to visit the grave. The stone was already weathered by then, and it seemed strange, to say the least, to be there. There must have been a thousand crows in the trees on the mountainside above, all calling at once. The flag on the grave had faded most of its colors. There seemed no connection between that little graveyard on the hill, and the Troy I had known.

Finally I did get a report from the National Archives, but it told me very little, except that the body after the crash had been identified "by fuses in the pockets." And there were thirteen people on board the plane when it burned. What they sent was just a xerox copy of a little typed form. It didn't amount to much. I couldn't decide if I knew more or less after I read it.

But just that little bit of information made me curious to know more. I was teased by the meagerness of the report they had sent. There was an address on the form for directing further inquiry to the Air Force Historical Archive at Norton Air Force Base in California. I was beginning to get excited. I sat down and typed another letter to the address they listed.

The next day I drove over to Asheville and stopped in the library. One of the attendants showed me where there was a section of books on World War Two, and I sorted through volumes most of the afternoon looking for something on the Eighth Air Force. There were books on tanks, and books on

Russia, and books on the battle of Midway. And there were several big picture books, including one called "Flying Fortresses." I took that volume to a table and flipped through it. There were hundreds of photographs of B-17s, and crews standing in front of their planes, and wrecked bombers in wheatfields and broken across stone walls. There were lots of charts and tables, and a section called "Operational Diary of the VIII AF in WWII." There was a list of the dates and objectives of all missions from 1942 to 1945, with the number of planes and the units involved. I quickly looked down the calendar to November 10, 1943. There were fighter missions that day, but no heavy bomber raids. That seemed strange. How could Troy have been killed in a B-17 that day if there were no bombing missions? There must be some mistake.

"Mrs. McGraw, we're going to walk down the hall today," the therapist says. She has come to remind me of a basketball coach with her combination of friendliness and bullying. Or sometimes she seems more like a revival preacher trying to get you saved. She treats me like a sinner that has almost come to a decision.

"You're just about there," she says, lacing on the artificial limb. "A little more practice and you'll be jogging."

"I just want to drive," I say. It remains to be seen whether I can qualify for a handicapped license in a regular car. I will have to take a driving test with my artificial foot. Lately the state has been getting tougher on elderly drivers. There are so many retired people in the mountains, all of them driving their big Cadillacs or Mercedeses. It's dangerous just to get out on the road.

In fact it's been in the news lately, all the old folks who have been denied renewal of their licenses. There was one man from Florida who got so mad when they told him he had failed his driving test that he dropped dead of a heart attack right there in the examiner's office. And the examiner was sued by his family for manslaughter. And there was another man, a local man from way up on Mount Olivet, who failed the test and went berserk. He came back with his shotgun and wounded the examiner before the police subdued him.

I hope I don't get senile as I get older. But I may be just as bad as the rest of them. I do want to drive again, to go to town, and to the store when I need something, and maybe over to visit Annie. They have lunches for the old people at the fire station now, but they send a bus around the valley for those participating.

"You're an old hand at this now," the therapist says as she leads me across the room.

"Or an old foot," I say. She opens the door and I am out in the hall. It is the first time I have stood on my own in such a large space since before the amputation. The corridor looks a mile long, down to the front desk, with obstacles like wheelchairs and laundry carts all along the way. There are at least two people on crutches going up and down the hall. Sunlight falls through the front door on the desk, but the lighting in the hall is that peculiar gray fluorescent that makes you feel under water. And no matter how much they clean a nursing home it still smells like pee and alcohol. It must be the laundry in the carts.

"Well look at that," the therapist says. "You're on your own."

The front desk looks halfway to California. Once I reach there I will be at the edge of the earth.

"Just take a step, and then another," she says, and gives me the thumbs-up sign.

I take a step on the smooth floor, and keep my balance. But I see instantly what this is going to take. It is work, and I am weak from all the days of sitting, and lying in bed. It's all a matter of accommodation, of compensation. Since I can't feel the floor with my right foot I have to feel it doubly with the left. I will have to learn to walk awkwardly before I learn to walk normally. You don't take regular steps, you inch along

229

almost sideways.

"Look ahead, not down," the therapist says.

It is like working on a ladder where it tires you out just to keep your balance. But I can see that it is possible. It is not a matter of confidence. This is not melodramatic, but a lot of hard work. I'm already sweating a little.

"You'll learn not to drag your right foot," the therapist says. "But that's OK for now."

I limp past doors where old folks are sitting up in wheel-chairs.

"Look who's sauntering around," Mrs. Killian shouts from her doorway.

There is a new woman four doors down who wheels herself out in the hall in front of me. I hope she backs away before I get there. "We came from Florida to enjoy ourselves," she says, all in a rush. "But my husband had a stroke and he don't know nothing sometimes. And then his head is clear as mine or yours."

"Mrs. Klotz, you're blocking the way," the therapist says. "Mrs. McGraw is walking on her new leg."

The woman wheels back, almost out of the way, and I edge past her.

"Some days his mind is clear as a bell," she says. "And the next day he thinks he's Franklin Roosevelt. He's just down the hall. You can talk to him if you don't believe me."

I nod in an ambiguous, noncommittal gesture, and keep going in my shaky way. I make it to the front desk after ten or fifteen minutes, sweating and trembling, but happy. The therapist lets me use the walker to get back to my room.

"We came here from Florida to enjoy ourselves," Mrs. Klotz says as I pass her room.

I am completely exhausted by the time I reach my own wheelchair.

Once I had started my inquiries, the pace seemed to

accelerate on its own. The Air Force personnel center in St. Louis sent me a xerox of Troy's file after I filled out several forms and got Annie to sign a release. And the History Center at Norton Air Force Base sent me a declassified history of the 482nd Bombardment Group. The personnel report said his plane crashed while returning to Alconbury after an "operational mission." The history of the unit told me his plane was the first American bomber fitted with H2S radar scanners. A further chapter explained that the radar scanner tried to identify a fogged-in target by the profile on the radar screen. For the first time I realized Troy must have been on board as a technician in charge of the equipment. That was the top secret project he had said he couldn't tell me about. It seemed likely he had flown on several missions before the crash of B-17F 42 5793 on November 10, 1943.

It's hard to explain the excitement and sadness I felt in this search. Perhaps I was like somebody picking at an old wound or scab to feel the sting or the itch again. But every bit of information I uncovered made me hungry for more. I felt like a scholar. My days were filled with writing letters and making phone calls and waiting for the mail. I wrote letters to the *Air Force Magazine*, and to the *482nd Bombardment Group Newsletter*, asking for anyone who might have known Troy to get in touch.

It was at that point I began to think about Robert Trammel again. I could remember the look on his face when he stood up that day and walked out past Charles, who was holding the door. If I could just find him I could start over again and set it all straight. He was the only one who could tell me the things I wanted to know. I would pay any amount of money I had or travel anywhere to see him.

Two more addresses I had gotten in the packets sent me by the Air Force were the headquarters of the Veterans Administration in Washington and the locator service of the Retired Personnel Office in Dallas. I wrote to both, and both answered in about a month, sending forms and asking for a three-dollar fee. The rules were that you paid a fee for their services whether they found an individual or not, you enclosed a stamped letter to the individual which they would forward on if they found the address, and in no case would they give out the address themselves. If the individual wanted to respond that was his business.

I spent hours typing and retyping the letters and sent them in with the fees, and waited. Both organizations said it was easier to locate people who had stayed in service after the Air Force became a separate organization in 1947. There was a good chance Trammel had left the service in 1945, about the time he stopped by the house.

It's hard to explain the thrill and sadness I felt in my search, partly because it was so different from anything else I had ever done. As I read the forms and typed the letters I realized I had missed my calling. I should have been a researcher, or at least a bookkeeper. I even got a pass to use the library at the university in Asheville, though they told me at first I could not. I ended up writing a letter to the president to get the pass. But there I found a number of other books about Flying Fortresses and bases in England in World War Two. And for the first time I saw pictures of the old bases in Suffolk and Bedford, at Alconbury. I talked with Hayes Fairfield at the fire station about England. He had been stationed in Suffolk with another unit during the war.

"Did you know Troy was flying missions?" I said.

"Sure, didn't you?"

"Why didn't you tell me before?"

"I thought you knew."

Hayes had lived five miles down the road all my life. He had once told me he tried to get to the site of the crash of Troy's plane, but it was all roped off. He couldn't get within miles of it.

One day I was peeling peaches and the phone rang. It was a man from the VA, and he said he was calling to say they had my letter and he had found Robert Trammel.

"Is he the same Robert Trammel who knew Troy Williams?" I said.

"Yes, he says he is. I will forward your letter to him."

"Thank you," I said, "thank you very much."

I was so excited I forgot to write down his name, or to ask him for Trammel's address. He sounded so friendly he might have given it to me. But I just assumed my quest was almost over, and that I would hear from Trammel within a few days. I'd included my phone number in the letter and told him to call me collect. Surely after all these years he'd get in touch. I was so excited I had trouble finishing my run of peaches.

Every day I went to the mailbox hoping for a letter from Trammel. When the phone rang I flushed with excitement, but it always turned out to be the Social Security office, or a neighbor who wanted to rent the fields next year. A week passed, ten days, another week. The Elbertas ripened, and then the Georgia Belles. By the time summer was almost over I realized Trammel was not going to reply. There was no way I could make him reply.

I wrote another letter to him, and sent it to the VA again, hoping to start the process all over. But this time there was no reply, either from the VA or from Trammel. I had reached a dead end.

I began to think about going to England myself, to look at the remains of the air bases where Troy had been stationed. I had never been abroad, but the idea fascinated me. I even talked to a travel agent about the price of tickets. But just then the pain in my leg began to get worse. When I stood up it took minutes for the feeling to return to my foot and leg. And sometimes the leg would swell and throb.

"It's the circulation," the doctor said. "The veins in your foot may be closing up."

"Is there any way to reopen them?" I said.

"I'm afraid it's an irreversible process," he said.

"How bad will it get?"

"We could have to amputate."

"We tried to call your son Jerry," the secretary says. "But so far we haven't been able to find a phone number."

"Then he must have an unlisted number," I say. "And he's forgotten to tell me what it is."

I don't want to tell them I haven't seen Jerry in over a year. Last Christmas, when I mailed him a Christmas present to the last address I had in Spartanburg, it never came back, so I figured he had gotten it. Will told me he heard Jerry was married and had a child, but he has not informed me. I told the woman from the county not to bother him or Will. I will get myself back to the house when the time comes.

"The county prefers that you be released into the care of the next of kin," the woman said.

"I don't see why it would matter to the county who takes me home," I said.

"It's the required procedure," she said. "Every possible effort should be made to secure the assistance of the family at the time of release from the nursing home." It sounds as though she is reading the rule. She must have said it so many times she has memorized it.

The sound of the word "release" makes me think of someone getting out of jail. I will have served my time and they want to make me somebody else's responsibility, release me into the custody of the next of kin.

"Can you tell us where he works?" the secretary says.

"He's a salesman and is on the road a lot," I say.

"Do you know his company?"

"It was one of those new electronic companies in Spartanburg," I say. "But he may have moved up to another job."

I can't bring myself to say the last time I talked with Jerry he was unemployed. He was fighting an indictment for selling drugs, but he *had* worked for a while as a salesman in electronics, and then in mobile homes.

"He's probably out on the road," I say.

"We'll have to get in touch with him by tomorrow," she says.

"You mean you can't let me go home?"

"We'll have to do different paperwork if the county takes you home. It could take a few days longer to get that through."

"Try again this afternoon; he might be there," I say, knowing Jerry could be anywhere, in Florida or Seattle.

"Don't you have another son, Mrs. McGraw?"

They must have looked into my records pretty carefully, for I haven't mentioned Will to them.

"He's living out of state," I say.

"But maybe he could come and sign the papers," she says. The secretary plays with her beads as she talks. She must deal with this kind of problem every day, because you can tell she doesn't care about the outcome. But if the county has to take me home she will have to fill out the extra forms and make some more phone calls.

"Do you have his address and phone number?" she says.

"I must have left it at home," I say. Actually Will keeps in touch better than Jerry. But then he can't move around, and he has more time to write letters. He's in the federal penitentiary in Atlanta for writing bad checks. But at heart he's better than Jerry. That may be why he got caught. I think it was the drugs he took in Vietnam that weakened him. He could never get started at anything after he came out.

"Can you tell me what town he lives in?" the secretary asks. "Maybe we can get his number from information."

"It's near Atlanta," I say. "But it's one of the suburbs. I can't remember the name exactly."

The secretary stands there for a minute looking at me and playing with her beads. She holds her pad and pen with one hand and twists the beads with the other. She knows I'm not telling the truth, but does not know what she can do about it. She just wants to get on with her work.

"If I can't get hold of them we'll have to do the forms for

the county," she says. "It will take several days. You never know how long they will take to process the forms."

"I'm sorry to be so much trouble," I say.

She lets the beads drop on her sweater, and takes the pad in both hands. "Do you have any other relatives?" she says.

I don't want to say I was an only child, that my sons are gone, that my second husband is dead, my parents are dead, my fiancé was killed in the war, and that I have no close friends. It sounds awful when you put it that way.

"Annie will pick me up," I say.

"Annie?"

"Annie Powell. My friend who came to visit me."

"Will she sign your release forms?"

"Will she have to pay anything?"

"No, but she will take the responsibility for seeing that you get home and get established safely in your house again."

"I'm sure she will." Annie is my best hope. I have not been in a hurry before, but suddenly now that I can shuffle around, I want to get home to my typewriter, to my research, and to my garden.

It had been raining for a week with no letup. The rain started in late October, and there hadn't been a day free of rain though there had been spells of fog and drizzle. You could take off in drizzle and even rain, but fog grounded all but a few fighters and weather planes. Luckily they didn't have to worry about linking up and flying formation themselves. That was the job of the bombers following. But if the bombers were grounded they were grounded also. It was usually OK once they were above the cloud cover, or out over the North Sea where wind broke up the clouds. It was their job anyway to mark targets that were fogged in.

The weather in England seemed strange in part because the days were so short. By November it was getting dark by three-thirty or four, and with the overcast it never seemed to get light until late morning. There was hardly any day. For a deep penetration mission that meant leaving in the dark and returning in the dark. That partly explained why so many pilots went to sleep on the return flight and nudged into their neighbors in formation.

Last year had not been as bad, because he was still discovering the strangeness of England. And they had said then the war might be over in a year. He was at Bovington in Buckinghamshire, and then at Alconbury in Huntingdon-shire. The countryside looked all the same to him, like pictures in a book, of hayfields and hedgerows, stone build-ings and villages, clustered churches and pubs. But every road was just a traffic jam of trucks and jeeps. The roads were so narrow that even driving on the left-hand side was usually not a problem, at least until you met oncoming traffic. He had seen a number of stone walls knocked down by big army trucks trying to turn corners without slowing down.

It was also the mud that got to you. Every foot of ground off the pavements and hardstands was mud churned up by tires. He had been given a bicycle to ride around the base, from the motorpool to the messhall, but most of the lanes were too muddy to drive on with thin tires. The ground was a kind of cream, gray in places, black in others. It squished and sucked when you stepped in it. At the crossroads between the messhall and recreation room the ground got flung in ruts and ridges, in twisted ropes of slime. Four-wheel-drive jeeps would bury themselves up to their axles. They put boards across the worst places, and then the boards sank out of sight. Finally someone put down a section of iron portable runway, and that worked for a while, even though the iron lace sank out of sight in the clotted and curdling mud.

The first winter, at Alconbury, he had been too busy to worry. The 92nd was short of B-17s and the mechanics had to keep the few they had flying. Even before Eisenhower requi-sitioned some of their planes for North Africa they were desperate. Often he and other members of the squadron

237

worked around the clock, retuning engines, taking parts, sometimes whole motors, off disabled or crashed planes, working by lantern and flashlight in the cold, rainy night. For several weeks he was a member of a crew that raced around to crashed planes to knock down the engines for parts, or even remove whole engines to take back to Alconbury. More than once they got to a crash to find it already stripped by another crew from their own or another group. The MPs standing guard just smiled when asked who had done it.

He had seen Fortresses that skidded across fields and across highways and smashed against stone walls. He had seen one that ended up leaning against a tree. He had seen B-17s that were burned or partly burned, and the charred and mangled bodies of the crew thrown out in the weeds.

"You can't help them," Driscoll, the head mechanic, shouted. "Don't look around you. Just get the goddamned fuel pumps."

He had seen B-17s with the rudders shot off, or half a wing. He had seen the bodies of turret gunners crushed to a stew of glass and blood when the bombers belly landed. Once he saw a bomber coming in low with its engines on fire. It exploded just as it touched down, flinging metal and bodies all over the runway. The other planes coming in low on fuel had to try to dodge the debris.

They found B-17s in the countryside crumpled like old sacks against barns. Many times he had seen the blood and brains of the crew splattered over the plane he was dismantling.

There was one crash over in Cambridgeshire they had rushed to on the night before Christmas Eve. The vultures from another group were already there picking the engines apart.

"Get out of there," Driscoll called as soon as they got out of the truck.

There was a floodlight on a truck and the boys just kept working.

"I've got a .45 here and I'll kill every son of a bitch that keeps stealing our plane," he hollered.

The floodlight went off and in the dark they couldn't see a thing. "Bring the lantern," Driscoll called.

By the time they brought their own light the other crew had packed up and were leaving. They never even knew what base they were from.

"Maybe they was Germans," Trammel said, his teeth chattering.

"Do you have a permit?" the MP said to Driscoll.

"You're goddamn right I've got a permit. We need every engine on this baby back at Alconbury by O400, and we're going to have them."

In the rain they got out their ladders and cranes. A floodlight like the other crew had would have made all the difference. Trammel went ahead of him.

"You don't want to look in there," Trammel said. "Let the medics worry about it." As he worked in the lantern light he could see the white face of the pilot or copilot against the window of the cockpit. All night as they worked the face never moved. Finally, just before daylight a rescue team came by and removed the bodies from the wreck.

He and Trammel had been together since mechanic school in Biloxi. Through the long, cold English nights they shivered and sweated over the big motors, to have them ready for takeoff. Black with grease and exhaust they talked through the rainy dark about the folks back home, about their girls, about Georgia and North Carolina, and about going home after the war.

"When I build my house in the pasture and marry Sharon you've got to come see us and stay a week. We'll go fishing every day," he said, as he had many times before.

"I'll drive up from Georgia with Sarah and our kids and we'll eat you out of house and home," Trammel would say. One reason why he and Trammel had stuck together was they were both from the mountains, Trammel from North Georgia,

Troy from North Carolina. "Never thought I would see such a spread," Trammel said when they toured the colleges at Cambridge one weekend.

Because the RAF had been doing the night bombing of Germany for many months, the British had invented a radar scanner to help locate targets. In the dark it was very hard for a pilot or bombardier to know exactly where they were. Troy didn't know that much about navigation, but when he transferred to the 813th Bomb Squadron the Brits had given them a two-week course in the use of the H2S radar unit. "The stinky" it came to be called, because it almost never worked the way it should.

"Of course your navigator will be measuring the mileage out to the target, and your radioman will try to get an angle on the two radio beams off the coast, and the pilot will try to locate the target visually. But if there's a cloud cover your only hope may be the image on the radar screen, the profile of a building, say, or the slope of a mountain. Some great tower or unique land form would be ideal. But most of the time you'll have to do your best with screen patterns that are partly ambiguous."

They put the unit right in the nose of the plane, so he worked beside the bombardier. Because there was nothing to do on the long ride out to the target he took one of the forward guns when fighters approached them.

But watching the screen to identify the target area was only part of his work. He had an assistant, a corporal, whose main job was to release flares as they approached a target. Ideally, as the bombardier took over the controls for the bomb run, and he found the target on the radar screen, they were to lay a trail of flares for the bombers behind to follow and sight-in on for their own bomb runs. And once over the target the bombardier tried to mark it with phosphorous bombs to make a big enough blaze for the other bombardiers to aim for in the fog. The Eighth Air Force bombed only in the daytime, but when it was overcast they weren't much more accurate with their "precision bombing" than the RAF was with its carpet bombing.

Never had he known such fear, such tension, such thrill. The first time he dove from the highboard at CCC camp he felt something like this. Before a mission you felt sick and watery inside. It seemed impossible that you had volunteered for this. You thought of going on sick call, of going AWOL, of asking for a transfer. You prayed and thought of home. You couldn't sleep, knowing you had to get up at 3 A.M. anyway.

Flying itself was so scary and thrilling he couldn't believe he was doing it. Their first practice trip had been up to Scotland to locate a castle on an island in a lake on a cloudy day. They were supposed to drop flares, and observers stationed around the lake were to judge their accuracy. On the flight north he was too nervous to concentrate. He sat in the nose watching the countryside, the churches, go by in the breaks between clouds. As a kid he often dreamed of flying, and here he was crossing the north of England into Scotland. He thought of Sharon, who was probably asleep at this moment, and of the weather back in the mountains. It was squirrel-hunting time there, and the night was probably clear with maybe a little fog drifting near the creek.

"Target approximately fifty miles ahead," the pilot said over the radio. "Bombardier will be taking over controls."

"Roger," McCall said beside him, and bent to his sight.

"We're flying at nine thousand feet," the pilot said. Storer, the pilot, had a Canadian accent and always pronounced his vowels funny.

"Roger."

"OK, it's your baby," Storer said.

The world below them was a glacier of clouds, with a rough-looking mountain poking up through, here and there. Sometimes there was a break and he could see the bleak countryside, all rock and brush, with fir trees and snow on the peaks. He switched on the unit and got a few blips.

"Target should be just ahead about twenty miles," Storer

241

said in the earphones.

The blips on the screen turned into wavy, frothy lines. That was the rim of the mountains, he assumed. He adjusted down as they got closer, and found a confusing mass of lines and specks, as the sweep circled. Could they be picking up geese or other airplanes?

"Watch out for the monster in the lake," Jones, the copilot, said.

"Got the flares ready?" he said over the radio to the corporal in the bay behind them, who should be standing with his hand on the release.

"Should be coming up," the bombardier said, his face against the Norden bombsight.

Troy could see nothing but rippling lines across the screen. He wondered if something had gone wrong with the wiring.

"We should be right over it," McCall said.

"No, wait," he heard himself say.

There were wavy lines and patches of emptiness on the screen. Was it the lake the sweep was registering? And then something tall apeared, like a building or a tower.

"Release flares," he shouted into the mike.

They saw the first flare go down, and then the second, third, and fourth. The fifth one, which should have been right on the target castle, came down on the peak of woolly brush that poked through the cloud cover below.

"Damn," McCall said. "I think we aimed for the mountain above the lake."

"I never even saw the castle," Troy said.

"Good work, boys," Storer said, as the plane began its turn. "Let's head for home."

On the report that night the pilot wrote, "Partial Success. The designated target was not hit, but the mistaken target was hit with remarkable accuracy." His assessment was confirmed by telephone by the observers even before they returned to Alconbury. One flare had been dropped in the lake, but the rest made a beeline for the mountain peak.

"We'll have to refine our technique for deep penetration," McCall said. He liked to use words that had sexual overtones without being explicitly dirty.

"Sex is like going to the bank," he would say. "It's all deposit and withdrawal."

They were not cleared for combat operations until late October, after the second great Schweinfurt raid on the fourteenth. If a Pathfinder had been used on that mission, perhaps the accuracy of the bombing would have been greater. All the published reports said the raid was almost totally successful. But Troy and Trammel knew men who had been part of it, and they said nearly half the planes that started out were shot down by anti-aircraft or Messerschmitts.

To use the colonel's terms, the air war was far from won. The new planes would not be arriving until after New Year's. Then they were promised shipments by the thousands, from the factories in Ohio and on the West Coast. In the meantime there was nothing to do but patch up and and steal parts from old Fortresses.

The theory that Fortresses could be self-defending was proving untrue in the most deadly way. Fighter planes with longer range would be arriving, but they were still in pieces and on the drawing boards in factories back home. B-17F 42 5793 was the only Pathfinder fitted with H2S radar so far. On it depended much of the success of the missions over the next two to three months. A million tons of TNT were useless if the targets could not be found under the clouds. So the colonel kept telling them.

The weather over Holland and the North Sea kept them grounded until November third. Because he couldn't sleep at all the night before, Troy spent most of those hours writing letters to Sharon and his mama and daddy. He couldn't really think of much to say, except to tell them he was fine and not to worry, that he had lost a little more weight, and not to send him much for Christmas because he had nowhere to put things in the hut. He wondered if they could imagine back home how crowded and cramped the space he lived in was, his cot under the curved roof of the quonset hut, with the trunk at the foot of the bed. There was a storage space at the end of the building, but it couldn't be locked and nobody but a fool would leave anything valuable there. He reminded Sharon that they would build a house in the pasture when the war was over.

Sometimes he realized he had forgotten her face. He would have to take the picture out of his wallet to remind himself how she looked. And then she seemed like someone he could barely recall. It was the fatigue. He had trouble remembering lots of things. Since coming to England he had been working fourteen- and sixteen-hour days for fifteen months. Since transferring to the 813th Squadron he had worked even harder to learn the radar technique. Nothing seemed real anymore. Day after day they ran through exercises with the H2S. When he closed his eyes all he could see were the blips and the sweeping straight-edge of light scraping over tell-tale blots and patches. Round and round the beam went. Pick out a mountain slope, pick out a building, identify the shape of a valley. It gave him headaches.

Lately there was a black spot wherever he looked. It was in his left eye. When he looked at a page the black hole was there, shifting. It showed up even at night when he looked at a light. Maybe the screen-watching had damaged his retina. He'd have to ask the doc one day.

When the wake-up came at three he had only been lying on his cot for a few minutes. It would be more than four hours before they were actually airborne. But he had to get up and have breakfast with the crew. All over eastern and central England crews were waking up, eating breakfast, going to briefings, driving out to their aircraft.

He and Corporal Lewis and McCall were briefed by the colonel on the target. They would be flying fifteen minutes ahead of the main bomber force and marking the oil refineries with flares and fire bombs.

"When you see this gap in the mountains you'll know you're close," the colonel said. "The refineries are off-center, about a third of the way from the left ridges, east of the center of town." He gave them photographs, and a grid configuration of the town. If there was cloud cover they wouldn't even be using the bombsight, only the radar and the navigator's calculations.

"You'll go in at eight thousand feet," the colonel said. "So flak may be heavy and accurate. On the other hand we're hoping they'll concentrate on the big force behind you. Maybe they won't even notice a single airplane, especially if you're in the clouds." The colonel had a dry Boston accent. He had been a professor at MIT before the war, and he still seemed more like a civilian than an officer. For one thing, he almost never cussed. For another, he never seemed to notice whether you saluted or not. Partly that was due to the small size of the group, and the frantic work they had been doing. Every man in the unit had been picked by the colonel for his record of skill and dedication.

"This is the test," the colonel said. "All our training has been for this day. And I don't need to remind you that the future of daylight precision bombing may depend on the results you achieve."

Troy was so cold he felt numb all through warm-up and takeoff, even in his flightsuit. The leather and sheepskin could have been paper for all it helped his nerves in the damp morning air. Their plane was the only one taking off from Alconbury, though all over the island squadrons and groups were warming up and waiting for the flare that signaled takeoff. He was so frightened he could hardly believe he was seeing the North Sea under them an hour later, and then the coast of Holland. It was happening like it was supposed to, but it was happening to somebody else.

"We're climbing now. Put on your oxygen," Storer said.

"We'll descend again as we approach the target."

He hated the oxygen mask, the sweaty, sticky feeling it gave you around the mouth and nose. He could smell the coffee he'd had, and the sour tension in his stomach was caught in his breath, and condensed inside the mask. He had to think of home, of his canoe, of Sharon. But he could concentrate on nothing. If a fighter spotted them he'd have to man the left gun in the nose. They passed over patches of cloud, then open country, and patches of cloud. The fields were scraps of canvas, painted on by tractors and winter wheat. There was snow on some mountains he couldn't name.

"We'll follow the Ruhr and attack from the south," the colonel had said.

"That's Essen down there, I think," Storer said.

He turned the H2S unit on and the green pencil began to circle.

"Oxygen off," Storer said through the earphones. What a relief to get the mask off. They were tilting down.

With the charts in his hand he bent to the screen.

"It's all yours," Storer said to McCall, after they had banked and leveled out into the bomb run.

"Jesus," McCall said, "I've got it in my crosshairs." There was a break in the clouds, and the H2S was unnecessary.

"The refinery is a dead duck," McCall said. "Release the flares," he said to Corporal Lewis on the mike.

One, two, three, four, five. The flares went down like big sparklers. McCall pushed the bomb release levers. "Take that in the throat," he said.

If the incendiary bombs didn't hit the refinery, at least they damaged the railyards and warehouses nearby. And the bombers above and behind would have a target to aim for.

"Let's go home and change our diapers," Storer said, and the plane began to climb toward the north and west. The fighters would be busy with the formations behind them. Troy suddenly felt the fatigue come over him like a warm lead suit. He could hardly keep his eyes open as he turned off the radar unit. By the time they reached the North Sea he was asleep behind his oxygen mask.

The moon is so full and bright even the sodium lights of the parking lot can't obscure it. We think of bright moons as an autumn phenomenon, but the moons of early spring are just as dazzling in the mountains. The March rain and wind must have blown away every speck of dust and pollution. The moon floats fat and rounded, painted with radium, and the mountains are clear beyond the wing of the nursing home.

I took off my foot at bed time, and have to wheel myself close to the window to look for stars. There are a few points of light, but the moon and the outdoor lamps blot all but the biggest. With any luck at all it will still be clear when Annie comes for me tomorrow. The secretary finally got all the papers signed by county officials and I am set to be relased to my own responsibility.

I have been thinking about the asparagus bed that needs to be cleaned off, and the flowers I want to set out in the yard. I put in a few bulbs last fall, but that seems so long ago I can't remember how many were dahlias or daffodils or tulips. Limping shouldn't hinder me from working in a small space with a hoe, long as I don't have to stoop too much. I'm thinking of burning off the weedstalks by the branch to put in some sunflowers there. Daddy used to burn off the bank there every spring.

There's a look the mountains have in early spring, when the slopes are still lavender and blue, but the trees along the creek are budding out a yellow-green. A few dogwoods and redbuds are in bloom higher up and seem to be floating in the transparent woods like colored signals of smoke drifting around the mountain. The fields and pastures lower down have already turned green, and mustard in the fields is bright as the daffodils in yards and out by mailboxes.

On the road down to Saluda there's a place where you can see all the way down the valley, all the colors and seasons from winter up high to early summer down by the creek in the protected hollows of the thermal belt. I hope Annie will stop there on the side of the road and just let me look. The thermal belt is a zone in the valleys near the foot of the mountain where the springs come early and the autumn late. I've read the explanation, but can't remember it exactly. It has something to do with the cool air sinking off the slopes at night and the warm air rising. It's why the Florida people like Tryon and Saluda so much, and it's why gardens and nurseries do so well in the hollows down there.

When I turn away from the light-filled window I see the silhouette of someone standing by the closed door. I didn't hear the door open. He is so tall it must be one of the orderlies, except none of them is so slim. I wheel away from the window and some of the light reaches across the room, revealing zippered fur boots and leather flight pants. The pants have pockets and zippers around the knees. Though I can't see the face I know it's Troy from the height, and from the posture. I am not scared. Instead I, strangely, feel angry.

"You have come back," I say.

But the face in the dark above doesn't say anything. I remember the dead can't speak to us directly. Though we feel their presence, and maybe even their thoughts, they don't talk to us in words.

"Were you curious to see how I was?" I say. "To see me after all this time?"

The figure steps forward, but stops when the light reaches up to the waist of the flightsuit. I think there is a smell of burned leather and singed hair, but it goes away. If only I could see the face, see an expression.

"I was a pretty young girl the last time you saw me," I say. "And now my hair is gray and I have an artificial limb. And I can't see a thing without my glasses. The last time we were together I weighed ninety-two pounds and you could carry me with one arm."

The tears are streaming down my face in the dark, dripping hot off my lips and chin. But the figure doesn't move.

"You left me on my own," I say, surprised at the change in my voice, at the anger that comes welling up. "You left me and I didn't know what to do. I followed everybody's advice and married. Trammel was insulted and Charles never forgave me. You left me with nothing but a box of arrowheads and a young girl's confusion. And when I needed advice there was no one there."

I look for some sign, some gesture from the figure. But it just stands there like a leather statue.

"We thought you were fixing airplane engines," I say. "I never thought you would be flying. You hid that from us. So we had no warning. At least you could have said you might die."

It doesn't seem possible I am saying these things. But they come out on their own, with no thought from me.

"Why did you volunteer?" I say. "For the extra money, to show you were brave? To work with fancy equipment? You didn't even marry me. You could have married me before you went in, or in '42 before you shipped to England. We could have had a child. That might have kept you from flying."

The front of my gown is wet, but I don't even reach for a kleenex. For once I just let my nose drip. The figure takes a step back and I don't roll forward. There is more to say.

"I don't think you ever wanted to get married. I think you liked the idea, but you didn't want to make love to me. You liked airplanes better, and the thrill of the war. What woman could compete with a war for a man's attention? Or maybe I wasn't good enough. Were you looking for somebody better? Your family thought their glorious Troy could do better than little Sharon?"

I have gone too far. I don't know where these things are coming from. I never talked to anyone like this.

"I could see it in Annie's face that she tolerated me for

your sake. But I could never really be one of you. Maybe I wasn't religious enough, or blond enough, or tall enough? I think they were relieved finally that you never would marry me."

The tears stop as the words stop. I must be dreaming a bad dream caused by the chili for supper, and the excitement of going home tomorrow. And yet the nightmare leaves me strangely empty. I feel as though I have been working and need a rest.

If only Troy would speak and answer my accusations, not with denials but affection. The light has not risen above the waist, and he seems already to be retreating. He will not touch me.

"When I first saw you I thought you had the longest fingers I'd ever seen on a man," I say. "You could take both my hands and hide them in your fist. When you leapt between the rocks in the river it was as though you flew. I have never known anyone with so many talents. I realize now I was intimidated, and still too young and foolish to know it."

I am too tired to talk any more, and when I look up the figure is gone. There is only moonlight and shadow in the room, and I have done all the talking. The only thing alive is me.

The living do all the talking, I say, and laugh.

I will have a feast of sleep tonight, a long leisurely banquet of many kinds of sleep, many flavors and speeds. Every day, after I work in the garden, or watch television, I can finish with another course of sleep. There are as many colors of sleep as there are kinds of bread or flowers. I think what a privilege forgetting is. The fields where we work, and the mountains we look at, even the people coming after us, won't remember us at all. And it's better that way.